Eden,

First Lady of Sin

Storm

http://www.melodramapublishing.com

Eva, First Lady of Sin
Copyright © 2006 by STORM

For information address:
Melodrama Publishing
P. O. Box 522
Bellport, New York 11713-0522

Web address: www.melodramapublishing.com
e-mail: melodramapub@aol.com
author's email address: **stormrizing1@yahoo.com**
Library of Congress Control Number: 2006934898
ISBN 1-934157-01-5
First Edition

10 9 8 7 6 5 4 3 2
First Paperback Edition

Eva,
First Lady of Sin

For so long a tale
awaited to be told.
So many feared
the truth.
The knowledge.
The anguish.
The ever-present
biases that live
within all of
us.
Let this urban
tale educate
each of
us,
make all of
us
remember who
we aren't and how
so very close to
the edge we really are.
May we acknowledge
that some of Eva lives
either inside of
us
or may be lying
next to
us.

STORM

THANK YOU's

I thank God for his infinite wisdom, unwavering patience and unconditional acceptance. Who else, but the Almighty, could keep this STORM RIZING from self-destruction when so many roads got rough?

JayeGrey, you are my love, my muse and without you, there would be no Storm. There simply are no words and you know it. We know what it is. I feel for those who missed out on your legendary talents – above board and below. What kind of world would it be without you?

Thank you to my sons who put up with my absences, and my love, often from afar for the last 3 years. I love you for believing in my attempts to improve our lives. Thank you for allowing me to bring my work home and miss Tuesday game night cause *Eva* wouldn't act right! My love for you knows no bounds. Smooches ; -)

Meat Man, let's try getting out of high school, dude, please. Leave the grille's to those below the equator, okay. Hmm, let me think. It's 4 pm; do you know where your cell phone is?

D Oven, let's work on that handwriting, okay? And, stop missing the school bus! No more XBOX game cheats. Let's try to get thru 2 weeks without leaving your homework on the dining room table, please.

Kev, when you get to Central H, please teach your dad every thing you learn about relationships. Let's all say it together: You only get one chance with da kid!

Thank you to my original editors, KM & JB. You read Eva so many times, just on the strength of friendship. You kept me in line with your honest opinions and suggestions from the beginning. Thanks for motivating me, sometimes daily, when I wondered if *Eva* would ever go to print. GOOD LUCK WITH YOUR INDIVIDUAL WRITING ENDEAVOURS. Don't ever stop writing!

Sharm, thanks for lookin out early on & knowing that I could do this. RatBoy & WildBoy, ya'll got a part in the tale of the Ghetto Daycare.

Thanks to my family – Bowens, Phillips, Willis, Johnson, Vadel, Holt, Hayes, Cook - for conversing with my Dell Wyle E. Coyote laptop instead of me since October 2005. Even on the cruise to Hawaii! I bonded with *Eva* at every family function and didn't help to clean up, EVER!

Thank you, from the bottom of my heart, to everyone else who gave a damn and believed I had this book in me.

Thanks to the many Urban & Suburban readers for supporting books written by, you for you when the Pink's and Pale's thought we couldn't do it.

Lace, I can never thank you and Melodrama enough for giving this first timer the opportunity to showplace her skills and strengths.

Thanks to the readers who will love *Eva* as much as they will hate her.

I know you'll enjoy *Eva, First Lady of Sin*'s tale of passion with a twist.

Feel free to drop your comments at stormrizing1@yahoo.com

STORM

Chapter 1

Probably the most important memory from my reckless 20s was: feet in stirrups, hearing the doctor say, "You have genital her-pes." What?! I'm in the OB/GYN office and I'm trippin'. It took a minute to register. This can't be happening, I thought to myself. I touched myself gingerly, making sure that this wasn't a sick dream; or worse, a cruel joke. The itching and burning. Herpes? Impossible!

Who was this man? For a moment, the doctor looked like a menacing clown delivering the worst, most horrible, practical joke.

The only thing I was sure of was that my legs were spread haphazardly apart on this examination table, feet resting not-so-comfortably in the stirrups, and this man: was he speaking to me? I couldn't be sure. I looked again. Yes, it was my doctor.

The room was warm, there was noise and the lights were dim. Somewhere, again, I heard the word: herpes. It was then I knew. Now it all made sense. The pain and discomfort: the burning, stinging and itching. Brand had given me herpes.

When the hell had this happened?

My mind flashed back to the last time we'd had sex, about 3 weeks ago. I grinned before I could stop myself, thinking of how Brand had me bent over the dryer in the basement, pounding me from behind.

Then I thought of the word 'herpes' and grimaced.

We were in the basement, washing clothes and measuring the dimensions of the walls, trying to calculate the amount of paint we would need to brighten the unfinished room.

Looking through photo albums and school pictures, we were laughing at Brand with missing teeth and bad hair days, when I came across an unlabeled packet of pictures.

"Hey, what is that?" Brand asked me, reaching to snatch the pictures out of my hands.

"No way, mister, I found it first. With these, I'm gonna blackmail you for my car and my diamond ring." I held the pictures out of reach and turned my back to him.

I pulled out the pictures, shuffled through the first five pictures and loudly cleared my throat. "Make that a brand new BMW." I held one picture at an angle, "Damn Brand, I didn't know you got down like that."

"What the hell is it? Damn it, Eva!" He snatched the picture from me and whistled. "Oh, shit. Give me the rest of them."

"Oh, hell no."

There were pictures of Brand having sex with various women. Other pictures showed two men having sex with one woman. One of the men was Brand.

"You naughty boy. You never told me you could do that." I looked closer at one of the women. "Is that Tammy? The married one with the twins?"

A naked Tammy was on her knees, deep throating Brand, her eyes staring up into his face: no easy feat, trust me. Brand was looking down, grinning, but not at Tammy. Fucking Tammy from behind was Evan, Brand's friend, squeezing her breasts, grinning back at him.

Poor Tammy. But then again, maybe not. A few pictures later showed Tammy grinning with pleasure as Brand came on her face and hair. I hoped the twins hadn't been born yet.

Then I thought, who the hell was taking the pictures? I changed my mind. I didn't want to know.

The rest of the pictures were equally as explicit, showing Brand's dick in every orifice the women had.

Evan didn't appear in any of the other pictures. Damn. Just when I was getting turned on.

"Come here, Naughty Boy. How'd Tammy get you all in her throat like that?" I pulled Brand to me and got on my knees in front of him. "Let me show you what I can do."

We both knew I was talking shit. On a good day, I could only get Brand halfway into my mouth. But it was worth a try.

I pulled Brand's penis out of his shorts. It was soft and small. I sucked it softly into my mouth and throat; it was easy to deep throat it when he was soft. I felt him getting hard and automatically pulled back before I started to gag.

Brand didn't let me complete my mission. Somehow, we made our way over to the dryer. He sat me on the vibrating dryer and pushed his hard dick inside my dry pussy, ripping me on the sides.

We both cried out at the invasion.

"Don't stop." I grabbed his head, pushing myself forward, seeking the release only Brand could guarantee me. I lost myself in thought, kept seeing the pictures in my head. The sight of Tammy sucking Brand's dick, with Evan's dick in her ass, was turning me on and making me wet.

"Too. Fuckin. Tight." Brand gritted the words out between his teeth. He pulled out and turned me around, bending me over the still vibrating dryer.

He pushed himself into my now-wet pussy. I moaned with pleasure.

Two minutes later, he climaxed. "Christ, Eva. I'm sorry." He fell forward onto my back. "Damn. Eva…."

I stayed there, motionless. I couldn't remember the last time Brand had left me hanging this way. I always came. That was part of the charm; part of our magic.

I didn't even get the chance to come. It was over. I pushed Brand off me and went upstairs to repair myself. There was slight bleeding from him ripping into me. Great, just what I needed. And for what?

What a waste of time. Were we losing our touch?

"Eva." The doctor broke into my reverie. "Eva. It's very important that you adhere to these precautions. I need for you to pay attention to my directions."

I felt myself nodding affirmatively to the doctor, to show that all was well in the universe. No, of course I wasn't surprised. Yeah, this happened to me all the time.

But I wasn't listening. My mind was racing!

Brand, that miserable bastard. Brand, my boyfriend of 1½ years. Brand, that nasty, dirty bastard!

No, not Eva. This can't be happening. My God, I'm 21 years old. This type of shit doesn't happen to people my age. This shit doesn't happen to pretty, young woman who are only fucking their boyfriends. This type of shit happens to ugly, desperate chicks, and old women. I peered into the mirror, across the room, to make sure that I was all that I believed I was. I continued to stare at myself in the mirror. I looked at my light brown eyes, my naturally curly, light brown hair. An actual waist, slim legs and arms. A little short on height, but nice breasts (a small C-cup on good days).

Not some nasty-ass disease for Eva, the hottest, prettiest chick in Germantown. Not some funky-ass disease for Eva, who had been practicing being faithful, finally. Not Eva, who never had a STD in her life. And definitely not for Eva, the one who had been so careful in selecting her partners.

Okay, reality check. Now it all made sense. The burning pain "down there" that she tried to ignore; afraid to mention to her boyfriend; afraid that he'd think she'd been cheating. Well, what a damned revelation. He'd been cheating!

Okay, reality check. The clown/doctor was saying something about, "going home and using cream medication for topical pain. And please don't forget condoms for all future sexual encounters." The doctor went on to advise that I may be unable to give birth naturally, as there was a possibility of transferring the virus to a newborn baby. What?

Condoms? For whom? Yeah, I know that we're all told, almost warned, to wear condoms for unprotected sex; but wasn't monogamous sex with your boyfriend more like protected sex? This is fucking surreal. This type of shit only happens on MTV *Real World* episodes and in the movies. Who gets herpes at 21? It couldn't have been that easy to get herpes from Brand. Sex that last time in the basement? That's not possible! Why haven't I gotten it before? What the fuck is happening here?

I'm not even sure how I made it out of the doctor's office. I got into the car, unlocking the door without thinking. The pain throbbed between my legs. I kept thinking of my now-ruined life with Brand. Who else would want me? Who would understand, other than Brand, that this was not the result of countless sexual partners gone awry? How do you say, "I have genital herpes?" When is the right time to broach the subject with a potential life mate? What had I gotten myself into?

The word *herpes* kept ringing in my head. I felt dirty. I felt faint. I was angry and crying. I didn't feel quite like myself. Why me, I kept asking. What had I done? I felt like the only one in the world with the disease. I couldn't think of anyone I could talk to about this. How could I tell anyone? What would I say? Would they look at me different? What the hell went wrong?

Okay, reality check. On the way home now, driving the car that *he*, the dirty pig boyfriend, had bought for me, I thought of the babies I would never have. Was this the payoff? Get a few local trips, money in your pocket occasionally, and all the free apple martinis and appetizers you could ever consume; in exchange for a dirty little nasty disease that would stay with you forever? Some shitty-ass deal.

Okay, reality check. Making a small stop on the way home to the pharmacy to get the small tube of cream to combat the constant pain & itching "down there." Paranoid as hell. Okay, is it me? Is this pharmacist looking at me with a knowing look? Knowing what this cream is for, and what is this attractive, few sexual partners, young, able-bodied woman doing getting this "nasty people's medicine?" I raced from the store.

Chapter 2

Okay, I'm actually home now. A hot shower sounds really good. I'm wondering if the virus could be cured. Yeah, I heard what the doctor said: "No cure, just a way to relieve the symptoms." What the hell did he know? Would it really stay forever? What if I scrub "down there" really well? Honestly now, is this the payback for the shitty things I've done in the past? What goes around, comes around. You know, you could have been a little more honest and possibly nicer to people. But this? This is a crappy-ass payback.

Ok, you're an intelligent chick. Call him. One doesn't talk about these things over the phone. What would I say? How would I do it? Where would I do it? Where do I start? I wanted the confrontation to be sensational!

I could imagine it. Brand, the rich, golden boy, brought down to his knees by little Eva. I imagined confronting him at the community college. I imagined going to his home, accusing him in front of his family. It would be particularly embarrassing to catch him with his friends.

While I was playing out scenarios in my head of contacting the *Philadelphia Daily News* and saving money for a full-page ad alerting the public of a communicable disease on the loose, the telephone rang.

"Hello." I was almost breathless, my mind continued to race. I could only see triumph and victory for me; slander and humiliation for Brand.

There was a female voice on the other end. It wasn't familiar and I couldn't quite make out what was being said. I asked her to repeat herself. I couldn't believe what I was hearing.

"I'm sorry, who is this?" I must have been hearing things. I thought I heard Brand's name coming from the other end of the line; on my phone, a female.

"Hello," she repeated, "I'm looking for Brand." I took the phone away from my face and peered at it. This was unbelievable. This was absurd. This was turning into one hell of a day.

"Brand? Who is this?"

"My name is Sheila and I'm looking for my boyfriend. Is Brand there?"

"Your boyfriend," I sneered into the phone. "If this is supposed to be some kind of joke, sister, this is the wrong damned day." I was ready for a fight. Whoever this was, she was barking up the wrong tree today; or maybe she was barking up the right one. So what, she had nothing to do with what was done to me? I would whip her ass for gp.

Then I stopped. Maybe she had been the one to give herpes to Brand.

Sheila continued, "Look, I don't know who you are and I'm sorry to call you like this. I called Brand's house already; some guy claimed he wasn't there."

This was too much. "No, Sheila, Brand is not here with me right now." I took the phone away from my ear again and looked at it. I almost expected it to fly away. I could not believe I was having this conversation, on this day, especially. I decided to play along with Sheila. "Does he usually call you back?" It was a nasty little slight.

"Yeah, he does. He won't answer his cell phone and he won't call me back." Sheila paused for a heartbeat. "Look, I don't know who you are. I just want to talk to Brand. Wait a minute. Who is this?" She paused as if trying to figure something out or come up with an appropriate comment. She started to say something several times and then stopped. "I need to talk to Brand. I think I'm pregnant."

Just like that. She dropped the bomb on me.

Yeah, well I had one better. It was time to drop MY bomb on Sheila.

"Yeah, well, Sheila, I'm pregnant and my fiancée, Brand, isn't here. I will be seeing him soon, though." I stopped to let her stew in what I'd just revealed to her. Yeah, I'd be seeing his ass soon enough. I'd make sure of it. (For the life of me, I don't know why I'm lying to this child this way.)

"Your fiancée? Pregnant? You can't be. I don't understand. I've been seeing Brand for five months and we're looking forward to having our baby."

"Well, Sheila, I don't know what to say to you. It seems that your boyfriend of five months is actually my man of 18 months. And I'm due in 6 weeks. We know the baby is a boy and I'm naming him 'Brandon Maxwell DeLoache II." (You know, just in case she didn't know his full government name, I was rubbing it on nice and thick.) There was silence on the other end. "Look, this is as much a surprise to me as it is to you. If you're telling the truth and you are pregnant by my man, that's between you and him and your poor bastard baby. I don't have shit to do with that. Are you sure you have the right Brand?"

Why was I defending him, hedging with this girl? I knew, just assuredly as I knew he gave me herpes, that this was the same Brand. Why wasn't I shouting from the rooftops that he was one nasty bastard? Was I crazy?

I was crazy. Instead of hanging up on her, going to find him and bash his empty head in, I changed tactics. I would use this girl the same way Brand was using her: I would take her information on Brand and use it against both of them. Now that I had the upper hand, I decided to roll with it.

"Sheila, honey, how did you get my phone number?" I could hear poor Sheila sniffling into the phone. Brand *was* a good catch, minus the herpes. She was probably thinking that it was too late for her baby to become Brandon Jr. She was probably picturing her house on the hill fading away. Oh, well.

"The last time he was over, I went through his call history when he fell asleep. I saw your number a lot, so I figured the person must be one of his friends or maybe family." She choked back a sob. "I knew something was wrong. He used to make time for me. He used to spend the night." (Oh, really? When was this?) "I don't know what I did wrong. I was supposed to meet his dad and his brother. We were going to Jamaica..." Sheila rambled on for a while. "Wait a minute. Is this Eva?"

I didn't even hear the question initially. My mind was racing. Sheila mentioned a brother and not his sister. I wondered if she knew about the entire family, including Tasha and Angelique. How close had they been, really? Had she been to the family home? I couldn't believe Bethany, Brand's sister, knew this girl and knowingly assisted Brand in deceiving me.

Sheila apparently had very little patience. I heard her sigh loudly and ask me again, "Is this Eva?"

¡Aye carumba! She can't be serious.

"You got it, girl." I almost felt sorry for her. It wasn't her fault she picked my unfaithful boyfriend to like. It wasn't her fault she was sniffling pitifully into the telephone.

Apparently, Sheila wasn't too upset. "I don't believe this. That sneaky bastard told me he dumped you six months ago. And to think I was feeling sorry for him. I let him take your calls when we were together, 'cause he said you wouldn't leave him alone; wouldn't stop calling. He didn't want you to hurt yourself again and I didn't want that on my conscience."

I didn't bother to reply. This was fucking fascinating. I thought quickly of hundreds of things I could say to make her day worse. The nasty, vengeful side of me wanted to make her squirm. That evil, devious side of me wanted to make her cry and leave Brand so that he would be mine, alone. I caught myself. This couldn't be the same Eva who was just questioning her past behavior and wondering if the herpes was the payback for it. I decided that Sheila, whoever she was, wasn't worth it.

"Well, Sheila, you just hang in there if you really want Brand. He should be free, single and available in about 1 hour. I need to go. Watch yourself, though." It wasn't my place to mention his affliction, was it?

"What are you talking about? Watch what?"

"Talk to Brand about that. Look, sweetheart, I've got calls to make and a fiancée to break up with. Don't worry, Brand will call me back. I'll tell him to call you."

I hung up on her protests.

Chapter 3

I *thought about my* conversation with Sheila for a little while. I wondered if she would call me back. I considered a tag team confrontation with her. 2 against 1. Brand wouldn't stand a chance.

I chucked that idea. I didn't need help to destroy this little man.

I left Dirty Boy a voicemail. He called *me* right back.

Once I got Nasty Boy on the phone, I simply said that I needed to talk to him concerning something the doctor told me. Ok. So did he ask me what the doctor said? No. I'm sure Dirty Boy already knew what I was talking about. Or maybe he didn't.

"I'll be there in a minute, Brand." I was going to his house. I would destroy him on his own territory.

On my way over I considered, how one starts a conversation like this? And, crazy enough, why am I suddenly feeling uncomfortable? I didn't do anything wrong, right? Now I'm starting to panic. What if he didn't give this to me? What if I had herpes (the word was so difficult to say!) all along, for years, and didn't know it? Had I given it to him?

I'm finally at Brand's house. My heart is thumping. I suddenly don't feel so brave. I'm feeling tongue-tied and foolish.

Now that I am here, I'm ready to leave.

As he opens the door, Nasty boy blurts out, "Eva, what did

the doctor say?"

Breathe in. Breathe out. Then I get an instant attitude. I mean, shit, I was only having unprotected sex with my boyfriend, right? Then I think about Sheila. Poor Sheila caught up in this nasty shit. Two of us caught up in his nasty shit. Maybe one of us could be saved. I mustered the energy to be angry enough for both of us.

"Look, I went to the doctor because Gena (my vagina's name, of course) had been burning and itching for a week. I hadn't said anything to you because I didn't know what was going on. I didn't want you thinking anything crazy."

Okay, reality check. Nasty Boy is not crying, is he? He can't be. Damned shame, he sure is. He actually said, "Oh, my GOD. I'm so sorry. I can't believe I gave it to you."

What the hell is Dirty Boy saying? Is this happening? He went on to say, "I got it from Jeanine (who?) three years ago. She gave it to me and never explained anything to me. I never gave it to anyone else, so I thought you would be okay. I'm so sorry."

Okay, I'm dizzy at this point. What is he saying? "What do you mean; you're sorry, that you didn't mean to give it to me?" Now I'm pissed. "You gave me this shitty disease that I'll have for life and you never thought to tell me, until now. How many other people did you do this to?" Now I'm on a roll. "You nasty-ass bastard, I should kill you." Now I'm seeing red. "You're so busy fucking these nasty bitches and you give me some nasty bitch disease. I was so careful all of this time! I can't believe this shit."

At this point, I storm out of the house. Anger does not begin to describe what I was feeling and I had a point to prove. I jumped in the car. Yes, he did follow, apologizing profusely. "Fuck it. Fuck you. Don't ever call me again, you nasty bastard. I can't believe you did this to me." I paused for effect before pulling off. "Oh, and call Sheila. She wants to know what you intend to do about your bastard baby."

At this point, I'm angry enough to kill someone. Call me naïve, but I was half hoping that he would deny it, or have some type of explanation. Something other than sorry. I mean, my life is over, right? I'm still itching and burning. Who will want me now? How am I to tell prospective suitors?

I went home and sat in despair. I hate being a damned statistic. Yuck.

I am way too cute for this shit. And this nigga got some gutter bitch pregnant on me?

Fast-forward approximately two weeks later. "I can't believe I'm saying this, but yes, I'll go to the movies with you." Yes, that's Eva talking to Brand. Dirty Boy never stopped calling and I started to get weak. I know you're thinking, how? How could you take him back? How could you so easily forgive him for that ultimate betrayal? What about Sheila? Believe me, I've thought of nothing else.

At least the pain had lessened over the last week. Plus, I'm damaged goods now; who else will want me? We have it together and at least I won't have to tell anyone else about it. Messed up thinking, right? Daddy, where are you?

We called Sheila together, from his house, and he told her that he couldn't see her anymore. They both confirmed that they hadn't had sex. There was no baby. At least I don't feel quite as bad for lying to her. Sneaky bitches. Yeah well, my lie trumped hers. At least that was something.

Fast-forward two months later. Nasty boy and I are officially back together, with our dirty, little secret. I'm there with him, but not quite there. I'm still hurting inside and I still feel tainted. I'm suspicious, jealous and angry. At times, I can't stand Brand and other times, I feel hopelessly connected to him. It makes me angry and resentful, but the relationship has its perks.

Like this weekend, we're off to Atlantic City to gamble, eat, drink and have drunken sex. Actually, we're already drinking as I drive the Audi along Route 42. The reckless 20s remember? You have to be reckless and crazy to drive, while drinking, through New Jersey. Sort of like a black man taking the chance to drive, soberly, through Maryland.

Guess what? He's asleep as usual. Apparently, a girl can't get live company, conversation, entertainment, or head during the 1-hour drive from Philly. His snoring and the silence give me time to reflect back to the early college days, when we met.

Rewind two years earlier.

Chapter 4

My best friend, Taylor, a popular sort with the guys, and I were scoping out the available gents in the CCP (Commu-nity College of Phila-delphia) cafeteria. One floor above, looking down through a long, plated, glass window, no one in particular stood out.

"There he is," she said, pointing downward to a sea of guys. "He's the one in the light brown leather jacket." Squinting, I don't see much.

"Come on, I'll introduce you to him," Taylor said. I hesitated. "Are you coming?" I didn't move. Taylor pressed, "Didn't you say you wanted to meet a guy with money? Well, there he is." Not convinced, I didn't budge. "Look, his family has money. In a few years, he'll join the family firm and then live off their money till he makes his own fortune." I still wasn't convinced. "Okay, he just sent his last girlfriend and one of her friends to Mexico, financed the entire trip, including spending money for both of them." Okay, I was convinced.

When I think about it, there were warning signs all around. I really should have known better. Why was my friend so pressed to hook me up with this guy and his money? Did she know something specific and wasn't telling? What was I missing? Don't be like me, ladies. See the flashing red lights and run, far and fast.

Oh, well, at this point, I was too intrigued to stop myself. Taylor and

I head to the down escalator to meet Brand.

In the cafeteria, we head for the center tables, where Brand sat with a few other guys. Taylor introduced us. "Brand, this is my friend, Eva." Taylor stood in between us and oversaw the introductions. "Eva, meet Brandon." Initially, I didn't think he was much to look at, but attractive enough and nice eyes. The proverbial jock: tall, dark, brooding and bald. I could do this!

Brand was dressed rather nicely, in addition to the brown lamb hugging his body. I thought I caught a hint of a Tag Heuer watch on left wrist and a single diamond winking in his left ear. My first thought was, No. Please, not another drug dealer. I looked into his eyes as he extended his hand. Whatever. I might be willing to take the chance. Apparently, he liked what he saw and I definitely liked what I heard because we exchanged phone numbers.

After we left Brand and his friends, we went to grab lunch and discussed all Taylor knew about him, which wasn't much, other than he treated his women pretty well.

"But what's wrong with him, Taylor?" I needed to know. I bit into one of my chicken fingers. "Why isn't he in a relationship right now? He's twenty-three, right? Why is he sending 'regular' girlfriends on exotic vacations, all expenses paid for them and a friend? I mean, if she was wifey, I could understand. Something just doesn't sound right. There has to be something wrong with him; we just don't know what it is."

"Eva, really! Why are you all paranoid and worried already? Damn, you just met him! How about you concentrate on what you'll get from this dude, and make sure you take me on your first trip out the country. I'm thinking Miami first, and then Brazil." Taylor snickered and bit into her cheese steak, loaded with fried onions, mushrooms, ketchup and mayonnaise. "I'm serious, Evie. You better remember who introduced you to this paid-ass nigga when a sista is in need of a few shekels." Taylor cracked up at herself. She really thinks she belongs on Comedy Central.

"Yeah, well, I just know that he better not be hidin' in the closet with his boys on the down low or no shit like that. I'm serious, Tee. Something has to be wrong with him. He probably has a little tiny baby dick or something. Or one tiny ball up in a shriveled scrotum sack. His breath probably stinks or he has some serious B.O. Either that or his tiny dick is oozing some shit I don't want to know about. Maybe he's addicted to porn or Internet sex. I swear, Tee, I'm gonna disown you if he turns out to be fucked up somehow."

"Stop worrying, please. Let's think positively here. Let's look forward to the money and nice things comin' your way, on the strength of your new rich boyfriend. Shit, girl, even if ya'll don't hook up like that, you could still be side jawn material and get paid. Fuck it, if you only get new boots in the winter, a few bills paid and your hair tossed once a week, it's a come up. What you got right now? Not much, from where I sit. Girl, look on the bright side. Dude stays fly and pretty as you are, you gone have his head spinning and once you put that legendary mouth on him, as you say anyway, he'll be putty in your pretty hands."

We tossed a few more ideas around until we were done eating. I kept my eyes on Brand, wanting to see how he interacted with his friends and the many females who walked over to talk to him. He seemed to be popular and I wondered how that would play into whatever we were going to have.

Who remembers who called whom and how many times we spoke, but shortly thereafter, we went out for a date to Mirabella's on City Avenue. Okay, I was impressed. Mirabella's is a slightly ritzy, almost classy Italian restaurant. Low light. Soft music. Good food. But in a new Audi. Brand confided, almost bragged that he just traded in a 3-year-old Jeep Grand Cherokee for the Audi. And that was the beginning of us. Okay, we had sex about five weeks later and it was pretty good; probably an 8.5 on a scale of 1-10. It was even better when we were drunk, which was most of the time.

Brand and I spent most of our nights eating, drinking and going to the movies. When we weren't out spending money, we were eating, drinking and sleeping at his house. After a while, his family expected to see me and looked forward to me being there. I felt secure knowing that no other women would be welcome in my place.

Brand lived at home, in Chestnut Hill, with his father and an older sister and brother. Bethany and Brighton worked for the investment firm and weren't interested in moving out. Their primary residence was a four-story single; a mini-mansion with a three-car garage and an in-ground swimming pool. A maid service cleaned their house, cooked dinner and washed clothes three days a week. There were six bedrooms on three floors, in east and west wings, each with its own bathroom and den. There were too many fireplaces in the entire house to count.

The home was decorated with priceless antiques and heirloom furniture dated back to the 1800s. Between the estate furniture, the porcelain lamps and polished silver, I was afraid to sit down, turn on lights and eat in their house. I felt much more comfortable in Brand's rooms, where the furniture had come from Macy's and Sears.

Brand's father, Wayland, was a single parent to three grown children who refused to leave the house. His wife dumped him years before and I don't think any of them had gotten over it. Before Wayland made a fortune in investing, the family was normal, middle-class folk, struggling to make ends meet. Brand's mother Trish, however, had delusions of grandeur and wasn't satisfied with a small house, struggling husband and three clinging children. Trish left four months before Wayland made his first $500,000 in the stock market. Their divorce finalized on Brand's fifth birthday and his dad forgot to get a cake and presents. Brand didn't mention his mother and barely remembered her. He once mentioned the disastrous birthday and blamed his mother's absence for it.

Trish moved to Las Vegas to find wealth, fame and fortune at the casinos. What she found was Teddy, an assistant supervisor, pretending to be the floor manager, at the Resorts Casino. He promised her the fortune and fame, but left her with a one-bedroom apartment and two additional children instead. When Brand heard from her last, she was working as a dance choreographer at the Palms Casino and Hotel.

Wayland didn't mention Trish. In fact, Wayland didn't mention much of anything. He was often away, traveling for business and when he was home, preferred the solitude of his third floor, west wing abode. Wayland's private life was just that: private. He brought no women home and answered only the private telephone line in his living suite. He offered his children no information on his personal life and asked them very little about theirs. Wayland's first love was money: making money, investing money, saving money. Money was Wayland's life and not even his children came before it. Brand secretly thought his father was afraid of women and avoided them, along with any possibility of having to share his money with them.

"Eva," Bethany, Brand's sister grabbed me coming out of Brand's bathroom one afternoon. "I know Brand told you about the girls. Can you believe this shit? What the fuck is my father thinking about? Who knew he could still get it up?"

I'm looking at her as if she's grown another head and it's trying to kiss me. "Um, no, Beth, Brand hasn't told me anything about your dad. What happened? Wait, if this is about your father's sex life, please — let's stop the conversation right now. We're going to eat soon and I'd like to be able to keep the rib sandwich in my stomach."

"Oh, damn, can I go? I haven't had real ribs since we were in South Carolina last summer. Anyway, my dad got a call from some woman who says she has two toddlers by him. Can you believe that? Little girls! Not big kids like us. I could better understand it if they were around our ages but according to this girl, she just had them a few years ago.

"Of course, Wayland's claiming that he knew nothing about them, but none of us believe him." Bethany's eyes looked glazed. "Little girls young enough to be my daughters. Who knew my dad was still having sex, let alone, making babies? I cannot believe Brand didn't tell you. It's all we've been talking about. Brighton almost had a coronary and stormed out of the house. We've been tripping for weeks." She scowled and added, "Next time, I'll call you myself. Obviously, we can't depend on Brand for shit. How could he keep something so important from you? Sometimes I hate him!"

Sure enough, a few months later, two young girls came to stay with the family. Wayland briefly explained that they were his children with an ex-girlfriend. There hadn't been much of an explanation for their existence, prior living situation, the location of their mother or why, suddenly, they were there to stay. Brand didn't mention them much, other than to complain that they were always in his bed when he got in at night.

I think they were 2 and 3 years old; too young for school, so his father hired a live-in nanny to take care of them. Brand mostly pretended that they didn't exist. After the sisters moved in, Bethany and I talked about them for hours, often late into the night: brainstorming, as we contemplated who their mother was, where she was and if they were really their father's biological children. There was an almost 20-year age difference between Brand, the youngest, and the sisters. Bethany briefly mentioned court dates and testing for paternity and that was the end of the conversations.

When I wasn't with Brand and his family, I was home with my aunt Mirabelle, with whom I lived. Mirabelle was my favorite aunt and my father's older sister. We lived together in a small, two-bedroom house in Somerville. Not quite Germantown, not quite Mount Airy/West Oak Lane, Somerville rested somewhere in between and was not nearly as well known as other parts of the city. The house was old, dilapidated, and in need of great repair, but it was a safe haven and my favorite place to be. The old, tired house offered more than just a roof over my head: it gave me access to a father whom I didn't know and information that I couldn't attain anywhere else. Mirabelle had pictures of them as children and glorified stories of growing up with the father I only knew on paper.

I had not lived in my mother Mavis' house in five years. She is a fanatical Christian type who knew the entire Bible the way most people knew the alphabet. She spent six evenings a week and most days in church. Mavis cooked at church, sang at church, prophesized at church. Almost every conversation with her began and ended with the Bible. Mavis and I had a difficult, strained relationship and it had been that way since I was a small child.

I have three older brothers, two of whom still lived at home with our mother. My brothers were her perfect children: Ethane, Christopher, and Marcell. They did not disappoint her or cause her shame. Mavis' perfect sons did her bidding, faithfully attended church services, and headed youth ministries. I moved out in my junior year of high school, due to personality and lifestyle conflicts with our only parent. I'm sure my refusal to accept and adopt her Christian way of life had something to do with our continuous rift. Somehow, Mavis and my brothers got along famously.

My father had not lived in our house, with us, as far back as I could remember. As a child, our household was unbalanced and divided, missing a man, missing the buffer and protector between Mavis and me that only a father could provide. I was convinced that not knowing my biological father was the bane of my problems, now and later in life. Somehow, my father managed to come around, get Mavis pregnant each time, and then disappear before performing his magic trick all over again. He did his magic one last time, resulting in the only female child, and got ghost for good. Hmm. Now, could that be the reason why Mavis hated my guts? I'm convinced that she did and does. But, that's her problem.

Aunt Mirabelle was my savior and the love of my life; she was an ageless and timeless wonder who understood my aversion to Mavis and her rules. She'd taken me in when Mavis' holy-roller attitudes and mandatory five-day-a-week church attendance were more than I could bear. My aunt was the biological link between my missing father and myself. With Mirabelle, I learned about my father, Anton, and their upbringing on Wharton Street in South Philadelphia. Their parents were deceased and there wasn't much left of their family. The few members that remained were distant and aloof. Therefore, I lived vicariously through Mirabelle's memories and faded pictures of my father as a child and later, a man.

I believe Mirabelle knew where my father was, but she wasn't telling. I think she was scared of Mavis. I couldn't really blame her. I should have been scared of Mavis as well. I was just stubborn and refused to be bullied into a life of bibles and repentance. I knew, from others and pictures, that my father was a fine-ass male specimen. He appeared to be of average height and size, but the face: GORGEOUS. Olive skin and dark, wavy hair was most of what I could make of his features in the faded pictures. I knew that he had spent time in the Air Force and worked in construction. I guess that made him fairly intelligent and good with his hands. He must have been good with something else, too, because he surely poked up Mavis four good times and ran out on her each time afterward.

There was never an explanation offered for my father's absence, why we didn't see him or if he was even alive, and Mavis refused to discuss it. Apparently, I was the only child of the disastrous union, who was concerned with our absent parent. My brother's were on my Mavis' side; they didn't bother to inquire.

I was convinced that my missing father was the reason that I had problems with men. Why I didn't trust men. Why I believed that every man, in my life, would cheat on me and leave me. Why I wondered if any man could love and worship his woman and children, and not desert them. Mavis obviously didn't have good taste in men and probably passed her dumb-ass genes down to me. Would I have the same bad luck when it came to men? Would I fall for the slick lines and gorgeous face? Aren't you supposed to talk these things over with your mother?

Sometimes, I really hated Mavis.

In turn, I grew closer to Mirabelle, who was always there for me and somehow understood when I needed extra space, a hug or $20. Mirabelle and I have a real, live, Hallmark card-type relationship. I mean, really. She's Italian, kind of old fashioned, and she's older than Mavis. She'd never been married and never had children. What did we have in common, you say? I'm not sure, but when we got together, it was like older and younger sisters living together. I often wondered why I bonded with and was closer to my paternal aunt than I was to my own mother.

Yeah, sometimes, I really hated Mavis.

Chapter 5

So, Brand with his absent mother and I with my absent father some-how managed to build a relationship, attend classes at CCP, eat, and drink a lot. After one more year at college and 66 credits total, I was moving on to Villanova University, a four-year liberal arts college in Villanova, Pennsylvania. Brand was staying behind to finish more classes and pull up his grades. Knowing that he had a guaranteed position with his family firm did little to motivate him to work and study hard. He wanted to transfer with me but Wayland balked and insisted that he complete his A.A. degree.

Brand and I were total opposites, in many ways. Brand was used to money and nicer things while I was a poor, struggling college student. I was from a modest home, raised by a single parent and expected to make my own way in life. There was no wealthy parent and family investment firm waiting in the wings if I fell. There was no inheritance or trust fund to be distributed at ages 21, 25, and 30. I was a full-time student with no money and no wardrobe. I got excellent grades, but that didn't account for much in Brand's circle of friends and acquaintances. I wasn't one of them and no one let me forget it, especially Brand. Luckily, his family didn't seem to mind that my clothes weren't made by designers.

Initially, spending time with Brand was adventurous and exciting. He

introduced me to shopping malls, department stores and designer shops I
didn't even know existed. Occasionally, he'd make fun of the way I
dressed and then make up for it by giving me money or taking me shopping. I was used to wearing rolled-up jeans and Bucks. Brand and his
friends shopped at the Polo shop in Macy's, Bloomingdale's and small
boutiques on Walnut Street in Center City.

He bought me my first pair of designer boots; they were on sale at a
boutique on South Street. I didn't care. The shoes made me feel like I
belonged in their crowd. Now, at least, I looked more like him and his
friends. At that time, Brand's opinion of me and the public persona I
displayed as his girlfriend was extremely important to me; at times, more
important than my education. When I was with Brand and his friends, my
motivation was to bridge the gap between us and make the financial differences less noticeable.

A major attraction for Brand and me was the fact that we were both
driven. We were driven to succeed and, initially, to be together. Of
course, my drive was stronger; it had to be. Unless I married Brand, I
was doomed to work a 40-hour week for eternity. We were young but
we dreamed of a life together and how we'd spend the money I intended
to make and he would inherit. I was steadily becoming accustomed to
having Brand take us out, buy anything we wanted at the mall and then go
to the bank for more money the next day.

Despite our social and financial differences, however, Brand and I
gelled in bed. When we were arguing and fighting, one of us made the first
move and we ended up in bed. When I felt slighted because of something
that was said or done by Brand, he made it up to me by giving me orgasms that shook me uncontrollably and made me lose consciousness.

When I didn't think I loved Brand, he gave me orgasms.

When I didn't even like Brand, he gave me mind-numbing orgasms.

When I was angry, jealous and unforgiving, he gave me orgasms.

When I found phone numbers in his pockets, fought him, and screamed
obscenities in his face, I eventually relented and let him give me orgasms.

There were times when I couldn't tell whether it was the sex or if there
were feelings involved: actual emotions there, hiding in the dark, seemingly present only when we were moving together in the bed, on the floor,
in the car. Our relationship was never static; it was a rollercoaster of up

and downs, dizzying days of good and bad. There were moments so tender and sensual that I cried wondering what I did to deserve this man who was so young, so giving, so everything I ever wanted. Then there were moments so cruel, so heart breaking, so everything Oprah said not to accept from any man in your life.

Taylor told me I was confusing sex with emotions. Wasn't it called making love? There were times when it felt like neither. Sometimes, there was desperation to the act, to us. Sometimes, I felt that there was only him in the world; that he was the only man for me, that I would never love another. Other times, I cursed him. Other times, I cursed myself. It was like a sickness, the sexual hold he had on me. Maybe we had it on each other. I didn't know what to think or do about it, so I did nothing, except accept whatever he gave to me.

Hearing myself say the word *sex* in my head sounds so unfeeling and casual. It wasn't like that, I told myself. It was beautiful. It was warm. It was erotic. Sex was everything Brand told me it would be and everything I had hoped for. But isn't it always like that in the beginning? What the fuck happened?

I had turned into a fucking sap and a wimp for the dick, just like older, casual friends told me not to. I should have listened and started selling this pussy to the highest bidder. Who knows where I could be right now? Married to a baller or something. Professional football, basketball, hockey, handball player — I didn't care. Certainly someone who did not have herpes, or some other dreaded disease. What I wouldn't give to go back.

I don't know what happened to me. I don't know when or how I became such a wimp for men. I used to be at the top of my game: money, dudes — you name it, I had it. I was young, pretty, had a body made for sex and entertainment. Kept my hair tossed. Bought clothes two sizes too small. Wore them as if they were custom made for me. Gave bitches the evil-you-know-you-wish-you-was-me-eye. No wonder Mavis and I knocked heads ALL the time. I had to leave her house when I felt like I was going to snap, cuss her the fuck out and spend an eternity in repentance and eventually burning in Hell. Hopefully, I'd make it to Heaven ½ hour before the devil knew I was dead.

My mind began to wander and I could feel my thoughts drifting away as I remembered the first day I had sex. I don't really recall the times that led to THE momentous event. I do know that I was frustrated and irritated by, tired of, and disgusted with Mavis, her rules, her beseeching eyes. I simply turned to the third boy who asked me for a kiss. Well, he got way more than a kiss, and so did I. He got to cum and I bled for 15 minutes.

My very first sexual encounter was with a boy I barely knew, enacted on Mavis' beloved blue sofa and right in Mavis' living room as she slept one floor above. What was his name? Oh, it doesn't matter. What mattered was the *coup de grace* I felt when the deed was completed. The initial exhilaration I felt to have been deflowered, soiled right under Mavis' nose. It seemed so much of what that I did then was to get back at and get even with Mavis.

Hot damn!

Forget the bleeding. Forget the missing orgasm. What I learned that day was about the Power of Pussy. This hot-ass pussy that had that boy panting, groaning and calling my name. He must have flipped and tossed me in every direction, and came at least four times, but his dick wouldn't stay soft and he kept fucking me for what seemed like forever. (I like to think that it was my hot, natural, virgin sex appeal). He kept saying, "Kym, you about to make me …" and "Kym, you feel so fuckin' …" Things like that.

Okay. Let's set the record straight. This dude was calling out the name I gave him when I met him at a party in South Philly one Saturday night. What did he know? When he approached me, the party was hot and crowded and I didn't want to be bothered. He walked up on me after someone had just spilled my drink on my friend Sandra, with some real 80s shit like, "You got a minute, beautiful?" Of course, I responded, "No." His response was, "That's okay, cause I got five minutes and I'll loan you some of mine." Then he cracked the fuck up, as if he was starring in his own one-hour HBO comedy special.

Ladies and gentlemen, there was a true PIMP in my presence. He laughed so hard and long, that I caught it and started laughing along with him. So, I did give him my alias (Kym) but refused to give him my phone number (who wanted Mavis screaming that I was going to burn in Hell because a boy called me?). I just went along with the program, pretending I was interested in his conversation and accepted more Seagram's coolers. And did I care? Hell no. I wasn't planning to see him again. He got what he wanted and I got mine. He popped my cherry, called me the wrong name and never called me again.

Of course, while he was fucking me senseless, I didn't know what the hell was going. What I did know was that my pussy was sore and I was dry, but I didn't want him to stop. I didn't know SEX would feel this damned good. I loved the feeling of having this boy whisper in my ear, telling me how pretty I was and how good I felt, and I loved the feeling of him between my legs.

When he stopped fucking me momentarily and buried his face between my legs, I thought he was crazy, that we were doing something illegal and that I was going to die or be arrested. His tongue was moving up and down on my clit, slowly, sucking it into his mouth gently. My hips were doing an exotic dance all their own, moving to a rhythm inside my head that only I could hear. Fuck it. I was going to enjoy this SEX thing before the cops came to arrest us.

I was completely inexperienced and didn't even know what he was doing to me. I didn't know what I was supposed to do. He was moaning and slurping my pussy juice, his face wet and slick. He came up for a breath and kissed me with that stuff from down there on his mouth. I kissed him back. What did I know? I was 15 years old. I'd lived with a relentless Christian tyrant and could barely watch TV or listen to anything other than what I called "Bible rock." But fuck that. I felt good. He felt good. I don't think I came but then, I didn't really know.

And then, he was gone. But it was cool 'cause I didn't really want HIM there and I didn't think I wanted him back, whatever his name was. I wanted to see if I had the same kind of power over other boys. Where the hell had I been? How long had this SEX thing been going on? Why had no one told me about this glorious thing called SEX/making love? Mavis, that BITCH. She always kept the good information to herself. Well, no longer.

I was bursting from excitement as I walked the three blocks to M. L. King High School on Monday morning. I was checkin' out the scene from a completely different perspective as I strutted down the street, my thick hips swinging extra hard from side to side. I'm thinking, Yeah, niggas, ya'll know ya'll want this shit. Out of nowhere, I felt sexy, sexual and wanted to fuck. I was checkin' out the guys checkin' me out. It was like a new world. Suddenly, I was noticing men looking and staring from their cars. I wanted to know how many more guys I could make moan and cry out in my ear. I wanted to lose myself in this thing called SEX. I planned to pick out a few new dudes at school and see what I could see.

I had on my usual fare: tight jeans, fitted tee (no matter what the weather), and a pair of Steve Madden loafers. It was my uniform, but no one knew that it was what looked best on me and was relatively cheap. I mean, I was pretty and had a nice body but couldn't afford well-made, expensive clothes. At least, not at first. I was the queen of TJ Maxx and Marshall's.

I couldn't wait to tell my best friend, Dee, the news of my non-virgin status. The momentous news almost gushed from me in school the next day, at lunch, where I munched on my usual fare of barbecue potato chips, pretzels and a Pepsi. Dee, alias Deidre, was my best friend in high school. Of course, I felt the need to give her a nickname and called her "Dee" from day one. We were very much alike when it came to our childhood and lifestyles. Dee was actually two years older than I was but had failed the third grade and started school late. That put her in the same grade and most classes with me. Her birthday was December 23 and I remember always being jealous as she got birthday and Christmas presents within days of each other.

Dee had her own apartment and had worked the welfare system so that they paid her rent and gave her an Access card with food stamps and cash. I think she had them believing that one of her sister's kids was her own, and she was going to ride the wave out until Welfare busted her and prosecuted her for fraud. As Dee put it, it would be worth it to be out of her mother's house and away from her other eight siblings and some of their kids. Her mother was similar to Mavis, except that she was a Jehovah's Witness. Damn, somebody in the world actually was worse off than me. I couldn't even imagine what Dee went through, going to her classmates' houses, handing out the WatchTower *Awake!* Sounds depressing. Dee left home at 14 and never looked back.

Chapter 6

"Dee," I *almost gushed* in homeroom, "wait until I tell you what I did over the weekend. I swear, I was going to call you right after but I seriously wanted to see your face when I said the words to you." I looked around the room conspiratorially and pulled her to me. "I got fucked by some guy at Mavis' house."

"What?!" Dee screeched and had everyone turning around to look at us. Damn, couldn't she see that I was whispering? "When? I can't believe you. We swore that we'd tell each other before we did something. I can't believe you. That's not fair, Eva." For a seventeen-year-old almost-woman, Dee was a virgin and flipping clueless. I guess that Witness thing had gotten to her and she was saving herself for marriage. I still didn't see the difference in fornication and lying to welfare for benefits, but hey…who was I? I had almost let that Christian thing get to me and look what the fuck I had been missing. Great for her. I had other plans.

"Wait, just listen. Dee, it was fucking amazing. This guy was cute and came over after Mavis and her angels went to bed. I was in my room and had to sneak downstairs to the kitchen to call him. Girl, he got to my house in about an hour and started kissing me before he was barely in the door. I met this guy last Saturday at a party in South Philly, when I snuck out of the house and went with Sandra, from chemistry. So anyway, I told him that my name was Kym 'cause he was cute and had a nice body. But I knew Mavis wasn't going to let me out of the house to go out with him, so I got his phone number and gave him that bogus name."

I almost laughed at the memory. "So anyway, girl, he played with my pussy and kissed me to death, his tongue was all over my mouth, making me feel a bunch of shit I didn't feel when I was kissin' the other two guys in the past. I was wetter than when I play with myself and I didn't even know I could get that wet." I tried to ignore Dee's incredulous look when I mentioned masturbating. What? Didn't she? Well, whatever. "He was screaming out, 'Kym,' and I almost laughed in his face except he was moaning and shaking and I was lovin' every minute of it. The best part was that I was doing it in Mavis' house while she was asleep and I got away with it." I wouldn't admit that I was ashamed to look at Mavis' large Bible, opened to Psalms 139:1 on the coffee table.

Dee was just looking at me, kind of in shock and a tiny bit of envy; I could tell, though she wasn't saying it. "So then he stopped fucking me and went down in between my legs and started licking me down there like a dog. I almost stopped him 'cause I didn't know what the hell he was doing, but it felt so damned good." I paused for a few seconds to get my words right. "I don't know how to describe it, but I heard him moan when he put his dick in and lifted my hips off the couch, he put my arms around him and started moving real slow. I wasn't impressed at first, but then he grabbed the shit outta me and started saying 'Kym,' repeatedly. He was sweatin' and makin' noises in my ear and suddenly, I was movin' my hips and kissing him.

"Girl, when this guy finally came, after fuckin' me and flippin' me all over the couch, I got this feeling of power and some kind of coochie hold on him. I wanted to do it again with somebody else. I need to know if this guy is just a lame, or if my shit is that good. Fuck it! I'm going to the varsity basketball practice today. Plenty of fine-ass dudes there." I could see Dee's eyes glazing over. I didn't know if it was from hearing me speak about fornication or if she just wasn't interested in my newest hobby. "You hear me, "I added as a parting shot, "I'm gonna do this again tomorrow. Today is Monday. I promise you that I'll have sex again on Tuesday. Watch me."

And I did. Oh, I knew the next guy's name: Tyrese. Oooh, Tyrese with the big dick. Short, thick and captain of the football team. When I wasn't getting the kind of attention I wanted from the varsity basketball team, I tried varsity football. Twenty minutes after practice, Tyrese fucked me in the gym, bent over the pummel horse. Told Dee that non-believing hater. I think I almost came that time. I remember looking at the size of his dick and wondering how the hell he was going to fit that monstrous thing inside of me. Well, it took a lot of finger fucking and kissing, but he turned me around and rubbed his dick up and down the crack of my ass. I started feeling a tingling sensation in my asshole and wondered what that meant. Tyrese was in my ear, talking, saying nasty things to me. I loved it all. Even though the size of him made me wince each time he pushed his dick way up inside of me. We parted afterward with a lingering kiss and I promptly forgot about him.

I couldn't wait to do it again. I didn't think one time about STDs or pregnancy. All I cared about were the words the guys said to me when they were inside me. The way they hugged and kissed me, telling me how pretty I was, what they wanted to do to and for me. I mean, it was over, right? I was no longer a virgin. No saving myself for marriage. I decided to make the best of it.

There were several more over the next few weeks. I shared SEX once more in Mavis' domain with Jorge, a real cutie from French II. Jorge had me flat on my back on the kitchen table, but that was making too much noise so he bent me over a kitchen chair. Jorge was okay, but he wouldn't put his fingers inside me and out right refused to kiss me down there like my first, the guy from the party. What was his name? Oh, never mind. Anyway, I was mad that Jorge wouldn't do as I asked him, but I let him flip flop on me 'til he was done. Okay, so it felt good. We parted without a kiss or a goodbye. Who needs that attitude shit from somebody getting FREE pussy?

I had SEX with one really cute guy named Mark, who had graduated the year before. He got me in his car and let me ride his dick in the passenger seat. I didn't even know you could fuck like that. Then I realized that I liked having SEX like that: I could control the movement, the depth of his dick in my pussy. Plus, I know for a fact that I finally had an orgasm with Mark. His dick was of average size but between the two of us, we worked that shit out. He surprised the shit outta me when he started rubbing my asshole with his fingers. That just intensified the feelings his dick was making inside me, causing me to cum almost instantly. Hmm. There might be something to this asshole/guy thing. I didn't quite forget Mark as soon as we were done because he did give me my first cum, but we parted ways and I moved on.

Then I did SEX with Overton from Algebra I. We cut seventh period and met at Sandra's apartment. O paid Sandra $5 and we had use of the pull-out couch in her living room. O was okay, though his dick was a nice size. He fucked me missionary style and then I had to flip it on that nigga; I flipped him over and sat on top of his dick. I was riding his dick like Mark taught me in the car. Of course, he was goin' crazy while I was tossin' my hips, ridin' his dick as if it was the last one on earth. When he told me he was coming, I jumped off his dick and told him to masturbate while I watched. He did as instructed and I watched, fascinated, as his semen squirted out of his erect penis and shot in the air, above his head. He was completely soaked by his own juices as I left with a quick kiss and a quaint goodbye. O wasn't completely forgotten at our departure, mostly because he was, at least, interesting. Maybe I could get with O again and we could masturbate together.

This was too much. There was so much to learn, and so many guys to learn from. I needed some sound advice from a seasoned SEX fiend. I needed a fucking friend who could give me tips on how to do this SEX shit right. Dee might soon be replaced by Sandra. Sandra was down with SEX, even though it was just with her boyfriend; but at least she was having IT. I don't know what Dee was doin'; probably reading *Awake!* or talking to Christians about going blind from various sins.

I told Sandra my SEXual tales in homeroom. "Girl, I'm exhausted. But my pussy is on fire and happy. We never knew we were so popular." I laughed like an idiot. "I must've fucked 10-12 guys this month. Where have I been? Why didn't you tell me sooner? How could you keep this shit a secret? I thought you were my girl. You, Sandra, should've put me down sooner!" I looked at Dee across the room, reading a thin pamphlet. Maybe she was considering going back to the Witness program. I slowly shook my head and added, "But, I must be doing something wrong. I haven't talked to most of them again. Should I be talking to them, on the phone or something? Anyway, I'm still broke. I don't have any money and I need another pair of Steve Maddens. What am I supposed to do now?"

"Eva, sometimes you can be so dense. I thought the answer was obvious. What you do now is find some guys with CREAM. Get the money, girl. Don't let niggas get that shit for free. Don't let that dick whip you. You gotta whip that pussy on the dick and all over the man. Make them niggas love you and want you." Sandra smiled and fingered her 1.5-karat studs in her ears. "You work that pussy right, and you can get any and everything you want."

So that's what I did. I think David was the next one. I scoped him out after school, picking up his sister and my best friend, Deidre. Everybody knew that Dave owned three restaurant/bars in North Philly. He was one of the well-known young entrepreneurs in Germantown. No one knew where he lived; not even his main girl. He drove three or four different cars and was constantly switching up his look. I don't know if he did all these things because he had something to hide, if people were after him, or if he just liked his privacy. Whatever; I was going to find out. I just hoped Dee didn't find out first.

I left gym, my last class, early. Why bother, really? We would need what we learned in gym, later in life like when? I went outside, waiting for Dave to pull up to the curb. Well, I didn't have to wait long. Dave's smooth-ass Lexus 450 rolled to a stop in front of me. Damn, I wondered if I would get the chance to run my tongue over his smooth-ass, chocolate skin. He whistled at me, long and loud. "Sexy Eva, come on, take a ride with me. I told Deidre that I would be early and meet me out here, even if she had to leave the last class early. She never listens to me, but you seem like the type to do what I ask."

I always thought Dave liked me. I don't know. Maybe it was the way his brown eyes washed over me whenever he was over at Dee's apartment. Maybe it was the slightly-longer-than-necessary-hug he would give me each time I saw him. Maybe it was the way he ran his fingers through his long dreadlocks when he was concentrating on me. Maybe I was looking for a man with money and he was it! Dave was 23 and had graduated from West Catholic High School, some years ago. He got money from somewhere (I'd probably prefer not to know where from) and bought his first bar two years later. Now he owns three bars that sell excellent mussels and crab legs. Maybe I'd been secretly lusting for Dave and wouldn't admit it, because why was I suddenly wondering what it would be like to lick his skin?

"So where are we going?" I asked as I climbed into the luxury SUV. Dave reached over to give me a hug. The only time I'd been in the Lexus before was the time he dropped Dee and I off at the Borders bookstore on Germantown Avenue. But that time, I was in the back seat and I wasn't up close to David. Dee and I were going to have a latte, decide on a book to buy, and later have a book club meeting by ourselves. I couldn't fucking believe I used to be that boring! Before I found SEX, that is.

"Not too far. Don't worry." Dave's eyes were on me and not on the road. "Damn, Eva, you sexy as shit. I don't know how I missed how pretty you are, all of this time. Are you sure you're the same Eva who's always hanging around my little sister, who's afraid of her own shadow?" He kept looking me up and down.

"I guess that's me. And stop it; Dee's not that bad. She's just afraid of your mother and believes the things she was taught by your faith. Even though she basically ran away from home and never went back." I thought about how ridiculous I sounded and laughed at myself. "Okay, she's a little scary, but that's just how she is. And she's my friend. You're evil." I turned in my seat to look at him, with a smile on my face. "Are you going to be evil to me, too, David?"

"First of all, it's not MY faith. I was already out of the house when little Deidre decided to fly the coop. My mom is crazy and I've been on her bad side since high school. But enough about them. And be evil to you, Eva? I couldn't do that. I wouldn't want to do that."

We stopped in front of a house on Hunting Park Avenue. I didn't recognize the building and watched as Dave jumped out. "I'll be right back. I just need to pick something up and we'll go back for Deidre, okay? Wait for me, please, pretty Eva."

Dave ran around the back of the house and disappeared. I hoped this wasn't what it was looking like. Please don't let him come back here with a drug pack. I'd have to have Mavis bail me out of jail because technically, she was still my legal guardian. The government didn't know that I didn't live with Mavis and her angels. Even then, she probably wouldn't come and get me. That BITCH! Get a grip, Eva, I told myself. This could be perfectly legal and innocent. But what did I really know about Dave, other than he was Dee's brother?

Dave sprinted back to the truck and got in. He had a manila folder in his hands that said April 2005. "Hold this for me, would you, sexy? I told you, it wouldn't take long. Were you okay here, by yourself? Did some crackhead try to sell you a used broom?"

I guess the fear of going to jail was clearly written on my face, because Dave took one good look at me and said, "Don't worry, Eva. I got you." He leaned closer to me. "You believe me, don't you?" He leaned in even closer. "You know that I'll take care of you, right?" His lips were almost touching mine. "Do you want me to take care of you, Eva? You know I'll never let anything happen to you, don't you?" I think I moved forward to close the small gap and we were kissing. A light, teasing kiss at first, and then I opened my mouth and licked his tongue with my own. Oh, my God. I was kissing a real man. A real, grown man; not the little boys who had been poking their little things into me over the last few weeks. I got scared and pulled back.

"Eva, you're about to make me say, 'forget my sister.' Damn, girl, I thought you was a little girl." Dave put my hand on his lap and I felt his arousal. Damn, that was easy! Is that all it takes? Then, almost talking to himself, he muttered, "Let me get away from this little girl before I catch a case." But he smiled at me and said, "Put your seat belt on."

We made it to the school without further delay to pick up Deidre. Before we pulled up to their meeting place, he leaned over to kiss me again and slipped me his phone number. "I wanna take you out with me one night to see what I do, Eva. I want to show you me, without Deidre. I know she's your friend, but I wanna get to know you away from this high school shit. Call me when you get a minute."

Hot damn! These men are going to be the death of me. Well this man, and these boys. Dave was the only real man, and the boys don't qualify as men unless we've fucked and I've reached my minimum and cum three times. Three multiple, elongated, mind-shattering orgasms. You know where you lose your breath and briefly lose consciousness. Where you come to with skin under your fingernails, hair matted, your heart pounding and you hope you know the name of the dude you just fucked the shit out of.

Chapter 7

I *called David two* days later on a Friday night.

"What's up, Shorty?" He sounded cute and thugged out on the phone. "What you tryna do wit' a brotha? Is you tryna see me or what?"

Ok. Great. He obviously hadn't spent much time in school, but who cared? This here thing was all about sex. I put on my sexiest voice and curled up in a kitchen chair. This was our only telephone, other than the one upstairs in Mavis' bedroom and she was out. At church, where else? The "angels" were in the basement practicing for an upcoming Nativity scene at church. I felt like I had my own apartment.

I tried to match his dialect. "I'm cool, *papi*." I felt like a jerk saying the words, but whatever I had to do to get into his pants. "Yeah, I'm tryna see you. What's up witchu?" If I had to continue talking this way, I was going to hang up and find somebody else to fuck.

"How old are you, sexy Eva? Are you old enough to do the things wit' me that I been dreaming about? You ready for this grown man shit?"

Okay. I was scared and shaking on the other end of the phone. Oh God, could I do this? I bypassed the first question and put up a brave front. "I'm ready for what ever you got. I know all about chu, David. I know about the type of chicks you get wit'. I'm wonderin' where I fit in." I was so nervous I found myself stuttering. I had to get this over with before I made a complete fool of myself. "I'm ready for whatever you got. I just don't want Deidre to know, alright?"

"Yeah, I got chu, ma. When can I see you? Can you come out tonight?"

I had to play it off right. I couldn't let David know that I was held captive in my own home by Mavis the Christian tyrant. "When you tryna see me? I'll come to you wherever you want. Let me know what time." I was straight playin' myself and Mavis was going to skin me alive.

"All right, then. I'll pick you up at 8 and we'll go to my house." He blew a kiss in the phone and sent shivers through to my toes. "I'mma grab us somethin to eat. Whatchu like to drink, ma? I need to know if I need to get you something special."

How did I know what I liked to drink? Alcohol was forbidden in our house. Mavis told us that alcohol would kill our brain cells and stunt our growth. I played it off. "Why don't you surprise me? And make it good."

After we hung up, I sat in the chair and contemplated my future. How was I going to get out of the house and get with a grown-assed man, without Mavis resorting to Christian violence and knocking my teeth out?

As it turned out, a sick-and-shut-in church member took a turn for the worst and required an all-night vigil and prayers by her bedside. That must have been a sign. I convinced the angels that I was going to Sandra's house to study, and thanked my lucky stars that they were so stupid and gullible.

I strolled out of the house with my book bag, wondering how I was going to explain it to David. Never mind. I would pretend it was an overnight bag. I saw the Lexus sitting at the curb and prayed that the angels were not watching from the windows. I did not want to have to explain to Mavis how Deidre's brother got into our studying equation.

Damn, he looks good, was my first thought as I jumped into the truck, leaning over to give him a sexy smooch, as I'd seen older girls do to their boyfriends whenever they got into the car. I was not tryna act like some highschooler. David surprised me by grabbing the back of my head and deepening the kiss, damn near pulling me onto his lap. I was going willingly; I would have curled up in his lap, right in front of my door, if that was what he asked of me.

So naïve, and dumb as shit. Well, we all had to learn. Some sooner than others, unfortunately.

"Damn, Shorty, you got my dick all hard an' shit. I'mma stop by Bilal's on Stenton Ave. and grab some fish sandwiches for us." (Hey! I didn't know I was a cheap date then!) Dave reached underneath his seat, pulled out a bottle of Rémy Martin and took a swig. "Here, take a sip. You lookin' all nervous and shit. Calm down, baby girl, I'm not gonna hurt you."

I took the bottle from Dave and took a small sip. I almost gagged from the strong taste. It was my first taste of alcohol and I briefly wondered if I was going straight to hell for lying earlier, and for what I planned to do tonight. I could see him watching me, so I put up a brave front and took another sip. That one didn't feel quite as bad as the first. This grown-up stuff was a lot more complicated than I'd expected.

"Stay here for a minute. I'll be right back. You gon' be okay without me for a few?" Ha. He had jokes. He pecked me on the cheek and bounced from the car to order fish for our dinner. I took another sip of Rémy. I felt like a pro now.

My thoughts were racing. "Wait 'til I tell Sandra about this night. She won't be able to stand it," I thought aloud as I watched David wait in line for our food. Damn, he looked so flippin' good. The more I sipped, the better he looked and the hornier I felt. I couldn't wait to get back to his house.

David hopped back into the truck, jolting me from my buzz and thoughts of what we'd do tonight. "Damn, Shorty. You hittin' that Rémy kinda hard, ain't you? You betta slow ya roll, sweetheart. I don't want you asleep for this. I want you ready to do this thang, ma. You got me?"

"Mmm hmm." Words eluded me. I closed my eyes and David lowered my seat from the driver's seat controls. Now this is what I'm talking about. Luxury, personified.

The next time I opened my eyes, the car had stopped and David was kissing me awake. We were in front of his house and his hand was on my right breast. I leaned forward into his kiss and tried to get my bearings. "Mmm. That's nice, David. I think I could wake up to that once in a while." I hoped I sounded sexy. I was feeling woozy and wanted to please him in the worst way.

"Come on, Eva, let me get you in the house. Can you make it, or do I need to carry you? How much do you weigh? Probably a buck twenty. Shit, I could lift about four of your ass with one hand."

I found my sexy kitten voice and pose. "I don't think I can make it, daddy. I need you to carry me in the house, please."

Without another word, David grabbed the bags and came around the passenger side of the truck, opened the door and lifted me out with his free hand. He gripped me firmly on his hip and slammed the door shut, strolling toward the house and up the stairs leading to the front door. His grip was strong and a little rough as I bounced around in his arm. This was like some real movie shit, and turning me the fuck on!

We got to the living room in one piece and he deposited me on a leather couch. I was still gripping the Rémy bottle and took a swig. My heart was pounding and I wondered what David was going to do to me tonight. He disappeared into the kitchen, returned with two glasses, and came to stand in front of me. Reaching down, he took the bottle from my hands and poured two glasses, handing one to me. I tried to take a small, feminine sip but my head was buzzing and I wanted to gulp the expensive liquor.

I watched David throw back the shot and wipe his mouth on his collar. For some drunken reason, I found that sexy and provocative. "What's up, ma? Whatchu wanna do?"

He was moving in on me and I found myself powerless to do anything remotely close to stopping him. My heart was beating I started wondering what I was so afraid of. This was only a man. Well, a real man, but what was really the difference?

"You what's up, *papi*. I'm tryna be witchu." I was going to gag! Who was this girl speaking? What the hell was she saying? I couldn't continue to speak this way just to get some dick. I absolutely refused to stoop so low!

But I was movin' in on him real sexy and I closed my eyes as my lips touched his body. I crawled onto his lap and straddled his legs with my own. My lips touched his collarbone and lingered as I took in his scent. I couldn't make out the particular fragrance in my drunken haze, but I liked the smell and continued upward.

His body temperature felt higher than normal. He was pleasantly warm and slightly damp; I consumed light moisture beads in my ascent toward his lips. I dawdled on his throat, lightly sucking, running my tongue around in circles, seeking damp skin untouched by my roving mouth.

My left hand trailed downward, expertly alighting upon his zipper where I used my fingertips as if I were a Braille reader, hoping to uncover signs of his arousal. My lips and hand worked in tandem, wreaking havoc on both of us as his sighs and moans excited me, causing my hands and mouth to work feverishly.

I stop to take a swig of Rémy. This shit was feeling good and I wanted it to stay that way. The liquor burned a slow trail down my throat and esophagus and worked its way down until it exploded in my clitoris.

David's hands commenced a movement campaign of their own accord. Hands reached the waist of my jeans (unbuttoned) and tugged diligently. His fingers worked their way between my legs as the alcohol reached my clit and the combined efforts created an explosive orgasm that stopped all traces of movement and breathing.

And with the orgasm, my body was rigid and went slack. My eyes closed and my body settled into something reminiscent of beginning slumber. David felt my descent into oblivion and carried me to the bed. He lay me down on a black comforter and covered my body with his own.

I felt his hands run alongside my breasts, which were standing at attention and still tingling in the afterglow. I felt him slide down my body until his mouth was on my neck, sucking and licking a path to my pert breasts. My body shaper seemed to dissolve into his hands and mouth and my nipples were in his mouth; a stinging, tickling sensation that made them further stand up and salute the flag.

Seemingly lost in pleasure and almost wanting David to devour my entire breast, one at a time, I missed his pause for the cause. With his next movement, he was straddling my chest and rubbing his dick between my throbbing breasts. Back and forth, groaning, grunting, his penis was oozing semen, creating a slick surface for his penis to glide with ease.

Then he stopped suddenly and squeezed the tip of his penis for 30 seconds. I watched in silence as he held himself in one hand and continued to fondle me with the other. Two hands replaced one and his mouth swept my breasts, all over and between them. His lips were back on mine; forcing a sigh from my mouth as his rhythmic tongue challenged mine into a dance.

And with that, he was back up and titty fucking me (as I found out later). His legs gripped my torso in a vise grip, his head thrown back, and his mouth open. His hands alternated between painful gripping to feather-light caressing, his hips working feverishly; semen was running from his penis continuously, the cavern between my tits wet, and the bulbs of my breasts creating a tight, warm hole.

"Eva, I'm coming." It was growled out from between gritted teeth. His admission was an instant boost in my arousal. Part of me wanted him to continue his pursuit; part of me wondered what he was doing to me. I knew it felt good to him; for me, I wasn't so sure. I didn't know lovemaking could take on so many forms.

"Eva, kiss me." It was a command. I felt his body tense and stop. I tilted my head forward to meet his lips in a kiss. His orgasm met my open mouth where I expected to find his moistened lips.

My eyes flew open, my mouth slack, unsure how to respond.

"Drink it, baby." It was a command. "Lick your lips." He rubbed my lips with a finger, coating my lips with his cum. "This is for you; I gave it to you." His finger slid in and out of my mouth, rubbing my lips and on my teeth.

"Suck it." His finger moved swiftly between my lips. Apparently, there wasn't enough movement. His one finger became two, moving vigorously, stabbing my tongue. "Suck it, Eva."

I sucked his finger. It wasn't until later I realized that I was simulating fellatio. Wow. I'd asked for a man. Look what the fuck I got!

Kissing, fondling, petting, stroking and grinding ensued.

I came again.

David came two more times. The last one commenced with semen in my right eye. A sting beyond imagination.

He never penetrated me. Vaginally or anally.

He dropped me off at 2:19 am. I was $370.00 richer. The sick and shut in church member was still sick and shut in. Thank God. The angels were snoring.

I attempted to flush my reddening eye with water.

I didn't hear from David for eight days. When he did finally show up, I didn't care to see him. I had spent every last dime he gave me.

He sent messages through Deidre. She was wondering what was up and why, suddenly, he had the desire to speak with me. I feigned ignorance.

He caught me coming out of my chemistry class. Wait. Isn't there supposed to be security at all schools? Someone mistook this grown man for a sophomore? Can anyone say "stalker"?

"What's up, ma? You been avoidin' me?"

Oh, God, had I really let this dunce shoot semen in my eye? His familiar thugged-out speech once turned me on. When was that? What drug had I been imbibing?

"David. Hello, have you been looking for me?" I pushed forward, surprisingly impatient to get to World History II. "I thought you were through with me. You know, I figured once you came in my mouth and in my eye, you'd lost interest."

I could tell I was angry by my tone of voice and didn't want to talk to him anymore. At least, not right now. I wasn't really fond of grown-man lovemaking. I liked it better when I had control of the situation and knew what to expect.

"What you talkin 'bout, ma? I been busy, makin' moves and tryna get dis dough. I thought you understood. I ain't been avoidin' you, Eva. I'm tryna see you again." He stopped me in the middle of the hallway and lowered his mouth to my ear. "I thought you enjoyed yaself last time."

"David, I got to get to class, right now. I'll get with you later."

I practically ran to class.

I avoided his messages from Deidre.

I was so damned glad I couldn't give him my home number.

Stalker, anyone?

My mind shifted back to the present. I'm trying to remember the Eva I'd been before Brand ruined my life with one, unfulfilled, quick fuck.

After Dave and I ended our thing — and you know they all end, don't you? — I got with him again and made him eat my pussy in his jeep. I stood, bent over his lowered driver's seat and let cum drip into his mouth. I held onto his head and rubbed his face in my juices until it covered his face.

I came again, wouldn't let go, and didn't care.

I didn't call him again and avoided him until he got the message. I told Deidre that he had given me a ride home one day and was trying to give back a book I left in his truck.

Dudes were all the same. Some were just older than others were.

Chapter 8

I *was an older,* experienced Eva, not expecting to have feelings for Brandon or any man. This new Eva was cautious, wiser. This Eva was skeptical, a pessimist and a non-believer. Eva knew what men wanted and what they were capable of. She knew to use caution and to disbelieve most of what came from men, and that included Brand.

So, Brand talked me through my fears.

He kissed me through my worries.

Brand walked me through my tears.

He patiently waited for me. He simply asked that I let him know when I was ready.

How, I wondered. "How will I know?" I asked him.

Brand kissed my doubting face, my pouting lips. "You'll know," he whispered.

I didn't believe him but eventually, I did know.

I let him know by the way I spoke to him, with him.

I let him know by the way I moved for him, with him.

I let him know with everything I knew, when I knew it, as I knew it.

Brand was sweet, but intense. He listened and watched intently as I shed my inhibitions and fears.

With Brand, the new Eva learned to give, to trust.

With Brand, the new Eva wanted to give, to trust.

Soon, Eva was more than willing. She did learn to trust, with caution. She only hoped she didn't regret it.

And then, he made love to her; real love to her and made her forget. This older Eva forgot to doubt Brand for a little while. When Brand made love to her, with her (it sounds so much better than having sex) it was unrushed, unhurried, so unlike the degradation she helped inflict upon herself in Mavis' domain. Brand was an experienced and skilled lover.

From the beginning, there were orgasms; so many orgasms and an intensity of knowing Brand so intimately. The orgasms made me believe in him. The orgasms made me forget for a little while.

The new Eva learned to revel in her relationship with Brand. This new Eva learned to trust and believe. Brands' family acceptance of her only further increased her comfort with him, causing her to shed the last of her skepticism.

Then the telephone calls began. A few, initially, that could be explained away easily to a girlfriend in love. A girlfriend so comfortable in her trust. Later, there were too many instances and she could not deny the significance or their meaning any longer. Brand found clever ways to justify the inconsistencies and the ever-present other women.

"You are so much more than this!" I screamed to myself in the mirror.

"You deserve better than this!" I shouted to myself when I was alone.

And just when it was time to put up or shut up, to make a life with Brand or leave him alone, the itching and burning began.

Then she became the Eva I am today.

I learned to forget and ignore the women. But I didn't forgive Brand. I wonder if I ever can forgive him. Will I ever forgive myself?

I shook myself out of the haze of memories. The many, false memories of what appeared to be, and what really was. The truth and relevance of a STD that couldn't be cured. What was a relationship without trust? I wanted to believe that we had more than good sex and great orgasms together. I wanted to believe that I had not put my trust and faith into someone who would not cherish me. At times, I couldn't get enough of Brand; couldn't get close enough to him. Other times, I could take or leave him. Lately, I could gladly leave him alone.

On some level, I couldn't wait to leave the junior college and Brand behind. I couldn't put it into words at the time but Brand, and our relationship, was draining my spirit. It was actually Brand and his friends: They, a seemingly impossible posse of identical siblings, similar in so many ways and always together. They talked and walked alike. They sounded alike, their language and placement of words, a testament of how much time they spent together over the years. It and they were annoying at times.

Brand and his friends were rich, were used to spending money and compared themselves to other, less fortunate people too often. I was never sure if they did it purposely, knowing that I was not of the same ilk; or if I was simply defensive and too aware of the financial status that separated us. Either way, I was ready for a break from all of them.

Chapter 9

I *was able to* breathe a huge sigh of relief when I made it to Villanova, at last. Finally, there were people like me. There were hundreds of literate people milling around, seeking higher learning. People who rushed from class to class, more concerned with comfort than fashion. I finally belonged.

Villanova itself was an entirely new world, different from anything else I had partaken. The first few months were a difficult adjustment period, filled with endless studying and preparation for classes. For the first time, it was painfully evident that the Philadelphia public school system had failed me, educationally, on many levels. I was studying night and day to keep pace at a private university and with students who thought nothing of the assignments that kept me awake at night.

I don't know how it happened, but I met someone else. His name was Daren and he was a poor athlete, on scholarship, who played basketball and lacrosse.

Oooh, his body! Ridiculous! Incapable of being adequately described. He was long and hard. *All* of him. He had been around and already had a minor reputation with the ladies on campus. He, however, had not had Eva. Daren didn't stand a chance.

Because I felt I belonged, I got involved. I decided to try out for the lacrosse team. Hey, I played in the 8th grade. My form and speed were way off, but my bubbly personality got me the position of assistant manager. Well, it was better nothing.

Because I was the assistant manager, I was in charge of the team members. We traveled to away games together, sometimes spending the night in hotels in other cities. I suppose it was a breach of university ethics to be involved with a member of my team, but Daren and I couldn't ignore the growing attraction for one another.

Somehow, Daren and I started a relationship. How, you ask? What happened to Brand? Nothing happened to Brand. He was still there, too. He was a full-time student, a wealthy eligible bachelor, and —I'm sure — testing the limits, with the ladies at his school. He was only calling me as little as I was calling him. If he didn't complain, why should I?

Anyway, Daren. He worshipped me and followed me everywhere I went on campus. He wouldn't give me a reason not to trust him. If I wasn't with him, I was talking to him or going to see him soon. He made sure I saw him at least once a day; it was his assurance to me that his minor reputation with the ladies would not affect our relationship. Daren was great for my esteem.

Plus, the perks still existed. I had one boyfriend from the right side of the tracks who was willing to buy me the world, or so it seemed. I had another boyfriend who was educated and loyal, with the body of a god. One boyfriend whisked me away for long weekend trips, complete with shopping and all-you-can-drink, champagne. The other one lived on campus, helped me study and write papers. Who cared that he survived on financial aid and educational grants?

Being with Brand wasn't always enough. His obsession with money and his friends seemed unnatural at times. Brand wanted to purchase his first piece of property and traded the Audi for a Range Rover. If I had to listen to the description of his leather truck interior or custom rims again, I was going to kill one of us.

Juggling two boyfriends was tough for the first year, but I pulled it off with aplomb. I can't imagine how neither of the two knew or guessed about each other, but I was good at deception and they were smitten.

During the summer break, I decided to let Daren go for the season. He lived in Florida, I in Philadelphia. Plus, I don't believe in long-distance relationships and I needed to concentrate fully on Brand for a while.

About one week after I sent Daren packing, I started itching "down there" and in the morning, there were red spots in my underwear. Okay, I'll admit it. I gave Daren some "going away, we'll talk soon, and I still love you," sex before he left. Two days later, I could no longer deny Brand sex any longer. It had been about a month for us. I mean, I wasn't a complete whore and slept with each of them only occasionally, if I could help it. It seemed to keep them in check and wanting more.

That night I stood, horrified, in the bathroom and plucked a miniature spot from my pubic hair. I put it on the sink and it crawled! I started to swoon and barely caught myself before I smacked into the sink. I couldn't believe it. Now where the hell had I gotten the goddamned crabs? My mind immediately went to Brand, and then to Daren. Which one had done it? So much for playing it safe.

I took my chances and called Daren in Florida. Of course, he denied all charges. He cried and swore his innocence. I didn't care and continued my verbal barrage. I called him all sorts of names, told him where he could go and promptly hung up on him. He never even thought to accuse me.

But it wasn't over. Approximately 20 minutes later, Daren's dad called me! Can you imagine my face? Apparently, Daren was hysterical and confided in his dad about the entire conversation. His dad was calling to let me know how upset he was and could I please speak to him? Can you believe this? I should have known better. How could he tell his father that I accused him of giving me crabs? Can I pick a loser or what?

I finally talked to Daren and denied any wrongdoing. Eventually, I let him off the hook without admitting anything. At this point, I didn't believe he was the guilty one, but how could I get back with him after this fiasco? I mean, really, his dad? The dad I had already met and might have to face again? No way. Daren was history, for good.

Okay, I know I already said that I never had an STD in my life. But crabs aren't really an STD, are they? Well, I never had any of the majors. You know, syphilis, gonorrhea, herpes, and (don't say it!) HIV/AIDS.

I knew what I had to do. I had to call Brand. I was so sure of myself. It had to be him. There was no one else.

Of course, Brand denied everything. Sure, he had crabs in the past, (Really? When?) But he didn't have them now. Now that I'd mentioned it, where did I get them? Now I'm defensive, almost caught, but I wouldn't give in. I pretended indignation and promptly hung up, blaming the university toilets. Oh, well. It was my fault and I ultimately paid the price.

Okay, reality check. To the pharmacy, I go for crab shampoo. How embarrassing. I took my little cousin to the store, declaring a case of head lice to anyone who would listen.

Back at home, I opened the package. What a cute little comb! With a locked bathroom door, I put the lotion on my pubic hair, combed it through and killed all of them, hopefully. Good riddance.

Did someone say I had to microwave my underwear?

Chapter 10

Intense memories, indeed. I needed to get back into real time. I shook Dirty Boy to wake him as we started across the bridge leading into Atlantic City. As usual, the entrance into Atlantic City was brightly lit and beckoning, welcoming all potential gamblers to come part with their well-earned dollars.

Before I met Brand, the furthest north and south I'd been from Philadelphia were New York and Virginia. The Motel 6 and Red Roof Inn were the fanciest motels I've spent the night in, so any time in A.C. was, indeed, a treat. We had reservations at Showboat Hotel and Casino. The Mardi Gras Hotel was always lavishly and garishly decorated and inviting. It was our favorite place to eat and gamble in the city. After losing a fifty in the dollar slot machine, we checked into our suite on the 16th floor. We never got a single room during our frequent stays in case some of his friends stopped by.

Because I had so seldom seen such opulence, I marveled at the size of the rooms in the suite, which were ours for the entire weekend. There was a small bar stocked with beer, brandy and whiskey. No thanks; we had two bottles of champagne for each night of our stay. I opted to eat peanuts and chips instead; the bubbly was for later. I turned on all three televisions — two in each room and one in the bathroom — and every light in the suite. Somehow, I managed a nap despite the bright lights and blaring televisions.

It was approximately 10 p.m. and he wanted to have sex. No thank you. I wasn't drunk, nor in the mood, and I was hungry. Plus his breath stank.

Luckily, I was saved from any further sexual advances as there was a knock at the door. Relieved, I rushed to answer it. I glanced through the peephole and inwardly gasped. It was Evan, Brand's best friend. My panties got wet as I stared. I prepared my brightest smile and I was instantly in the mood for sex. I yanked open the door and frowned. He was not alone. There was some tomboy 'thing' with him.

"Sexy Eva," Evan whispered in my ear as he hugged me close to him. He dragged the tomboy with him and didn't bother to introduce her/him. I wasn't even sure if it was a girl. Damn, please don't tell me Evan was bi. Things would be so much nicer if he were alone. There I was, contemplating his sexuality while yearning for him, all because of this boy/girl with him.

Let me say that Evan and I had this silent, almost non-existent, flirtation thing going on. He was cute beyond belief and built like a demy-god. He was one of Brand's closest friends from childhood.

I met Evan a few weeks after Brand and I got together and had an immediate physical/sexual attraction to his gorgeous face and body. He apparently had a similar reaction to my looks because we stared at each other in the small, crowded club all night. I wanted him to know that I found him attractive and got a rush from my careless attitude. It was a huge slight against Brand and completely disrespectful, but I didn't care. I knew I would never act on it.

Later, I continued the flirtation, staring and eventually touching, because it was my way of getting Brand back for giving me an incurable disease.

We never ventured beyond knowing looks, staring, and casual brushes up against one another in crowded places. Once, I massaged his bulging penis under the table as we sat next to each other in a restaurant. He was hard and I was tickled. We'd been glancing at each other all night and rubbing legs when we could. It was a risky and shocking move for both of us, but that was the appeal.

We found each other mutually attractive and knew that we'd never do a damned thing about it but continue to flirt in secrecy. He would never tell Brand. He couldn't. He'd have just as much to lose as I, if not more.

Evan had no proof and Brand would kill him for, if nothing else, the disrespect.

Anyway, Evan's tomboy was dressed like a model. A short, mostly unattractive model, but she'd taken the time to put her clothes together and it showed. Evan must have spent a fortune on TB, trying to cover up her lack of looks. Well, it worked and compared to TB I was, again, looking like a bum.

I had a mini-wardrobe, but nothing in my closet compared to what TB had on that evening. Unless Brand bought my clothes himself, I spent a portion of the money he gave me and pocketed the rest. At the Villanova, you looked like a moron if you dressed above sweats and cut-off jeans. I had a growing money-market account that would make TB look like a welfare mother in a few years.

Evan and TB came in bearing gifts. Grand Mariner, Hennessy, and for me, a bottle of Moët. Evan always gave me little gifts when he saw me with Brand. I don't think Brand thought anything of it, but Evan and I knew what it meant.

Brand stepped out of the bathroom, shook hands with Evan and hugged TB. Oh, so they've met before. When, I wondered? I'd never seen her before. I stored the information away for later.

We started drinking, talking about people we all knew, and places we'd been. Evan and I started flirting and grew careless as the night continued. TB pulled a vial of cocaine from a gigantic Louis Vuitton bag and I immediately wondered if the bag was real. It probably was. Bitch.

I declined the cocaine and gave Brand the look to do the same. We were many things but drug users, we were not. I told Brand that I wanted to play the slots and to come with me. We left Evan and TB there to indulge in their mess, alone. I secretly hoped they wouldn't have sex. What if he got her pregnant?

We got to the casino floor and Brand handed me $100. Instant attitude.

"Is this it? Brand, you've got to be kidding." I stood in the middle of the casino floor, staring at the single bill. "What the hell am I supposed to do with that?" I was getting loud and attracting attention, but I didn't care; they were strangers. "Shit, Brand. I'll be broke in 45 minutes and then what? Come looking for you and beg for more money?" I was completely pissed and wanted to slap his face.

"Look, Eva. Evan owes me some money and this is all I have right now. Try to appreciate the fact that we're here for the entire weekend. I'm not made of money and I just spent $900 on the rooms." The bastard actually put the money away. "I'm tired of you always complaining about what we don't do and what you don't have, compared to everyone else."

Brand started to walk away and then turned back. "Either you want it or you don't. Take what I'm offering or go back up to the suite. This conversation is over."

I didn't believe he was short on cash. Maybe Evan owed him money. Maybe he didn't. Brand didn't come out of the house with less than $2500 in his pocket. He was being an asshole. Maybe I should have had some not-so-drunken sex, after all.

Swallowing my pride and cursing his very existence, I conceded and put my hand out. "Whatever, Brand, just give me the money. I can't believe you're acting like this." Sarcastically I said, "I'll take *all* of this money and get out of your way."

Of course, I lost it all in 20 minutes so I started looking for Brand, and found him shooting craps. He was up $500 and not quite ready to quit. I began whining and complaining of hunger. Fortunately, he started losing and down to $425, I finally got him to leave.

We went back to the suite where TB was passed out, thankfully, on one bed. Evan was watching college football. Or maybe college football was watching him. He looked high and disoriented when we woke him. He briefly glanced over at obviously cocaine-induced, semi-conscious TB. Evan looked even better minus TB attached to his hip. We let her sleep.

We called down for room service (burgers, chicken fingers & wings, mozzarella sticks, fries, mussels, potato skins; munchies food, you know) and when it was delivered, we ate like refugees.

At about 2 am, Brand and TB were passed out and Evan and I were tired of flirting in silence. I suggested that we all go down to the casino. Again, the money problems continued.

Once again, I had no money. Once on the casino floor, Evan handed TB $500. Brand pulled me aside and handed me $150. I had an instant attitude. What was this slight? He couldn't be serious. Hadn't we just gone through this a few hours ago?

I mean, seriously. I was Brand's main girl and I got $150. TB was Evan's flavor of the week and got $500. I was beyond pissed.

Okay. Here come the repressed feelings that I carried with me every day. I had never actually said it to him but Brand owed me, in more ways than one. No, we'd never spoken of the herpes incident since the day I came home from the doctor, with the news of it. However, in the back of our minds, it was always there. At least in my mind, it was.

Did he think I had forgotten? Did he think clothes and material items made it all go away? Did he think I'd gotten back with him because of love? (That damned disease came back once a month, at least, and this was how he repaid me?) Oh, no. He owed me big time.

Even on the quarter machines, I'd be broke in one hour. Then I would be forced to hunt him down, again, and wait patiently until he handed over more money; if he handed over more money.

I deserved better than that. With an incurable virus I'd be forced to carry for life, I'd earned better than that.

I stood there, in silence, looking at the money Brand was holding out to me, and watching TB happily count hers. I didn't think of embarrassing Brand in front of Evan and TB; I was too well schooled for that and Brand had trained me well. I said and did things to and with Brand in front of strangers that I dared not do in front of his friends...

The look in my eyes spoke volumes, yet I silently took the money Brand offered and thanked him. I sulked off to find the nickel and quarter machines, with TB in tow. I stretched the $150 out for 1-1/2 hours and kept giving TB dirty looks. Eventually she caught on and left. Pride and attitude kept me from finding Brand and asking for more money. I went back up to the rooms.

Chapter II

Guess who was in the suite alone? Evan was asleep on the couch and TB was nowhere in sight. Evan looked even better now that Brand was on my short shit list. I stood over him, watching, wanting to reach out and touch him. I suddenly envisioned all sorts of nasty things we could do quickly.

Instead of sexually assaulting him, as was my initial inclination, I decided not to chance it and sat down at the desk instead. Evan awoke and sleepily mumbled, "What happened, Eva? Lost all of that money?" Smartass. I really tried not to stare. Evan looked so damned good.

Suddenly everything was different. Normally Brand was with us; someone was always around. This time, we were alone in this room. My mind was wandering. I couldn't concentrate. I faintly heard Evan speaking and snapped myself into focus.

"What did you do with Brand, and where's Lisa? (Oh, is that her name?) Come here, sexy." I almost looked behind me for the person Evan was talking to. Surely, he wasn't speaking to me.

My heart and panties leaped at the same time. I licked my lips and thought about the condition of my breath and Gena. I mean, there was no way that Brand was getting sex tonight; maybe not even this weekend. Why was he asking me to come over to him? I was almost afraid to guess. Was I really walking over to him? Yes, I was! Evan grabbed my hand and pulled me, face forward, on top of his lap. I put my hand down first. Hard again. I smiled, slowly lowered myself on top of the bulge in his pants. I felt guilty and excited at the same time. I started grinding on his bulge, moving around in slow circles.

Was he going to kiss me? Looking at his lips and feeling his bulge, I hoped so. Instead, he reached into his pocket, pulled out some money, counted out ten one-hundred-dollar bills and handed it to me. One thousand dollars. Just like that. "Let this be our secret. Okay, pretty girl?" Transfixed, I could barely respond. Evan grabbed my hair and kissed me and without even thinking about it, I kissed him back. His tongue invaded my mouth and I thought, what am I doing? He then kissed my cheek and my left ear. He then pushed me up and toward the door. He grabbed his bulge and the remote at the same time. "Leave, Eva. Now."

I wanted to leave; I really did. I really meant to leave. Maybe I was tired of being treated like shit by Brand. Maybe I wanted to know what Evan was really all about. Maybe I had gotten with the wrong friend.

I told myself to get up and walk away. I heard myself say it. I glanced at the door and thought of locking it.

Instead, I lowered myself to the floor, on my knees, in front of him. I ran my fingers over the bulge in his pants. I licked my lips and put my mouth on his penis through his jeans.

"Eva, don't do this right here." Evan grabbed my head and pushed my face down as he said it. Apparently, he wanted it; he just wasn't sure where and when he wanted it.

"Shut up, Evan. Just let me do this. I've wanted to do this for so long." I pulled his hard penis out of his jeans and kissed the head. My mouth started to water and I licked the length of it. It was smooth, soft, and chocolate...

I put the head in my mouth and sucked softly. I stuck my tongue in the tip and tasted his semen. I grabbed the base of his penis and licked up and down, my tongue and hand following each other. Evan moaned his pleasure. "Eva..."

I was scared of being caught. I was excited. I wanted more of Evan. Brand, who? I briefly thought of the unlocked door.

I sucked Evan hard and fast, moaning and humming. I stopped sucking and pulled back. Then I sucked harder and massaged him with my hands, looking into his eyes. Evan grabbed my head and stuck his tongue into my throat. He pushed my head back down and guided his dick back into my mouth. Evan had my head in his hands and he was pushing himself out of the chair and further into my throat. I was gagging and choking and I loved it.

I felt myself getting wetter and my panties were soaked. I stroked my clit and pushed two fingers into my pussy. He pulled me up from my knees and onto his lap and kissed me, pushing his tongue deep in my mouth. I kissed him back and sucked his tongue into my throat. I giggled, thinking that his dick had just been in the same place.

Evan kissed me for a long time, breathing hard and moaning into my mouth. He pushed me off his lap and started pulling my jeans off my hips. Through my panties, he licked my clit with a soft, wet tongue. I pushed my panties aside and put my clit on his lips. My clit was swollen, hard, and big, like his dick.

Evan roughly pushed my legs apart. He grabbed my waist and pulled me forward. He licked his finger and pushed it into my anus. I leaned forward, kissed Evan harder, and pushed down further on his finger.

My legs buckled and I felt myself explode as my first orgasm rocked me backward. Evan turned me around and pushed me down onto my knees. With my ass in the air, he replaced his finger with his tongue. I felt myself falling into another orgasm when he stopped.

I was turning around to complain when he grabbed me by my throat and pushed me forward. When he yanked me backward, I felt his dick rip into my pussy and I screamed. Evan seemed oblivious to my scream, his face intense, his hips and body relentless as he pushed forward, filling me completely and then in retreat. He choked me harder.

During my second orgasm, I thought of Brand.

Evan said something like, "What the fuck am I doing…?" and choked me harder. He leaned forward and bit my ear. He fucked me so hard I thought I would split in half. I felt faint and when I thought I would pass out, that I couldn't be fucked any more or any harder, I came again.

During my third orgasm, I thought of Lisa.

Evan's orgasm rocked us both and I thought of nothing.

Though I'm sure it was only minutes, it seemed like hours later when

I was finally able to move. I slowly put my clothes on and remembered that we were not really alone.

I felt scared and excited.

The thought of being caught by Brand or TB was making me horny again.

I ran to the door and pulled it open, almost hoping Brand and TB were near by. I was so turned on and breathing hard, I had to lean against the wall in the hallway. I couldn't believe what had just happened. I couldn't believe what Evan and I had just done.

On the way back down to the casino floor, counting my money, I thought, that's the way a man's supposed to treat a woman. Brand, if you only knew. I'd find a way to get him back. I'd already started. I wondered if I'd end it with Evan.

On the elevator, I felt Evan's semen slide out of me and fill my panties. I giggled in delight. It was sinful. It was wonderful. We didn't use protection of any kind. I was thoroughly delighted. Maybe I would fuck Brand tonight and let him taste his friend in and on my body.

Apparently, I *had* picked the wrong friend.

Chapter 12

Brand and I spent a week in Atlantic City and two weeks in Maryland at the Baltimore Harbor. We amused ourselves exploring and shopping, running around town, drinking, eating and having drunken sex.

Then I missed my period. Okay. Meant nothing; just a little lateness.

I started feeling nauseated. Okay. Meant nothing; just bad food.

Then my breasts leaked milk. Okay. I could no longer ignore the obvious signs.

My initial reaction was to panic. I had slept with Evan, unprotected, and been having sex with Brand almost daily. Plus, I had been guzzling mixed drinks and tequila shots for three straight weeks.

I wondered who the father was.

What the fuck was I going to do with a baby?

I put it out of my head. It was easy to pretend that nothing was going on. Weeks passed and I'd still done nothing and told no one.

I decided to call Taylor; she'd know what to do. She and the abortion clinic staff were on a first-name basis. But did I want an abortion? Should I tell one of them or both? Did either of them have the right to know about the baby?

As usual, I didn't know what to do. Emotional and confused, I called Taylor.

"Taylor," I wailed into the phone, "I'm pregnant."

"Hello? Eva? What are you talking about? What time is it?" Apparently, I was waking her up, at 2:30 in the afternoon.

"I'm pregnant, Tee."

"By who? Girl, are you sure? How do you know? Did you see a doctor?"

I sniffled into the phone, "Not yet. Nevertheless, the test is positive and my boobs are leaking. I'm scared and I don't know what to do. Tee, how did this happen?"

"I can't believe you're waking me up like this and I'm more than sure you know how this happened. I can't believe this shit, Eva; what the hell were you thinking?" Taylor was awake now and not too happy about my announcement. "Why the hell am I asking you, by who? Does Brand know?"

"Nobody knows. I didn't tell Brand yet. I need to talk to him. But first I wanted to talk to you." I paused, not quite ready to reveal my secret from Atlantic City. I quietly added, "I think I should talk to Evan, too."

"What!" Taylor screamed so loud I had to pull the phone away from my ear. "When did you fuck somebody named Evan?" Taylor hesitated. "Eva, please tell me that it's not Evan, Brand's best friend. Damn it, tell me that you did not fuck Brand's Evan." She didn't wait for an answer. "Are you fucking crazy? I can't take this shit. You are crazy! Brand is going to fucking kill you, and I am going to watch."

"Taylor, please. I need you on my side. I'm sorry I didn't tell you about Evan. I was going to, I swear. It just happened one night when I was really pissed at Brand in A.C. Evan had this ugly girl with him and Brand was being cheap and it just happened."

"Where the hell was Brand when this 'just happened' thing was taking place? Where was the ugly girl? What the fuck were you thinking?" Taylor stopped and took a deep breath. "Goddamn it, Eva. You're supposed to be the careful, cautious one. Trust, me, this is not something you want to make a habit of. I know. I know. Who am I to talk shit to you, right? I think I have frequent attendee miles with the Elizabeth Blackwell Clinic."

"Tee, you're supposed to be on my side."

"I know, Evie. I just can't stand to see you come this far without getting caught up in the cycle, to start this dumb shit now. AND you don't know who the father is. Come on, Eva. Maybe I'd be a little more understanding if it were just some other, regular guy. But Brand and Evan?"

I would hate to see you play yourself out with Brand on some bullshit charge, like fucking his best friend." I could hear Taylor cursing to herself under her breath. "Okay, Eva, look. I know that I'm the last person you want to hear this from. I'm sure you've heard enough about this shit when you were home with Mavis. I'm done with preaching hour and I know you already feel bad enough. You don't need me adding to it. What do you want to do?" Taylor stopped again. "How long have you known that you are pregnant?"

"About 25 minutes. I'm still looking at the blue line on the test. And I haven't thought about anything. I didn't expect this to happen. Brand and I are usually so careful. A baby would be okay, if I knew for sure it was his."

"Eva, you've got to make a decision. Now, before it's too late either way. Evie, I hate to put it to you like this, but your options are slim right now. Are you sure, you can pull this off? Will you be able to get Brand to go for this, if you have this baby? Have you even considered abortion? I know this is a lot, but you have to get crackin' on making a decision. Believe it or not, before I had my first abortion, I was against women killing unborn babies. Yeah, well, Tom, Dick and Harry later, and I was an old pro."

"Tee, I can't tell Brand that I slept with Evan. You're right; he'd kill me. I can't have this baby. Evan and Brand look nothing alike. Brand would know." I stopped talking and started to cry. "Tee, what if I want to keep the baby? What should I do?"

"First, you're going to the doctor to get the test confirmed. Then you're gonna find out just how far along the pregnancy is." She paused and took a deep breath. "We'll wing it from there."

I loved Taylor. She always had the answers for my problems. She couldn't solve her own problems for shit, and was constantly wrong about the men in her life, but was always on point for me. Taylor was secretly scared that all of her abortions would damage her body, she'd confided in me one night. She was afraid that she'd meet Mr. Right and not be able to conceive or carry a baby to term. When it came down to me having unplanned pregnancies and abortions, she was more like my older, concerned sister.

As it turned out, I didn't have to do anything. The OB/GYN confirmed the pregnancy and I decided to keep the baby. I'd deal with Brand and Evan later. I stopped drinking and partying with Brand. I couldn't avoid him altogether but I did my best to hide my condition. I made plans to convert my bedroom into a nursery and picked out baby names. I was gaining weight and leaking more breast milk. I loved every minute of it.

College. Career. Owning my own home. A brand new car. Vacations to the Caribbean. Everything took a back seat to the thought of my own child. I talked to myself, convinced myself that I would not be like Mavis. This baby's childhood would not be like my own. This baby would have a mother and father who would love and cherish them. My baby would not have a crazy mother like Mavis, or a disappearing father like Anton.

I continued to hang out with Brand, secretly glancing at Evan when he was in the vicinity and openly giving his chicks the evil eye when one was present. Brand and I went to dinners, comedy shows on South Street, but I avoided going to bars, as we used to. I always pleaded a headache or being tired, anything not to be around alcohol, needing an excuse for why I wasn't throwing back shots of tequila.

The weeks were passing quickly and I still hadn't done anything other than go see the doctor every four weeks for a checkup. Even though I knew my life was in shambles, I knew the importance of having a healthy baby and that monthly obstetrician visits would keep me informed of my baby's health. Once I thought about mentioning herpes and then quickly banished the thought.

I worried constantly that my outward appearance was changing and wondered when others would start to notice the change in my body. I didn't know what to tell Brand and simply carried on as if there were nothing wrong. I mean, I was smart, right? I would figure it out as I went along. And maybe, just maybe, I'd be able to convince Brand that it was his child, even if the baby looked like Evan. Come on, now, stop it. We all know that folks only see what they want to see, even if it was obvious to everyone else. This would be Brand's first child. I could do this!

Then I miscarried the baby at 3 ½ months. It was probably what I deserved and it surely took the worry and stress off me. But I was sad. I'd gotten used to the idea of having a baby. And I thought I felt the baby move a few times.

I called Taylor as usual.

"Tee, I'm losing the baby."

"What!? Eva, what are you talking about? Is something wrong?"

"I'm bleeding and cramping. It feels like something's being pulled from inside me. I'm scared to go to the doctor's office."

"Eva, where are you right now?"

"I'm home, at my aunt's house in the bathroom. Aunt Mira is home but she doesn't know I'm pregnant. I didn't want her to find out like this." I was crying into the phone and starting to panic. "Tee, can you come over here?"

"Eva, calm down. I'll be right there."

I was on the toilet, doubled over from the pain, holding my stomach, legs wide open and watching the blood pour into the bowl. I was stifling my tears, hoping that Aunt Mira wouldn't need our only bathroom before Taylor arrived. This was a flippin' mess.

Taylor got to the house in 15 minutes, stuffed three Always pads in my underwear and we crept out of the house. She rushed me to the Chestnut Hill Hospital Emergency room in her '91 Nissan Stanza.

"Please, my sister needs help. We think she's losing her baby." Taylor lies well under pressure and I reminded myself to be impressed later. Intake nurse Benson looks bored initially but one look at my pale and perspiring face shifts her into gear.

Things speed up quickly. An orderly and a wheelchair appear before our eyes and I am whisked through the emergency room doors and down the hall to a private room.

I can feel blood pouring from my body and I say a silent goodbye and prayer to my vanishing baby.

Two hours and three doctors later my miscarriage was confirmed. I was admitted to the hospital for observation. An overnight stay and I would go home tomorrow alone, without my baby.

After mourning for a few weeks, I put it out of my head and decided that it wasn't meant to be. I worried about explaining to Brand that I wouldn't be able to have sex for a few weeks. What a joke. I didn't even see him until it was time to go away again. The summer picked back up as if it never stopped.

The rest of the summer was a repeat of the weekend in A.C., and one long week in Miami Beach. More of the same, hardly changing: suites in the hotels, shopping, eating and drinking.

Chapter 13

Thankfully, the summer was over and I was back at Villanova. I'd had enough of Brand for the moment. I didn't break up with him; I never did. I just took station breaks from time to time to get my life back on track and to focus on me. Sometimes I needed extra time to get over the anger and hurt that seemed to linger. At times, the money wasn't enough. I knew the money and lifestyle couldn't make up for contracting the disease, nor take it away, but I thought Brand could do a little better to help me get over the rough times that I still had.

I was also tiring of Brand and his lifestyle. Brand and his friends were rich, flashy and arrogant. Their idea of a good time was drinking all night, literally throwing money at admiring females and buying rounds at the bar for everyone. My idea of a good time was curling up with a cup of tea and a good book. I still don't know how we got together and stayed together.

I was finally a senior at the university. Studying was kicking my butt and I was grateful for the space I'd asked of Brand. That, however, wasn't going to last.

September merged into October and suddenly it was November. Brand's father called to inquire about Thanksgiving and our plans. I didn't even realize that the holiday was a few weeks away.

Aunt Mirabelle and I spent Thanksgiving Day at the estate with Brand

and his family. The sisters, Tasha and Angelique, blended into the family as if they'd been there the entire time. They kept us entertained with dance recital steps they learned in ballet class. Tasha was 10 months older than Angelique was, but they were about the same size and looked like twins. Most times, I couldn't tell them apart so I avoided talking to them when I could.

It was difficult to believe that Wayland was still making babies at his age. I could hardly believe he had fathered the two toddlers that were running around. I wondered if he had more kids we didn't know about. Apparently, Brand's dad was quite the stud and couldn't keep his hands or other body parts off their young mother.

I tried to picture a handsome, graying, Wayland making babies with a mysterious Christine, the "college student." It certainly made one wonder what was going on there.

Was Wayland robbing the cradle with a teenybopper? Was Christine an aging granny-type, trying to recapture her youth? Either way, thinking of a 50-something Wayland making babies at his age was a thought to behold.

Bethany grabbed me coming from the kitchen with my third mimosa. "Eva, this whole thing is really weird. Dad won't tell us anything about Christine, but we know she's young and the girls are telling us 'Mommy's in college.' We don't know whether than means she's a 21-year-old college student or what. We think she's somewhere around our ages. This is sick."

"Who is she? Where's she been?" I was more curious than concerned. This was like the soap operas. "Have you seen her yet?"

"Nobody knows who she is. Brighton swears he's going to slap her when he sees her and Dad isn't saying anything, as usual. He's acting like he has babies every day. As if we, his grown children, don't have the right to know about our younger siblings."

I felt for her. She looked worried about her dad and their entire family. The sisters had changed the dynamics of the family. They were either going to bond the family closer together or pull them apart.

"I don't know if Brand has mentioned it, but we're pushing Dad to use his connections to get a paternity test as soon as possible. What if they aren't even his kids? This is way too much, I swear. They are cute though, aren't they?"

I had to agree. I just didn't want them touching me with their sticky hands.

Thanksgiving and Christmas passed by quickly and suddenly it was a new year. My month-long holiday break from Villanova was over. I started the New Year on a positive note, armed with the knowledge that this was to be my final semester in college, as an undergraduate.

Chapter 14

Running late to class one morning, I was waiting for the bus when a BMW 745 stopped in front of me. As I got a closer look, I could see that the side doors were scratched and peeling. But it was a new BMW, so I decided to overlook that.

Warning sign, ladies. We all know what car scratches mean, right? A female is the only living being with enough balls to mutilate a man's car. I should have run far and fast.

The passenger window rolled down and this major cutie, with perfect white teeth, grinned at me. Caramel brown skin, light 'stache; almost beautiful. Oh no, I thought, way too cute for me.

BMW Cutie said, "Beautiful, let me be your chariot and whisk you off to…"

I cut him off. "Stop it, please. It is way too early in the day for this bullshit." This was my tough, I'm-not-attracted-to-you, speech. I'm thinking, shit girl, this man is gorgeous. Then I'm thinking, go away, I don't have time for this shit.

"You are way too pretty to curse so early in the morning. You sure you don't need a ride?" BMW Cutie needed to work on his pick-up lines.

I silently cursed Brand for not buying me a car and told BMW Cutie, "You're starting to resemble a stalker." I'm thinking, I really hate you,

Brand. I'd seen his friends' main girls. I was the only girlfriend who didn't own, or at least drive, a car.

BMW Cutie stated, "I know a brush-off when I hear one, but at least take my phone number, in case you change your mind."

It was early and I was tempted: He was too damned cute and I was trying not to respond to the entire gorgeous man/car package. Plus, I already had a boyfriend. But I couldn't resist. I stepped forward to take the phone number, which was written on a Sprint bill. BMW Cutie's name was Cory.

I made it to school and got into my studies. Cory's phone number was tucked away, into a zippered pocket in my book bag, and promptly forgotten.

School was getting harder and I was sorry that I hadn't gotten a better secondary education, after all. I was studying constantly, most times well into the night. Weeks passed and there was no let up. I was stressed out, Brand's weekend trips had become more infrequent and my financial aid grant had been denied. Graduation was looming for those who had paid their tuition in full and I was exhausted from studying every night, all night.

I was late again, waiting for the bus, when Cory's BMW stopped in front of me. This time, he got out of the car. Yummy, he was tall too. I barely smiled when he said, "Don't tell me, you lost my phone number."

I didn't say anything. I just patted the zippered pocket of my book bag.

"Well, say something," he said, "I've been waiting to hear from you. Didn't I mention that I don't bite?"

"Look," I blurted out, "I have a boyfriend."

"Yeah, I know. I saw you with him last week. You got out of his Range in front of your house." Oh, really. So he was a stalker.

I decided to be honest. "I'm sorry, Cory. I forgot about you. I put your phone number away and got immersed in my studies. School is really rough right now and I've been stressed out."

Cory just stared. I could tell he wasn't used to being brushed off and forgotten. He apparently didn't like it.

He looked up the street. He saw my bus was coming. "Just tell me to go away and I won't bother you again." He was annoyed and I was intrigued. I couldn't resist.

I wrote down my phone number and handed it to him. Oh, shit, I thought. What if he knew Brand? I reached for my number but he was already grinning and backing away toward his car. If this was a set up, I was busted.

As if he could read my mind, Cory said, "Don't worry, I won't tell Brandon." Oh, well. Shit happens.

Mr. BMW Cutie Cory didn't call for five days. This only added to my stress as I waited for Brand/Cory to bust me. Then he called. He thought it was funny, making me wait, knowing I was stressing.

Yes, Cory knew of Brand. He didn't actually know him, however. What Cory did know was his reputation; of his fondness for the ladies. Really? "You look much better than Brand's last girlfriend." Gee, thanks.

Cory didn't want a girlfriend. He'd just broken up with one. Maybe this girlfriend was the one who scratched up the BMW, I considered. I wondered if she was okay with being broken up with. It didn't look like it. Cory became a little vague when I asked about the reasons for the breakup and the damage to his car.

As it turns out, Cory just wanted to take me out. As it turns out, I wanted him to take me out. I couldn't resist, so I agreed.

Chapter 15

We went to a small restaurant in Manayunk, with patio tables. It was chilly, the menu was in French and I was impressed. It was obviously expensive (no prices on the menu) with few patrons. I'd seriously doubt that Brand or his friends would be there, ever.

We talked about our lives, families and friends. Cory lived in Glenside, PA, where he owned a townhouse in a gated community. Since he did not live in the city, when he was there, he spent most of his time at his older sister's house in Logan. His younger sister lived in Lindenwold, NJ with her boyfriend and children.

Cory worked for PECO, Philadelphia's only electric company. He was 26 had a small son named Corey. Oh no, I thought, a kid. Of course, there was always something with the cute guys. That's why I usually stuck with the not-so-cute-guys. The knowledge that Cory had a child was a complete turnoff and something I didn't think I'd want to deal with.

After an obvious lull in conversation and apparent lack of further interest, Cory asked if I was okay with his being a parent.

I told him I honestly didn't know and that it was a first for me. I had never dated or even gone out with a man with kids, and wasn't sure how I felt about it. I did, however, appreciate his concern. He was winning points in my book.

Cory volunteered information about the non-existent relationship with Corey's mother. They had been broken up for 6 months and things were not going well between them. She, apparently had a jealous streak and wanted them to get back together for the sake of their son. Way too much information. This was dinner and drinks only. I decided that it didn't matter that he had a child. Really, who was I to complain? I had a boyfriend, right?

Who remembers who called whom and how many times we spoke, but shortly thereafter, Cory and I were inseparable. Cory was a much-needed diversion and I was happy to be with him. We didn't wait long to be intimate and we moved quickly from small kisses to almost daily sex all over his house.

Sex was good with Cory; not great like Brand, but more than adequate. Cory had an ass fetish and couldn't keep his fingers out of mine, whether we were in private or public. At the movies, Cory insisted that I wear short skirts so that he could fondle me at will. During a horror movie or comedy, I began to look forward to the eventual invasion of his fingers stroking my pussy into an orgasm. Other times, he would slowly insert a wet finger into my anus and finger fuck me for the entire two hours of the movie. I would be out of my mind, wet and so horny that we rarely got out of the parking lot before I was straddling him at the wheel of the BMW.

Cory patiently introduced me to anal sex on the sunroom couch. I'd had plenty of fingers in my ass over the years but no one even attempted to put a dick up there. Cory had been talking about it for weeks but my denial was always quick and the subject dropped. Then one night, after he served me dinner of garlic, angel hair pasta with mussels, shrimp and scallops, he brought it up again. I was slightly drunk from the red wine he purposely served with dinner and my denial was slow in coming. Cory took that as a sign of acquiescence and slowly pulled off my clothes while he kissed me breathless.

After more wine, I found myself naked and kneeling on the all-weather couch, in the sunroom. Cory slowly rubbed the opening of my anus with his penis, applying gentle pressure and then replacing his penis with his tongue. I could feel his tongue up in my anus, licking softly and then harder, tickling me on the inside. I felt myself responding to the pressure of his tongue by moving my hips backward, riding his tongue, thinking that Brand could take a few lessons. I could feel an orgasm building, the involuntary movement of my body to the rhythm and pace of my hips. Then his mouth and tongue were replaced with his penis.

The pressure wasn't all unpleasant initially, as I felt the head of his penis enter me, slowly moving in and out. Bold now, feeling the orgasm again on the horizon, I pushed backward and was shocked; feeling pain and pressure as the widest part of his penis stretched my asshole wide and immediately moved forward in retreat. Cory hugged me tight, murmuring words of love and appreciation, how good I felt as he slowly pulled me backward again telling me, over and over, to "relax."

I could feel his penis pushing forward again and this time, prepared myself by relaxing my entire body, bracing for the pain. Cory impaled me an inch at a time until I could feel his pubic hair on my ass cheeks. I slowly rocked myself around, enjoying the moans and words of pleasure as Cory held himself still, waiting for my body to accommodate the seven inches of penis in my asshole.

"Fuck me," I heard myself say. I couldn't believe I said as much but I didn't have to wait long. I could feel waves of pleasure as I slowly rode his dick in my ass. With a long moan, Cory withdrew his dick, pulling it almost completely out of me and then pushed his dick as far into me as he could. The pain and pleasure combined was enough to make me jerk my hips into a fast rhythm with Cory as he fucked my ass as if it was my pussy.

Minutes later, without warning, I felt him swell inside me, urging me to come with him. I was moaning and riding, caught between pain and shock to my system and the desire to reach the elusive orgasm. I reached down to rub my clit and surprisingly felt it engorged and extended. I masturbated, riding Cory in my ass, stroking my clit vigorously, reaching orgasm as Cory let out a long, moan and came in me. I felt his semen shoot up into my ass and sighed with satisfaction.

Cory pulled out, moving up and down my body as he kissed my neck, shoulders and back. He held and caressed my body, telling me that he couldn't believe I took him that way, that he'd never felt anything like the feel of my sphincter muscles gripping him, pulling an orgasm from his body.

"That was intense and painful," I whispered to Cory, wincing, as I caught my breath, the lingering pain more evident as we lay on the couch. "I'm glad you enjoyed it."

"I'm sorry, Eva, I didn't want it to hurt you." Cory rubbed my back and cheeks, whispering that he was sorry, asking what he could do to make the pain better.

"Just rub down there, 'cause it stings."

Cory surprised me, moving down my back, licking and kissing as he moved toward my ass. I felt his tongue enter my stretched anus, licking and sucking slowly. His soft, wet, tongue continued to work magic as I felt his semen slide out of me. I thought he would stop and wondered if he realized that he was licking his semen as it ran from my anus into his mouth. Cory slowly licked, sucked and massaged with his mouth until the pain diminished and I started to fall asleep.

My last thought, as I fell asleep, was what kind of man had I hooked up with that licked his own semen from my ass, after he so willingly put it there?

Chapter 16

Brand gave me a car in February. It was a used, gold Mitsubishi that I named the Gold Coast. It wasn't much to look at, but it started when I turned the key and I no longer had to catch the bus. I felt really guilty for taking the car when I was fucking Cory on the side, but that didn't stop me from driving it to Cory's house when Brand thought I was studying.

Honestly, I thought I deserved a new car. Brand was being elusive and often difficult to catch up with. I started to believe that the car was a gift designed to distract me from his disappearances and the time we no longer spent together.

I started to really consider my relationship with Brand and all that we were and were not. I thought I loved Brand, but now I wasn't sure. We didn't talk much and saw each other even less. The sex was great when we had it. Honestly, without the amazing sex, we may not have been together as long. Despite the physicality of our relationship, having sex with Brand often reminded me of that fateful day, so long ago in the gynecologist's office. I was still hurt and angry about the disease and his unwillingness to discuss it.

I felt myself pulling away from Brand for the first time. I attempted to talk to him about my feelings, about our situation, but he refused to discuss it. His attempts to downplay the situation angered me even more. He acted as if we could pretend that the disease hadn't happened, that he hadn't given me herpes and affected my entire life. I was angry, confused and in need of someone to talk to.

I thought, for the first time, about leaving Brand and our past behind. I worried about our commitment to each other. I knew the lack of communication was the key to our problems. I wondered how much further we could go and if we had anything to sustain our relationship. So often, with Brand, everything came back to sex; sex and great orgasms. Sadly, sex was what kept us together initially and a sexually transmitted disease was what connected us now.

I was angry and confused because I felt dirty and guilty for keeping a secret from Cory. Didn't he have the right to know about my disease? I felt like damaged goods and good enough only for Brand. I knew the disease could be controlled with proper hygiene, condoms and medication. What I didn't know was how anyone else would feel about taking risks, sexually, with me.

I didn't have anyone to talk to about my feelings. Brand wouldn't talk and I was too embarrassed to tell any of my friends. Not talking to Taylor about IT was killing me. I talked to Taylor about everything, all day, every day. We kept no secrets from one another, except this. I had to tell her; I just had to muster up the courage to admit IT to someone other than my OB/GYN and primary physician. Somewhere I read that 7 out of 10 people have the disease, though no one I knew was admitting it.

I tried to imagine telling someone about it. How would I start? If I told them before sex, would they continue to see me? If I told them after we'd already had sex, would they be ready to fuck me up? I knew they had the right to know. I would want to know. What would I have done if Brand had told me up front? Would I have called him? Would I have had sex with him?

I knew the answers to all of my hypothetical questions. I would demand to know about any diseases up front. I would not consider a sexual encounter with an infected person for one minute, if they told me up front. I know it sounds horrible and selfish compared to my own oxymoronic standards, but somehow I justified it in my mind. I was playing with fire and I knew I was wrong. It didn't, however, stop me.

I called Taylor.

"Tee. What's up, girl? You busy?"

"Like that ever stopped you, Eva. What's up? This better be good, 'cause you know I'm busy and I have company."

"I don't know, girl." I sighed, thinking that I had too much going on in my head. I wanted to be able to talk to Taylor. I mean, really talk. I needed a shoulder to lean on, to cry on. "I'm fuckin' trippin' and goin' through it over this Brand and Cory thing. I'm goin' crazy, I don't know what to do."

"Eva, what do you want to do?" Sometimes, Taylor made thing seem so simple.

"I'm not sure what it is I want to do. I like Cory a lot and I think I still love Brand. But then, I think that Brand and I have gone about as far as we can go."

I stopped talking. "You sure you got time for this? Look, you said you had company, so I can call you back."

"Eva, don't worry about it. It's only Chris and I just put his ass to sleep. Plus, you are way more important than he is. What's the deal?"

"I'm confused 'cause I don't know who I want to be with. I feel committed to Brand for the time we've put into our relationship. But then, I'm feelin' Cory for what we have right now." I was going back and forth, in my mind, between Brand and Cory, trying to figure it out as I went.

"For one, Cory's a talker. We communicate on a completely different level than Brand and I ever have. And we talk about everything. We've talked about marriage, having kids, education, family. I could go on all day. We connected right away and I love who I am with him." I could feel myself smiling just thinking about him.

Taylor broke into my daydream. "Okay and Brand's an asshole. He ain't been putting the thang down right, lately. You haven't been happy at all. Ya'll been going through somethin'. I just can't figure it out and you ain't really talkin about it." I could almost hear the sneer in her voice; see the grimace on her face. She was probably feeling guilty because she was the one who introduced me to Brand. But I let her finish.

"Sounds like a slam-dunk winner for Cory. I know you been with Brand for a while and it's probably easier to stay where you are, but why put yourself through the hassle and heartache? Maybe it's over. Maybe it's time for a change. Obviously, Brand ain't all you thought he was gonna be and all this Cory shit is a sign."

"I know, Tee. I want this to be a sign. I'm hoping for a sign. I love everything about Cory. I love the time we spend together. I love the compliments he drops on me. I love that he does exactly what he says he's going to do. I can depend on him." I stopped and laughed at myself, hearing my own words. "I guess I pretty much know what I want to do. I guess I have to make up my mind to do it."

"Which I knew you would." Taylor wasn't impressed and said so. "I don't know why you do this to yourself, Evie. You always have the answers. You just need to hear yourself say the words and move on from there."

I don't even remember the rest of the conversation. I listened to Taylor; I always did. I heard the wisdom and truth in her words but she didn't know the whole story. I'd never confided in her about the disease and since she didn't know, she couldn't give truly accurate advice. I wanted to tell her right then. I wanted to scream out the truth and get it over with. This shit was going to kill me. For sure.

I continued to see Cory almost everyday. We carried on as we had before. I spent all my free time, and some that was a little more costly, with him. I was ignoring Brand, plain and simple. My attention and affection were elsewhere. I knew what I was doing, and at times, didn't especially care. I called myself pouring my soul into my burgeoning relationship with Cory. Apparently, I didn't know what the hell I was doing.

Cory didn't talk much about his son and I didn't ask. It was as if he knew I didn't want to be bothered, I'm ashamed to say. I should have paid closer attention to Cory's lack of commitment to his only child. I was with Cory almost daily and rarely saw his son. Selfishness prohibited any self-acknowledgement of how much of Cory's time I monopolized. Least of all, I should have questioned the small amount of time Cory spent with his son. Any other woman would have demanded answers.

I ran wild with Cory in my free time. Most times, I thought little of Brand and our fading relationship. My time with Cory represented the carefree Eva I wanted to be again. With Brand, I constantly had to face the disease I so desperately wanted to forget. With Brand, I was angry, confused, and tired of the controlled lifestyle that revolved around not spreading herpes, trying not thinking about herpes. I was saddled with

Brand's sexual branding, intentional or otherwise. Cory represented the carefree Eva I was when I met Brand. I didn't know her anymore, except with Cory.

I thought I still loved Brand and attempted to spare him any unnecessary hurt and humiliation. I didn't initially flaunt Cory or any other man in and around the city of Philadelphia. As I'd mentioned, Brand had trained me well. I wasn't goin' out like a nut. I was torn and unsure of my actions but I wouldn't play myself. Cory and I began and commenced our relationship like any other, only in secret. We went to Delaware and places in southern New Jersey to be together and not be seen.

Then I lost my mind. We got bold and careless and started going to local malls and movie theaters. We were bowling at the Thunderbird bowling lanes in Willow Grove the first time I ran into one of Brand's friends. Initially, I froze. Then I spoke and moved on, acting as if it wasn't a big deal and I wasn't busted. I was sure I would hear from Brand shortly. I braced myself for the eventual confrontation.

However, Brand didn't mention it, so I didn't mention it either. I wondered if his friend told him that he saw me with someone else. I thought about avoiding Cory for a few weeks, and then quickly dismissed the thought. I thought about all I had been through with Brand, my newfound happiness with Cory, and decided to chance it. I waited for the eventual confrontation from Brand and continued to see Cory.

Cory and I enjoyed sneaking around and texted each other with secret codes. Out with Brand, I'd get a text from Cory with his secret code. It resembled a telephone number but it was to let me know he was thinking of me.

The extra attention was flattering and a definite distraction from Brand. I started looking forward to my time with Cory and the attention we drew around town. We were an attractive couple and constantly drew attention from the opposite sex, even when we were together.

Cory wanted to buy me some new lingerie. Of course, I had to visit Victoria's Secret. No average mall would do. I wasn't going back to Willow Grove, though the mall has a Vickie's. I was putting time and distance between Brand, his friends and myself. The King of Prussia Mall, at the end of I 76 W, is an oasis of designer boutiques and every major department store imaginable. Louis Vuitton, Gucci, Coach,

Movado. For the underprivileged, there was Guess, Limited, Express and Aldo.

Cory and I strolled through Neiman Marcus so I could eye the shoe department and make my wish list. I felt safe and uninhibited. We were openly affectionate, giggly and chased each other through the men's department. Then we ran into another friend of Brand's. This time, I knew I'd have to say something to him. He wouldn't take two acts of indiscretion lightly. I had some thinking to do. I needed to make a decision.

Chapter 17

I *decided to break* up with Brand.

Needless to say, Brand wasn't very happy about my decision. Amazingly, he asked me if I told Cory about having herpes. I reminded him that he hadn't bothered to tell me. Brand was hurt and asked me if I was sure about my decision. I honestly couldn't say that I was, but when I attempted to draw Brand into a conversation about my feelings about us, he cut me off.

It was a typical Brand conversation, talking about only what he was comfortable with. In an attempt to hurt and embarrass me, Brand told me that he had slept with sixteen women during our relationship. I was shocked and outraged. I wondered if he was telling the truth.

With that information, my decision was swift and surprisingly easy. I told Brand it was over and was momentarily stunned at my actions. What was I doing? I had just given up my safety net. Cory knew nothing about my herpes. What if I gave it to him? Was I making the right decision? Who would I talk to about the disease? No, Brand wouldn't talk about it but we knew about each other. The herpes was an unspoken link between us that I had just broken. I hoped that I didn't live to regret it.

At that point, I simply walked away from Brand. Apparently, I was doing the right thing after all, now that he'd confessed to bringing sixteen women into our relationship without my permission. I hoped he'd been using condoms, for their health and mine.

I entered into my full-time relationship with Cory, guilty and worried about giving him herpes. I had broken down and talked to my primary doctor about the disease so there were new pills and creams to help the outbreaks. There were times when I thought very little about the disease and times when I thought of nothing else. I played out scenarios in my head of Cory confronting me with the knowledge and, at other times, I pictured myself confessing about it.

Soon the outbreaks were less frequent and I put the disease out of my head for months at a time. Then there would be the inevitable signs, like the tingling in my left leg and swollen glands in my pelvic area. Some days the outbreaks would come on strong, with a vaginal discharge and severe pains that affected the way I walked. Other times bumps would appear and be barely noticeable. I could never guess the severity of the outbreak; I just had to be ready for whatever happened upon me. I did research on the Internet and learned that avoiding stress was a major factor in keeping the outbreaks at bay. The stress, however, was much harder to avoid as I finished my senior year in college.

Then in a matter of two weeks, my life flipped and things quickly changed. My grant appeal was denied a second and final time for various, unsupported reasons. The fast pace of the private, Catholic university and a full course load was finally catching up to me. Stress was hounding me from all sides and when I should have been focused on my studies, I was worried about ways to battle the disease.

My senior year in college was difficult in many ways. I'd opted to live on campus, for the true college experience, despite living 10 miles away. What was I thinking? The tuition, however, was more than I could ever afford and without the needed grants, it appeared that I would not graduate with my class. That knowledge, coupled with an 18-credit course load, was apparently more than I physically could tolerate.

My body changed rapidly and without warning.

I was breaking out almost weekly and the stress and pain became almost unbearable. The disease was driving me crazy. I was months away from completing my B.S. degree, yet nothing seemed to be going right. I was snapping at Cory and picking petty fights and I didn't know why. It became harder and harder to continue the pretext that all was okay in my life.

There were times when I was hysterical in private. I would have multiple crying jags for 10 to 15 minutes at a time. I would then go to the bathroom, wash my face, and then carry on as if nothing happened. These sessions took place all too often.

I thought I was going out of my mind. Was this what I had to look forward to for the rest of my life?

Where had the real Eva gone? I almost couldn't believe that I was the same fine-ass chick who had my pick of men a short time ago. I wasn't taking pride in my appearance; I was letting myself fall apart.

I had not told Cory about my disease and, truthfully, not intended to do so. I told myself that I loved him and then immediately questioned my actions and myself. If we were truly in love, wouldn't he be accepting and forgiving? I told myself that he deserved better. Instead, I learned to pay close attention to my body and its reaction to stress and foods. When I felt an outbreak approaching, I would immediately reject Cory sexually. There were many ways to get out of having sex without making it obvious. I became a master at them all.

There were times, however, when I made mistakes and didn't protect us as diligently as I should have. I learned to have sex favoring a particular side to avoid Cory coming in contact with an area that I thought was contagious. I read books and articles on ways to avoid spreading the disease and made every attempt to spare Cory the horrors I lived with daily.

There were other times when I really didn't care about any of it. I took careless chances, sexually, with Cory too often. I wasn't angry with him and it wasn't that I didn't care. I was too tired of living my life worrying about sex, condoms, positioning, having babies and spreading herpes to someone I cared about.

I wanted to be normal again.

I wanted to curse Brand, to embarrass and shame him. I wanted to hang outside his house or follow him in his car and warn every available young woman to watch out for him; I didn't want any unsuspecting woman to be swayed by the façade of the healthy, eligible bachelor. I wanted someone else to know; maybe every woman should know about Brand's affliction and the havoc it would wreak on her life. I was still so angry and wanted to strike out at someone, anyone for the unfairness of what happened to me.

Apparently, I hid the disease and the guilt well. I seemed to be a mastermind at deception, but what choice did I have? I wanted love and adoration from Cory, not fear and revulsion. I wanted our lovemaking to be spontaneous and uninhibited. I didn't want him to hesitate when it was time to make love, fumbling for condoms, wondering if this was the time that I would infect him. The guilt was mounting and it got to a point where I thought of leaving Cory and simply being by myself. I wanted to be with Cory; I just needed to figure out a way to do so and be honest with him.

Cory and I discussed our relationship, our life together and the possibility of having children. I knew that I wanted to wait until I finished at the university before having a child. I also knew that there was the possibility of passing on the disease to a newborn and wondered how I might explain that to Cory if it happened. There was too much to think about; too much to care about while I was busy living.

I wanted to be normal again.

Chapter 18

After discussing my financial dilemma with Cory, he offered to borrow $6500 from his mother to pay my tuition so I could graduate on time. I was elated when Cory told me to concentrate on completing my studies and not to worry about the loan from his mother; he would pay it back as a graduation present to me.

Our sex life had improved steadily since Cory introduced my anus to his penis. It hadn't taken long to realize that this was Cory's preferred method of lovemaking. After a few months, my body adjusted to his penis in my mouth, vagina and anus, sometimes one after another, all in the same night. I could honestly admit that I enjoyed Cory in me, in every hole and could easily reach orgasm with him in my mouth, ass or in my pussy.

Cory's sexual appetite was wide and varied and I enjoyed every aspect of it. Cory was what I called "nasty" in every way possible and I discovered a side to myself that had been waiting for a man like Cory. I stopped questioning his sexual methods, and wondering why seemingly, atypical sex excited him, and simply accepted him for who he was.

I would sit atop Cory, riding his penis in my ass or pussy, bringing him to a swift orgasm and then stand over his face as his semen dripped from my body onto his face and into his eagerly awaiting, opened mouth. Once

I knew what he wanted, what turned him on, what he liked; I gave it to him at every opportunity.

Cory would fuck me missionary style for 45 minutes, fingering my asshole, moving back and forth from my pussy to my mouth with his penis, only to withdraw when he came and spill his semen onto my stomach. He would then move up my body to kiss my mouth, invading my mouth with his tongue and now-flaccid penis. He would then kiss down my body and lick his semen from my stomach, eyes closed, apparently enjoying the taste of himself in and on my naked body.

Cory's favorite fellatio position was to sit me on the floor in front of the couch. He would then lean my head back on the seat of the couch straddle and my face with his knees on either side of my head. Using the back of the couch for support, he would fuck my mouth for an hour, grinding in and out, often smothering and leaving me gasping for breath, while cleverly maneuvering my head in rhythm with his hips. Then he would come into my mouth without warning, only to immediately kiss me, pushing his tongue deep into and around my mouth to share the taste of his seed before we both swallowed it.

Cory's appetite for his own semen became commonplace and I stopped questioning it: I simply got used to Cory coming into an orifice on my body, only to immediately lick and suck it from it's hiding place. Sometimes he wanted me to taste his semen, to suck it from his tongue, other times he was content to imbibe alone. At times, he forced his semen-laced lips onto mine, holding my arms down, unable to escape his grip. Cory could come again, immediately after the first, as he sucked and licked himself from me, sometimes grinding on me, sometimes simply grinding into the air, just the movements enough to arouse him and bring him, again, to orgasm.

Because I enjoyed myself as much as him when we shared our juices in the bed, I did as he pleased most times without complaint. There was one circumstance, however, where I put my foot down and refused to budge. I didn't care if Cory loved the taste of his seed as it ran from my anus, and he came there often, but I refused to allow him to come near me until he brushed his teeth, which was oftentimes the next morning. I had my own limits to his freakish, sexual behavior, even if he didn't.

Chapter 19

In March, I got my annual Pap smear and there were precancerous cells on my cervix. I needed outpatient surgery to freeze the cells and fight off any possibility of cervical cancer. Great, just what I needed.

Cory drove me to my pre-dawn appointment at Women's Medical Hospital and was there when the doctors successfully removed the cells. After an hour-long surgery, I was given the okay to go home. I needed to be immobile for 6-8 hours so Cory and I decided that I would recover at his house and return to school the next day.

I slept for several hours and awoke to intense cramping and pain in my lower abdomen. I was also covered in blood. Cory's bed was covered in blood as well. Great. The discharge papers mentioned slight bleeding; not the bloody Niagara Falls that had befallen Cory's bed. I took the prescribed pain pills, showered, and began searching for more sheets. I found them in the hall linen closet and after applying them to Cory's king-sized bed and washing the dirty sheets, I found myself exhausted.

After sleeping for several hours, I awoke and really looked around Cory's bedroom for the first time. I looked in the closet at his gorgeous clothes and shoes. Cory could have been a model and I often wondered why he wasn't.

I found myself walking around Cory's room, opening dresser drawers and looking under the bed. I perused Cory's two bedroom closets that were filled to capacity with clothes and coats. There appeared to be dozens of shoeboxes along one wall and way in the back, there was an orange milk crate.

The crate was completely out of character compared to Cory's bedroom furniture so I pulled it out and looked into the envelopes that were stuffed inside. At the time, I told myself that I wasn't looking for anything specific or really anything at all. I can admit now that I was seeking information about Cory, some dirt, evidence of another woman.

Well, I found it.

There were letters and pictures of Cory and a woman in his house, dated within the last month. There was a card from a woman named Therese, thanking Cory for a great time. The other comments stated that his lovemaking had not changed since their college days. Oh, really? There was a picture of Cory holding his penis on the stairs and a self-taken picture of them kissing. I was devastated.

I checked my calendar for the specific day to match the date and realized that Cory and I had sex the same day, approximately 2 hours later, at my house. I felt dirty and betrayed. Then I felt stupid. I had been worried about giving Cory herpes, thinking that he'd been faithful. He didn't even deserve my concern or appreciation. He'd been sneaking women in from out of town, having sex with them and pictures taken of the penis. This is what I left Brand for?

Therese was tall, nicely dressed, and attractive. She lived in Mechanicsburg, PA. I didn't see what he saw in her. I sat on the bed, looking at the pictures of Therese with Cory and named her Zimbabwe.

Why is it that men cheat, in private, with women that they wouldn't take out in public? As I've mentioned, Cory was an extremely attractive man. I couldn't imagine him dating this woman, at all. She did not seem to be his type. I couldn't imagine what he saw in her. It must have been sex.

I sat on the bed for a minute, alternately staring off into space and then, at the pictures. I was scared. It was difficult to admit to myself. Fear wasn't an emotion that I was used to. I didn't know what to do with it. I didn't know how to handle it.

I knew I wasn't looking at the woman in the picture through clear,

unaffected eyes. I was jealous, plain and simple. I didn't want to imagine
that he'd be attracted to her; that he'd like her over me. That he'd choose
her over me. I'd never considered the possibility of Cory cheating on me.
Maybe I should have.

Maybe I should have watched Cory closer. Were there signs? Maybe
I should have watched out for signs of infidelity. I was so concerned with
betraying Cory the way Brand betrayed me. Well no longer.

I took the pictures, card and letters and went home. When Cory
called after work, I didn't mention the pictures, Zimbabwe or the reason
I had left so soon. I called Taylor, cried over Cory's betrayal, and questioned what I had done wrong to make Cory cheat with her. Were there
others? I tried to think back to other times when Cory had been alone
and wondered if he was cheating every time I wasn't there. Cory's betrayal gave me the perfect excuse to lean on Brand, so I called him.

Chapter 20

Brand was happy to hear from me and didn't ask why I was calling. I was ashamed to say and didn't offer. He had a new apartment in Chestnut Hill and wanted me to come see him later that night. I was excited to see Brand and pushed thoughts of Cory and Zimbabwe from my head. I went to see Taylor instead. Taylor and I celebrated the reemergence of Brand over shots of tequila and frozen strawberry daiquiris.

The alcohol, however, only intensified the images of Cory and Zimbabwe in my head. At some point, I couldn't think of anything else. I showed Taylor the pictures of Cory's penis and of them kissing. Since the card was inside the envelope it was mailed in, Taylor suggested that I call Zimbabwe at home in Mechanicsburg PA.

I called information and asked for Therese Matthews in Mechanicsburg. There was only one T. Matthews listed and I called the telephone number, nervous and wondering what I would say to her if she answered. Well, Zimbabwe answered the phone on the fourth ring. Her voice was soft and confident and didn't match the semi-ugly chick I saw in the pictures.

I introduced myself only as Cory's girlfriend.

I asked Zimbabwe if she had been to see Cory lately. She answered, yes.

I asked Zimbabwe if she had had sex with Cory. She simply answered, yes. I asked Zimbabwe if she knew that Cory had a girlfriend. She answered, yes.

I asked Zimbabwe if she and Cory used a condom. She simply answered, yes.

Zimbabwe offered that she and Cory had been sex partners in college; never in a relationship. She said that she had been in town for one day and wanted to see him. She stated that Cory invited her over to his house and once there, they had sex. Zimbabwe said that she asked him not to wear a condom but he insisted. She stated that it was simply sex and she left his house shortly thereafter.

She stated that she took the pictures of Cory because she thought of him from time to time and wanted a reminder of their day. Zimbabwe said that she called Cory since then but he made it perfectly clear that he was in a relationship and the encounter would not be repeated.

And yes, she knew about me before she had sex with him.

Zimbabwe then asked me why I was calling her if I had the pictures, physical proof. I didn't know what to tell her. She told me that this is what Cory does and always had. He'd had a girlfriend in college when they started having sex. Zimbabwe stated that their sexual relationship had no emotional ties and hadn't since the beginning.

She advised that their brief, sexual encounter should not matter to me or affect my relationship with Cory. She then asked me again why I was calling her instead of questioning him. I didn't know what to tell her. Zimbabwe said that she would sleep with him again if he called her.

"How could you just have sex with someone that you haven't seen in 5 years, someone who you knew had a girlfriend..." I cut myself short. I tried to get angry but I really had nothing to say to Zimbabwe. Cory was the one who had hurt me; the one who was in a committed relationship with me.

I tried, again, to get upset and say mean, nasty things to her but I couldn't; she was too civil and obviously not to be deterred. I told myself that I was ready to drive to Mechanicsburg to defend my relationship. I told myself to shut up.

I hung up with Zimbabwe, confused but no longer as angry with Cory. I think I was equally angry with both of them. I didn't know what to think about Cory, our relationship and why he had sex with Zimbabwe and me on the same day, two hours apart.

Chapter 21

But, I didn't have time to dwell on it because I told Brand that I wanted to see him and drove to his new apartment, post haste. I made it to Brand's apartment and was impressed with what awaited me. He had purchased the building, a duplex, and lived in the top apartment. The living room was decorated with cream-colored, leather furniture and black accessories. The kitchen was mostly bare except for a refrigerator and freezer filled with frozen pizza, bread and liquor. The bedroom had a king-sized bed and was decorated with rich, mahogany furniture.

Brand and I talked over drinks and I admitted that I missed him and wasn't so sure that I made the right decision by breaking up with him. I told him that Cory and I were having problems but I still cared for him and wasn't ready to end our relationship. Brand said he missed me and asked me to come see him when I had a chance. Brand was so familiar and understanding that I let my guard down and enjoyed his company too much.

We christened his new couch by having loud, passionate sex. It was surprisingly good, but we were drunk, of course. Guilt never entered my mind and I didn't think of Cory or Zimbabwe. Brand asked me to tell him my sexual fantasies as we cuddled and watched television afterward.

I hesitated, not willing to admit to Brand what really turned me on. I wasn't sure why he wanted to know or what he would do with the information. I told Brand that I'd have to think about it.

"Come on Eva," Brand said, "I know you, girl. Don't think that pretty face is fooling me. I know there has to be something else you'd like to do besides eat, drink and fuck me when lover boy's not looking."

I wasn't willing to admit to anything right now. I wasn't sure where Brand was coming from and why, now, he was asking me about my sexual fantasies and what I liked.

I figured I'd give him a little information and then he'd leave me alone. I pretended to think about it and told Brand, "Well, porno's turn me on, especially two women having sex."

Brand seemed to like that idea and asked me if I ever thought about having sex with a woman. "No," I said too quickly. It was, honestly, the one thing I thought of constantly. There had always been something about a female body that turned me on. I admitted to Brand that I had thought of sleeping with another woman once or twice.

Brand didn't say anything else on the subject. We slept for a while and then he kissed me at the door when I left. I figured he'd forget about the conversation, as I did, the minute I got in the car. I thought of Brand for a while on the ride home. Being with him was fun and definitely familiar.

I talked to myself, aloud, on the way home and kept the conversation going for miles. Being a psych major, I questioned my behavior, mostly having sex tonight. Despite Cory's behavior, I felt whorish for my actions with Brand. And because I was on my way to understanding the human psyche, I knew that his behavior should not shape my own.

I attempted to place myself in the position of a professional therapist and tried to self-diagnose. What would a therapist say? What type of mental condition was I in? Was my behavior indicative of a normal girl/woman my age?

I mean, really, did twenty-something women masturbate? So often? Did they have herpes? Did they sleep with multiple men in one week? Did they think of other women's bodies in a sexual way? Did normal women fantasize about eating pussy and liking it?

I thought of Cory and Zimbabwe again. I wondered if what she said was true; that their sexual encounter was nothing to worry about, that it meant nothing to either of them. Honestly, I was happy that Cory used protection with her and that was much more important than any feelings he had for her.

I didn't call Cory for a few weeks after that, nor did I take any of his calls. I assumed that Zimbabwe told Cory about our conversation. Cory called my aunt to inquire about me when I refused his calls. She appeared to enjoy talking to him and that was okay with me. I wasn't ready to talk to Cory yet.

I also wasn't ready for what Brand was offering when I went out with him or to his apartment. Brand wanted us to get back together. I wasn't sure if I wanted to get back with him. I wasn't sure what I wanted at the time.

Eventually Cory wore me down. I loved him too much to continue to ignore him and I missed him more than I cared to admit. There was something about Cory's style and maturity that I couldn't resist. I loved the way he looked and dressed. I love that he gave me space and respected my need for it. Cory had dated women all over the country, including lawyers and an emergency room physician. I was flattered that he wanted me. I loved the way he took charge of me in the bed. Cory was a freak in bed and made me do things I'd never done or been asked to do. I loved all of it.

Being with Cory, however, scared me. I forgave him for Zimbabwe but I didn't forget the hurt and devastation I felt when I saw them in the pictures. He didn't have a reason for having sex with her, other than it just happened. I didn't understand that, nor did I accept it, but I wanted to be with him, so I dealt with it.

Chapter 22

I *also continued to* see Brand.

Brand was my safety net. I needed to be with Brand once or twice a month to feel safe and not love Cory too much. I was afraid of falling completely in love with Cory again. Being with Brand kept me from focusing solely on Cory and wondering if he was sleeping with the Zimbabwe's of the world.

One Friday night I went to Brand's apartment, as we'd planned, and he wasn't there. Oh, did I mention that I had a key? He called me from a restaurant (Chestnut Hill Grille) on Germantown Avenue, around the corner, and told me that he had a surprise for me.

"What is it, Brand? Don't do this to me. You know I can't stand the suspense."

"You just be ready when I get there. I got you what you said you wanted." Brand could be a real slick ass when he wanted to be. Then he hung up on me.

I went into the kitchen and poured myself an Absolut and cranberry juice. Then I thought about Brand's surprise and poured a double shot of tequila as well. I couldn't imagine what the surprise could be but I figured being drunk might help.

I heard the front door open and Brand walked into the kitchen where

I was still standing at the counter with the glass in my hand. Brand took the glass from me saying, "Eva, girl, I need you awake for this. I promise you'll love it." Brand pushed me toward the door, "Go in the bedroom and wait for me. I'll be right there."

I found myself walking toward the bedroom as I was thinking that I should be walking to the front door. The bedroom was dark and dimly lit with scented candles. The room was empty except for me. I sat on the bed hoping my surprise was a 3-karat diamond ring and matching bracelet.

The door opened and Brand walked in with a woman. She was short and slim with long dark hair. Her bright brown eyes were shiny with mischief as she stared at me. Her mocha brown skin was sparkling as if she was covered with glitter. I don't know what I was thinking. I don't think I was capable of thinking. I wondered if I was dreaming or if this was the effect of the alcohol.

She walked toward me, smiling. She had on a ¾ Burberry trench and 4-inch stiletto Gucci sandals. I just stared. She was attractive enough, though not really my type. But what was my type? She took off her coat and stood in the doorway in a matching bra and panty set. Vickies, I thought, nice. I just stared. Brand stood next to her, smiling. I wondered if they had slept together. Was she one of the sixteen? Was he trying to share one of them with me?

"Surprise," Brand said. He looked elated. I thought, damn, all of his fantasies were coming true.

"Eva, this is Kristal." Brand stood there continuing to smile. "I brought Kristal here for you." Oh. Some surprise.

Kristal walked into the room, stood in front of me and touched my hair. I immediately pulled back. Kristal smiled and glanced at Brand over her shoulder. I looked at Brand, and then Kristal. I didn't know what to do.

"Brand, give Eva and me some time alone," Kristal implored. "I'd like for us to talk and get to know one another. I think she'll feel better if we're alone. Trust me; we don't need an audience, or admiring fans about."

Brand paused in the doorway. He looked at me and though I was hesitant, I wanted him to leave. I wanted to talk to Kristal and find out what she was about and why she was here. She was obviously here for me, or maybe for us. I couldn't be sure unless I got the chance to spend time with her alone.

"Go wait in the living room, Brand," I told him. "I'll be okay here. Just stay close, in case we need you."

Brand backed out of the doorway, closing the door slowly. He was grinning as he left the room and I immediately thought of locking the door behind him. I didn't lock it; however, because I wasn't sure what I wanted Kristal to think of me then.

Kristal and I were finally alone. She sat next to me on the bed, looking into my face. Kristal lightly caressed my hand and moved closer to me. I wasn't sure what to think and I still wasn't sure why she was here. This time, I didn't pull away.

"Are you Brand's girlfriend?" Kristal asked me. She pulled my hand up to her mouth and began kissing my fingertips. She started sucking them, individually.

"No, not anymore. Not since about 18 months ago." I was talking to Kristal and wanting to pull my hand from her mouth. Her mouth was soft and warm. I closed my eyes and didn't think about the fact that this was a woman sucking my fingers.

Kristal rubbed my shoulder and walked her fingers down my arm. "Brand told me that you are a special friend of his. He says he loves you. He says your pussy is divine and tastes like a peach." Kristal leaned over and kissed my cheek. "Brand says that you have been looking for me but you didn't know it. He wants me to play with you, to teach you. Brand wants you to be happy."

"What else did Brand tell you about me?"

"He told me that you were pretty, smart, and had a nice body. He was definitely telling the truth about the body. He said that you had been thinking about making love with a woman. He thought I'd be nice for you."

I didn't know what to do. I didn't stop Kristal from touching me. I thought I wanted to touch her and wondered how she would feel. I stared back at her, my eyes roaming over her pretty face, slim shoulders and flat stomach. My mind began racing and I willed myself to calm down, to be patient. My hands found her stomach and began to rub softly. My fingers dipped lower and I lightly touched her inner thighs.

Kristal leaned over and kissed me. Her lips were soft on mine. Her mouth tasted like mint. Her tongue was soft, yet firm, as it invaded my mouth. I couldn't believe I was kissing a woman. Kissing Kristal was very much like kissing Cory, just softer, with no facial hair.

Kristal began touching my breasts, making circles on my hardening nipples. "Tell me, Eva, what you want me to do."

Instead of answering, my legs opened. They seemed to have a mind of their own. This girl was turning me on. I didn't say anything. I willed her hands to touch me everywhere. I wanted to touch her, again. I wanted to kiss her, again. I was excited to touch her body, everywhere. Mostly, I wanted to touch and kiss her breasts.

"Eva," Kristal purred, standing and bending in front of me. Her breasts were pushed up in the bra and inches from my lips. "Touch me."

I instantly thought of Cory. Then I thought of Cory and Zimbabwe. I wondered if this is what happened with them. Initially, an introduction or greeting: An intense physical, sexual, attraction, and then sex.

I thought of Brand one room away and what he must be thinking. I wondered if Brand would look at me differently later. Then I realized that I didn't care. This is what I wanted. Kristal, this opportunity, was something I wanted way more than I had confided to Brand.

I put my hands on Kristal's waist and pulled her onto my lap. I rubbed her lip-gloss off with my fingers. I stared at her lips, and then into her eyes. Suddenly I wanted this to happen. I didn't want her to leave. I wanted to say something to Kristal that conveyed how much I was looking forward to this. I closed my eyes, leaned forward and spoke softly in her ear, "I want you to fuck me, Kristal. I want you to make me want you and show me how it's done."

Kristal grabbed my face and kissed my lips. I adjusted my head and put my tongue in her mouth. Kristal sucked my tongue and pulled my hair. I sucked her tongue and rubbed her breasts. I sighed with pleasure.

Kristal placed my fingers on her clitoris and rubbed herself with them. She guided my fingers into her panties and I felt a silky wetness. I slid a finger inside of her vagina, shocked by the tight curves and warmth of her womanhood.

I removed my finger from inside of her and put it into her mouth: Kristal moaned with pleasure as she sucked her wetness from my finger. I put two fingers inside of her and then into my mouth. I sighed with contentment as I sucked her wetness from my fingers. I kissed her again, mixing our saliva and her wetness as our tongues met in a slow, exotic dance.

Brand and Cory were in trouble if this was how women made love. Kristal kissed a lot better than either of them could ever dream.

From that moment, things moved fast.

I poured myself chilled vodka from the kitchen because I didn't want to lose my nerve. I was enjoying myself and imagining the things I'd get to do with and to Kristal.

Brand was masturbating on the couch. I guess he was living his fantasies through the closed bedroom door.

Once over my initial inhibition, I moved with Kristal in the darkness as if she'd been my lover for years. She peeled off my clothes and kissed every body part she uncovered. She kissed my lips and face. She told me I was beautiful and she would love making love to me. Kristal told me that my skin was soft and made to be caressed by her mouth. She hugged me and pressed her breasts against mine, rubbing our nipples together and making them hard. I felt a tingle between my legs. I felt wetness between my legs.

Kristal grabbed my hands and helped me massage her breasts and body. She pushed me back onto the bed and knelt in front of me. My legs opened to her gentle nudge and she kissed my inner thighs, sucking the wetness and licking it from my skin. She was rubbing my breasts and making me moan and writhe in anticipation. I lifted my hips against her lips as she placed butterfly kisses on my clitoris.

Kristal stopped and looked up at me. "Are you ready, Eva?" She asked me, her lips wet and shining with moisture from my pussy.

I could only nod in acknowledgement as I grabbed the back of her head. I needed to feel her lips on me: wanted to have an orgasm in her mouth.

Kristal's wet, warm mouth sucked my clitoris for hours, it seemed. I remember screaming and having orgasm after orgasm in her mouth, on her fingers and all over her face. Kristal lifted my hips and licked my asshole. She turned me over, sucked my anus, and pleasured me with her tongue. Her warm mouth licked and sucked my ass the same way she kissed: soft, slow and wet. She fucked my ass with her tongue, going in and out, bringing me again, to orgasm.

I was out of my mind with pleasure. Kristal was on top of me, over me, behind me. Her fingers and mouth were on every part of my body. I could only think of Kristal and the sexual feelings she was bringing out in me. *I thought I wanted to marry her.*

Brand and Cory were in big trouble. At some point, I opened my eyes and saw Brand standing over the bed, stroking his penis, bringing himself to orgasm as he stood over us and watched. Brand continued to stand there rubbing himself, watching Kristal fuck me. I didn't care. I closed my eyes and rode the waves of pleasure.

I found myself flat on the bed with Kristal on top of me. I pulled her forward until she was kneeling; her legs were straddling my face. She positioned herself until her clitoris was on my lips and she moaned as I softly sucked it into my mouth. I ran my tongue around her nether lips, using my fingers to pull her lips open and pushed my tongue into her vagina as far as I could.

Kristal grabbed my head, pushing my tongue further into her vagina and started rocking her hips as I pushed my tongue in and out. I moaned involuntarily as her legs tightened around my head, her hips jerking as she pulled my hair and pushed her pelvis down further onto my face. With a low moan and a vise grip on my head, Kristal came, dripping warm, clear fluid into my mouth and nose. She continued to gyrate her hips, jerking and moaning, gripping my head to hold it in place. I pulled her closer, drinking her fluids, enjoying its silky feel on my tongue and in my throat.

I flipped Kristal, pinning her to the bed. I stared in her eyes, wanting her to see my face, slick with her wetness, willing her to feel the emotion coming from me. I rubbed my face onto hers, smearing her wetness onto her lips, kissing her softly, licking her lips, pushing my tongue into her mouth. Kristal licked my lips, into my mouth, into my nose, lapping up her orgasm, laughing into my eyes, as we playfully shared our experience.

Chapter 23

Later at home, I relived my first homosexual experience with Kristal repeatedly. I couldn't stop thinking of the things she did to me, and those I did in return. I thought of how Kristal coaxed me out of my tentativeness into some sort of reckless wanton, designed for sex. Kristal made me come more times than I could count. She had me crying out and begging her for more. She had me doing things I'd never done before and was ashamed to admit. Kristal made me wonder about my own sexuality for the first time.

Cory, who?

I returned Cory's house later that morning. He didn't ask where I was and I didn't offer. I briefly thought about confessing to Cory about my wild night with Kristal. I wondered if it would make a difference to him. It certainly made a difference to me.

Cory and I continued our relationship, as usual. I saw Brand when the desire struck. I ran back and forth between them and concentrated on graduating from college without driving myself crazy. I thought of my experience with Kristal often.

Then the unthinkable happened. I got pregnant.

I immediately stopped having sex with Brand, as if that would change anything. I told Cory the news and we were elated. We decided that I would move into his house and live in sin for a while. We spent our nights discussing baby names and the best hospitals to give birth.

The baby would be the first grandchild for our parents and Cory couldn't wait to tell his parents. I couldn't wait to tell Aunt Mirabelle. I was anxious, however, about my mother finding out about the pregnancy. Thinking about her set me on edge and memories took me back to the last time I had seen her.

Whenever I saw Mavis, the few times we occupied the same space at the same time, her disapproval was apparent. She rarely addressed me personally, opting to talk around me, and when she did, she referred to me by my full name. "Evangeline Arianna LoDolce, you shame yourself when you…." Or "Evangeline Arianna LoDolce, the Lord frowns upon your behavior…"

Mavis was a relentless adversary, delivering an onslaught of carefully chosen words, both venom and disdain spewing forth from her pursed lips at every turn. Disappointment and disapproval were evident in her body language and the dismissive way she addressed me.

I could imagine Mavis, on discovering my pregnancy, dropping to her knees and reciting countless Bible verses, hands clasped, begging for the intervention of her God. Her sermons (admonitions), to me, usually started with Sodom and Gomorrah and ended with the reborn whores Jesus saved from themselves.

I wasn't going to let her destroy my moment. This baby would be born in love, despite her ravings of fornication and bastards born in sin. Maybe we'd get married before the baby was born. That would satisfy, at least, part of Mavis' ranting.

I tried not to think about the other baby.

I concentrated on my relationship and burgeoning motherhood. I forgot all about Zimbabwe. I stopped thinking of Brand and Kristal. I started thinking about marriage and being with Cory forever. In my mind, I had already picked out which bedroom would belong to the baby. I saw myself decorating it in neutral colors and small furniture we'd buy from IKEA.

Cory had no idea that the baby might not be his and I felt guilty because of my deception. Brand kept calling and I didn't know what to tell him. Brand would know about the possibility of the baby being his and would demand that I find out. I decided to play safe and avoid Brand all together until I was ready to admit that I was pregnant.

On the exact date of the third month of my pregnancy, I talked Cory into taking me out for dinner to celebrate. He had been tense and preoccupied over the last month. I figured it was due to the pregnancy and his looming responsibilities. I attempted to question him a few times, but he always waved me off, too busy to talk. He had been working overtime and was gone until 9 or 10 at night almost every night. He said he was making extra money for our family and all the things we'd need when the baby was born.

"Cory," I whined one Friday evening, "the baby is 3 months old now, I'm getting fat and you've been ignoring me. I want to do something. I want to go somewhere. I want you to make love to me. Or, at the very least, take me to get something to eat; I'm hungry again."

Cory looked annoyed and distracted. He'd been on the phone again, as usual, and looked as if he didn't want me around. "Eva, please. I'm busy. Why don't you have something delivered?"

"Cory, you have been gone for hours. You're hardly home anymore and when you are, your ear is glued to the phone. You've been ignoring me and I'm tired of it." I had had enough. I would rather have Cory at home than have extra money for the baby.

"Damn it, Eva! I'm not in the mood for this. Can this please wait 'til later, or tomorrow?" Cory ran his fingers through his hair looking angry and frustrated. "Look, I need to talk to you, but not this minute. Give me some space, for a change."

Nevertheless, I was not to be deterred. "No, you listen! I'm tired of waiting here for you, tired of you ignoring me. I want to do something. You asked me to come here to live with you, I didn't ask. I'm pregnant with your child, and you're acting as if I mean nothing to you." I was near tears with frustration. I was crying all the time now. I didn't feel like myself. Maybe I didn't look like me either, and that was why he was treating me this way.

"Look, Eva, I'm sorry. I have a lot on my mind right now. Give me half an hour and we'll go somewhere where we can sit down and talk, okay?"

I happily agreed and went to the kitchen to make a cup of tea. I needed something to settle me and calm my nerves. I was getting vibes from Cory that all was not well with him, or with us. I wondered what we needed to talk about. I wondered if it was us. I wondered if it was the baby.

Exactly one hour later, we were on our way down South Street. I wanted to go to Copa Banana at Fourth and South, where they had the best margaritas and Buffalo wings. Of course, I couldn't drink margaritas, but I could pretend.

We sat down at a table for four in the back. Cory had asked for a table away from others. Our waiter brought Cory's Corona and my Pepsi and took our order for appetizers. Cory looked irritated and tired and I started to worry about the information he had to discuss with me. Cory waited until the waiter took our order for dinner before he started to talk. I was about to explode in anticipation. Cory hesitated and then spoke. At that moment, being struck by a speeding car, in the restaurant as I sat, couldn't have surprised me more.

"Eva, I've been thinking and I want you to have an abortion." Cory had tears in his eyes as he spoke those horrible, unbelievable words to me.

What? I was stunned into silence. Was I drinking margaritas after all? Apparently, Cory had a sick sense of humor, or was I imagining things?

"Cory, that's some crappy-ass shit to say. What are you talking about?" I couldn't even begin to digest what had come out of his mouth. The waiter came with our food and I began to eat. "Eat, Cory." I ignored him. Maybe he needed to eat something and we could begin again.

"Eva, did you hear me? Stop eating. We need to talk. I don't want to upset you, but I need to say this to you." Cory was looking at me as if I was the one saying stupid shit out of my mouth. "Eva, listen to me. I want you to have an abortion."

Apparently, I had subconsciously tuned him out. I began to hum as I ate and looked out of the window. Cory jerked me back into reality by grabbing my hand and preventing me from eating. Now he had my attention. I looked at him in bewilderment.

"Cory, what are you saying to me? I don't like this. I don't like what you're saying to me. How can you say those things? How can you talk like that? What do you mean abortion?" I shook my head at Cory as if one of us wasn't speaking English.

"Eva, are you listening to me? I want you to have an abortion. I don't want you to have the baby. I can't do this. I can't do this right now. I can't do this with you." Cory looked pleadingly at me. "Eva, please…" Cory started to say when his cell phone beeped. He looked at the number and silenced the ring.

I was openly crying now. The other patrons in the restaurant were staring at us. I didn't care. I began screaming at him, "Cory, what are you saying? I can't have an abortion. I am three months pregnant. I can't have an abortion. Why are you saying this to me?" I wailed at him and jumped to my feet. "I'm not going to stay here for this shit. You know where to find me, when you change your mind and stop talking like you're crazy!"

I ran to the bathroom because I had nowhere else to go. I wasn't driving. This wasn't like the scene with Brand, where I could easily get home. I was stuck, miles away from home and no way to get there.

I eventually came out of the bathroom. I was not going to spend the night in a restaurant bathroom to prove a point. Even if my boyfriend was crazy, I was not. Plus they were closing and a waitress had come in to tell me that it was time to go. I couldn't delay any longer.

Cory was waiting at the front door. I pushed past him and walked out. Cory trailed behind me as I walked to the car and waited for the automatic locks to open the door. We drove home in silence.

I wanted to ask him again what was going on, and why he was treating me like this? My pride kept my questions inside and I refused to ask him again.

Cory dropped me off at my aunt's house and said goodbye. I was again crying as I walked into the house. I had been gone for 2 ½ months and I was back home. I didn't know what to think. I went upstairs and cried myself to sleep, rubbing my stomach and wondering what was to become of my unborn child.

Chapter 24

Cory didn't call the next day. I sat around all weekend waiting for his call; waiting for him to change his mind and ask me to come back and to keep our baby. He didn't call. I waited for two weeks. I had an abortion on the 15th day.

Amazingly, Brand called me the next day. It was almost as if he knew that I was free of Cory and his baby. I didn't question it. I was happy for the distraction.

I had physically recovered from the procedure, but was mentally drained and confused. I wondered how the abortion would affect my body and reproductive organs. I wondered if I had done any permanent damage and if I would be able to conceive and carry a child later. My mind was going non-stop and I wasn't prepared to hear from Brand. I was still waiting to hear from Cory.

Brand, however, was relentless. He called all day, every day. He wouldn't take no for an answer. He asked me about Cory. He asked me about Kristal. He asked if he could see me again. Brand wanted to know why I had stopped calling him for three months. He was full of questions and inquisitive about things that I didn't want to talk about and was trying to forget.

Finally, I went out with Brand and surprisingly, I enjoyed myself. I still wanted to hear from Cory, but I was no longer waiting for him to call. It seemed that he had moved on and forgotten about us. I wondered if I would hear from him again, ever. I never called to tell him that I had the abortion and he didn't have to worry. I still loved Cory and knew that it would take time for me to completely recover from my ordeal and to get over him. Brand was helping, though.

It was May and I was concentrating on graduating from the university finally. I convinced myself to forget Cory for a while. I was still seeing Brand and as usual, he was a constant in my life. Brand turned out to be a great friend and we were happy being friends. We went to the movies and out to eat. No sex, just small occasional kisses and lots of laughs. It was as if none of the bad things had ever happened between us.

School was tough, but without a boyfriend to worry about, I sailed through finals and coasted toward graduation with a 3.6 grade average. I happily paid for my cap and gown and concentrated on graduation. I visited employment fairs looking for the right job for a college graduate.

I met with the FBI and ATF. Ms. Gomez, a Latina sista, was a representative from the FBI. "Hello, my name is Maria Gomez. I've been with the FBI for 22 years. I started out in fingerprinting and now I'm a supervising recruitment agent. We are recruiting agents willing to work any where in the world right now. Let me tell you, Eva, is it? You are the perfect candidate for our newest recruiting class. Of course we take all qualified applicants, but our minority numbers are low and as an African American female, you are our dream candidate."

I heard the same thing from the ATF. They were offering positions in Washington, D.C. and even hinted that I may be able to work locally. Alcohol, Tobacco, Firearms. The position sounded interesting but the thought of chasing gunrunners who were buying weapons from the Middle East and other poor, third-world countries willing to sell anything to anyone to make a buck, didn't appeal to me.

I made stops at the DEA and Pennsylvania State Highway Patrol recruitment stands. Their recruiters eagerly explained that as a triple threat, I was almost guaranteed a position of my choosing with their agencies. I tried to imagine myself outfitted with a bulletproof vest, running through the streets of the USA and the South American jungles, in search of elusive drug-carrying, gun-toting criminals. What a scary thought!

Instead, I applied for the position of Case Manager with Meadow Springs, a well-known mental health agency located in Fort Washington,

Pennsylvania. Way less money and surely less danger and drama, but I figured it would be safer. The agency paid a decent hourly wage for a single, childless, young woman and had good benefits. What more could I ask for?

Maybe I should have thanked Cory for the decision to have an abortion. What would my life have been like with his child? He probably would have expected me to spend more time with his son and include him in our family plans. Would I have to get to know his son's mother? Would his two children have to vie for his attention? Would there be enough money to go around? The questions were endless.

My short-term plans were to apply to the Temple University Social Work program for my graduate degree. An MSW would open many more doors in the mental health field and finally the big money. How would I manage with a baby and possibly no husband? That abortion may have saved my life.

As a graduation and employment present Taylor, my popular friend, took me to Friday's for dinner and drinks. Taylor was still enrolled at the junior college where I met Brand. Her popularity on campus was more important to her than a college degree. Taylor was interested in the men and wouldn't listen to my pleadings to join me at Villanova, so I stopped trying to convince her.

Over draft beer and chicken fingers, Taylor filled me in on the latest gossip among our friends and acquaintances. Her ex-boyfriend was in jail for statutory rape; her hair stylist, Kesha, was sleeping with two of her female clients; and her cousin, Corrine, was pregnant with her third child at 17, by her high school principal. Then she mentioned Cory and ruined my night.

"You know, Eva, I wasn't going to mention this to you because I didn't want to upset you. It's about Cory, and it's not good. I mean, I guess it's good for him, but you won't like it." Taylor paused to gauge my reaction.

"Taylor, please, you know I haven't heard from Cory in months and could certainly care less what he's doing now," I sarcastically said to Taylor, hoping she didn't see the pain and longing in my face as I waited for her to tell me something, anything about Cory.

"Well, you know the skinny girl in my English 203 class?" I shook my head no. Taylor went on to say, "Remember when you picked me up from school last Friday, the girl I was talking to at the bus stop? Well, according to this girl, her cousin is pregnant by Cory and the baby is due in November."

I was momentarily dumbfounded. I quickly counted the months in my head. Our baby would have been due in January. I suddenly felt sick. I felt tricked and stupid. Cory had gotten another woman pregnant at the same exact time I was pregnant. She, however, has to keep her baby.

Taylor read my mind and said slowly, "That means that he was sleeping with this tramp at the same time. Damn, men are such cheating assholes! How could he get both of you pregnant at the same time? Girl, have you been checked for anything lately? She's probably a nasty tramp! I wonder what she looks like. If she looks anything like her cousin, there's going to be one ugly baby born in November." Taylor paused to consider more information. "Evie, did you have any idea that he was cheating again? Was something going on that you didn't tell me about? I don't understand. You were practically living with him and rearranging furniture and shit. I can't believe he would make you have an abortion and let this other chick keep her baby."

I burst into tears and ran to the ladies room. Sound familiar? I was in a stall crying and choking and finally threw up in the toilet. I couldn't believe what I was hearing from Taylor. I couldn't believe how I had been willing to change my life for that lying idiot. Oh God, our baby. I had been willing to put off school and get married, to that cheating bastard!

Fifteen minutes later, I was back at the table with Taylor. I looked a mess with red, puffy eyes, but I was putting up a brave front. "Fuck Cory. Forgive me. I must be crazy. Let's pretend this never happened. I'm hungry, so let's eat." Taylor looked sad and slightly uncomfortable. I wondered if she was sorry she told me about Cory and his baby.

"I'm so sorry. I thought you were over him, Evie. I could have waited to mention Cory and his shit. I never meant to upset you." Taylor had tears in her eyes. "Let's go by his house and scratch up his car or break some of his windows." I shook my head no. "We need to do something! He can't just treat you this way and get away with it. He needs to pay. He has to learn."

"Taylor, just forget it. It's over now. Cory and I are over and the baby is gone. Maybe he'll be happy with this girl, and I don't care any more. Can we please stop talking about it and eat?" I was still upset but unwilling to let Cory affect my life any longer. I needed to move on and decided that today was the day.

Chapter 25

Later, at home that night, I thought about Cory and our relationship. I wondered what had gone wrong; what I had done wrong and if there was something I could have done to repair it. I wanted to call Cory and confront him with the information I now possessed. I wanted to ask him if it was true. I wanted to make him feel the pain I felt during the abortion.

I felt a burst of anger and frustration, different from the hurt I'd felt at the restaurant. Emotions and feelings were running through me that I couldn't quite identify. If I had kept Cory's baby, he or she would have had a sibling 2 months older. How do you explain that? I would have been branded a fool for life. I would have had to subsist with the deception each time I looked at my child's half sister or brother.

The thought was over whelming and disturbing.

For the first time, I wasn't sorry about the herpes. I wanted to use it to hurt someone; I wanted to hurt Cory. I thought about having sex with Cory when I was having a horrific herpes outbreak, giving the virus to him. I wanted him to eat my pussy and lick my ass, not knowing that his lips and tongue were coming in contact with a sexually transmitted virus. I wanted to hurt him badly and give him something to remember me by.

Later, I wanted him to be in pain and have bumps break out on his lips and his penis. I wanted the sensitive areas on his scrotum to burn and itch. I wanted him to wonder who had given him a disease and have it drive him crazy not knowing. I wanted to hold it over him forever.

I thought about it all night, but I knew I wouldn't do it.

I felt lonely and wished for someone to talk to about all the problems I faced. Taylor was great to talk to about problems with men, but she couldn't help me with the problems I faced when it was time to have sex with someone new, or how to tell someone about the herpes. I decided to forget about it for a while. I'd just put it behind me and wouldn't think about it. Fuck it. I didn't want to give anyone herpes but if it happened; it just happened. I put Cory out of my mind.

The month of May happened upon me and before I knew it, I was graduating from college. I couldn't believe it! I was the first one in my family and I felt like the smartest, most intelligent person on the planet. Few members of my family showed up for the ceremony, but that didn't stop my happiness. My aunt and brothers took me out for dinner and I didn't worry about Cory, Brand or anyone else. I was thinking happy thoughts and refused to let anyone ruin my happy day.

With school behind me, I began to think about working every day instead of going to school. School suddenly seemed like a luxury. Close in proximity to home. No real commitment except to get there and hand in papers on time. I had been spoiled by being with Brand and never having to worry about money. What kind of salary would I make? Would I like my job? Would my boss and coworkers be assholes?

I began considering what I'd like to do with my time and the money I had been saving when Brand treated me badly and sent me shopping to make up for his behavior.

I had been investing approximately $250 a month, on average, over the last two years and when I got my May statement, I was shocked to see that I had just over $22,000 in an aggressive mutual fund and money market accounts. I immediately thought about buying a car and clothes. I felt rich and could buy anything I wanted. I called Taylor, screaming as I dialed her number.

"Taylor!" I screamed into the phone when she answered. "Girl, put your fucking clothes on and meet me at Savannah's. Wait 'til I show you what came in the mail. You're going to love me and I'll buy you anything you want on the menu. Girl, we are rich!"

"Eva, you do realize that it is after midnight, right? Damn, you're inconsiderate, Girl, I'm tired as shit, plus I have company."

I immediately started in on her. "Who? Not Andrew again. I can't believe you. Taylor, I don't know why you continue to deal with that guy; he's married, he's fat, he's…" I was cut off abruptly by Taylor's next words.

"For your information, Eva, her name is Shawn and she's not married or fat. She's tanned and beautiful and she's got D cups that are in my hands right now." Taylor paused to make loud licking and kissing sounds as she bit Shawn's nipples. Shawn squealed on cue. "She smells like mango and apricot and her pussy tastes like cream." I could hear Shawn in the background whimpering and making noises. "She loves it when I'm fingering her pussy and, yes baby, you're coming right now, aren't you?" Taylor forgot about me and dropped the phone. She purred to Shawn, "Aren't you baby? Do you like this? Yes, I know baby. Let me taste you. Mmmm. I love it. Kiss me, Shawn. I want you to taste your pussy on my lips."

This went on for several minutes. Shawn was loud; Taylor got louder. I sat back listening and getting horny. I couldn't believe what I was hearing. Shit, I wanted to join in. I wanted some of that pussy on my lips. I didn't even know Taylor liked women like that. What the fuck happened to Andrew?

"Eva." Minutes later Taylor breathlessly picked up the phone. "Girl, forgive my indiscretion. Damn, I didn't mean to leave you on hold for so long. Wait, hold on." In the background she said to Shawn, "Shawnee, baby, go wash that beautiful body and come back to me."

I snapped back into it. "Taylor," I shouted into the phone, "Get Shawn off your mind for one goddamn minute and listen to me. I have a surprise for you. I want to go out. Fuck it, Shawnee can come with us. I don't care. Meet me at Savannah's in ½ hour and don't be late." I slammed down the phone.

Shit. I was horny and now I wanted to cum.

I got in to the shower and soaped my body, running my hands

over my breasts and ass, rubbing my nipples and hearing the noises Taylor and Shawn made in my head, envisioning their mouths on each other's bodies. I pictured me in between them, kissing one and then the other, their hands caressing my body from behind and in front.

With the water running over us, I was holding onto the wall in the shower with Shawn licking my pussy from the front. Taylor was behind me fucking me alternately in my ass with her finger and tongue.

I was rubbing my clit, fucking my own fingers when I came, savagely, a few minutes later, grinding into the air, and attempting to catch my breath.

Damn. Thank you, Shawn and Taylor.

Chapter 26

I *was still reeling* from the breakup with Cory and the loss of the baby. The thought of Cory and a newly made family made me physically ill. It made me want to possibly kill someone. It was definitely time to move on.

I threw myself into finding employment, now that I was a college graduate. I perused the Sunday newspaper and badgered friends for workplace insider hiring tips. I was finally hired as a case manager at Meadow Springs in Fort Washington, PA.

The hours were 8:30am to 5:00pm and the pay was slight, but it was work. I started thinking ahead to graduate school. The Temple University Masters of Social Work program was 15 months in length. I would get an MSW and then be able to make my own hours and schedule. I knew I was on the right track to earn between $80,000 and $100,000 in the next two years.

I needed to get my own place. Aunt Mirabelle didn't want me to leave and I didn't really want to, either. But I was a 23-year-old college graduate and it was time to move on. I wanted privacy and to live by my own rules. I was ready to explore my sexuality with men and women and could do so only in private. As much as Aunt Mirabelle loved me, I'm sure she would have been unable to deal with me bringing both sexes to her home for overnight stays. I also wanted peace and quiet and the ability to mourn the loss of my unborn baby and Cory.

At times, I felt as if I would never get over him and hated myself for it. Cory was long gone, probably living with his children and one of their mother's. He was certainly not thinking of me. I seemed to be stuck in a time where Cory was the love of my life, stuck with the belief that our baby would bond us together forever.

I found a small, one-bedroom triplex in Mount Airy. Two other young women occupied the 1st and 3rd floors. Heather and Desiree. Damn, they were cute. I threw a moving-in party and supplied pizza and beer for those who helped me move a bed, a 24-inch television, and a cable box. I needed to dip into that $22,000 quickly and get some much-needed furniture or no one of either gender would want to come see me.

My first official visitor was Taylor. She came bearing gifts, mostly of the alcoholic variety. Somehow, she had coordinated her arrival with the pizza deliveryman, paying and tipping him as I opened the door to greet her. Hauling in bags of alcohol to make mixed drinks and boxes of pizza, we stumbled into the living room and stood, staring at the empty room. Taylor laughed out loud. "Only you, Eva, would move before you had at least one chair to sit on. If I didn't know any better, I'd be hard pressed to believe I was your best friend. Friends don't let friends sit on the floor.

"So, anyway, girl. Subtract the missing furniture and this place is huge. Cute sunk-in living room; girl, please don't stumble down these two steps, coming in drunk. Nice little eating area. Kitchen's a little small, but then, you don't cook much, do you? Taylor thought for a moment. "What we really need to do is to run up to City Line Avenue and go to Pier 1. We can decorate this place in a hot second and make this place a batchelorette's dream. Girl, get one of those cuties from up or down stairs and impress one into your bed."

Taylor wandered into the bedroom, grabbing two comforters out of the closet. "But first, let's eat. We'll eat a slice here, take one with us and make the drinks when we get back. How's that?"

"It sounds like a great idea, of course. The only problem is that I haven't redeemed the shares from the mutual fund yet. I think there's a one day wire transfer available, but even then, I won't have it for two more days."

"Eva, eat please. Don't worry about money. Carlton's back and you know I did not let him out of my door without leaving me with something. Who knows when his flighty ass will be back? I have the gold MasterCard, so prices are not really a concern of ours today."

I was first out of the door, so Taylor didn't see the face I made when she mentioned Carlton's name. I hated him with a passion. He treated Taylor like shit, coming and going out of her life like the summer rain. I couldn't count the times Taylor took him back, only to have him cheat on her or simply disappear for months. Most times, she hated him too. Maybe I was glad Carlton appeared now; this time I wouldn't complain. Surely, I didn't hate him enough not to spend money on his MasterCard. I wasn't a complete fool.

We spent two hours in Pier 1, spending $4,276.79 on Carlton's credit card. We picked out lamps, tables, chairs, candles, glasses, artwork; the list was endless. And we didn't buy anything on sale. It felt great, sticking it to Carlton, right in his cheating-ass pockets. To add insult to injury, Taylor talked to Shawn on the phone the entire time.

After securing the delivery truck, date and time, we left Pier 1, laughing like jewel thieves. We contemplated going across the street to Lord & Taylor and spending more of Carlton's free money. Taylor, however, wasn't sure of the available balance and since obviously neither of us was Mr. Carlton Tyson, we didn't want to draw attention to ourselves if the card was declined.

Instead, we went back to the apartment to hang three portraits, put down two area rugs and plugged in three table lamps, minus the table and bulbs. It was a start. After two strawberry daiquiris and a Rum Runner, the apartment almost looked furnished. Thank you, Carl, baby.

I decided to come clean to Taylor about the herpes. Even though she knew everything else about me, it was proving to be difficult to say the words to anyone other than Brand. But this was Taylor, right? She didn't pass judgment on me, ever; we didn't do it to each other. She knew that Brand had been the only one I'd been fucking at that time. She would have to understand.

I could feel the effects of the mixed drinks as I sipped the last of the daiquiri. My head was light and my legs felt like rubber when I walked into the kitchen. I came back and sat next to Taylor on her red comforter (mine was light blue) and poked her arm; she appeared to be falling asleep.

"Tee, wake up. I have to talk to you. I have a confession to make and I need you up and awake to give me feedback and tell me that I'm okay and that I'll be okay if I have to tell someone else, and that I'm not some nasty bitch because this happened to me. I mean, this could've happened to anybody, right?"

"What are you talking about, Evie?" Taylor wasn't doing much better than I.

"Shh. Listen to me. I got herpes, girl. That nasty-ass Brand slept with some funky chick and got some foul shit from her, and now I got it too."

"Oh shit, Eva. Herpes? Are you sure?" Taylor leaned in and whispered, "Where are they? The herpes, I mean. Have you seen them? Can I see them?"

"No you can't see them and I don't have any right now. But yes, I am sure; too sure, in fact. This is what I'm trying to tell you. I've had this shit for months and months. I was too ashamed and embarrassed to say anything. I feel so dirty and nasty. I know that I'm not, but this thing got me fucked up every time I think about it or whenever I get that feeling in my legs or down there."

"How do you know it's Brand? What did he say? Did he at least say sorry? You know, he can be a serious asshole sometimes. Wait a minute; was he cheating when he gave this shit to you?" I shook my head no. Luckily, I had never told her about the sixteen women Brand brought into our relationship the first time. Taylor had sobered up quickly: Actually, we had both sobered up rather nicely, needing our sober wits as we conspiratorially trashed Brand. There's nothing like tragedy to blow a high.

"Yeah, he apologized, but what good was that going to do? It's too late for me now. Some chick ruined his life and, in turn, he ruined mine. I'm screwed for life and I probably need to stay with him and not have to worry about this shit any more. You cannot imagine what I have been through, on my own. I wanted to tell you sooner but I can barely make myself say those words: herpes. Herpes. I swear I hate him."

"Oh my God, Evie, I can't believe you've been going through this on your own! I feel like I should have known something and been there for you. I hate Brand for you, now. You are the very last person this should have happened to. You are too good for Brand or Cory! These assholes don't deserve you. Look at how they treat you. I should have known something. I should have been able to see through you. What kind of best friend am I?" Taylor belched long and loud after her emotional story. I felt like pulling out my miniature violin and playing.

"Look, Tee, it's over now. I feel like a weight has been removed now that I've told you. I've needed someone to talk to for so long. Brand wants to act as if it never happened and I've been driving myself crazy, worrying about my future. I'm just glad I told you."

"Do you want to stab him, Evie? We could probably get away with it and if we didn't, his giving you herpes will surely win a jury's sympathy. We would be free and he would be dead! Oh God, Eva, where's the bathroom?"

Taylor threw up in the toilet and briefly napped on the red comforter. We stuffed ourselves with pizza and coffee for the rest of the night. She left, giving me a hug and assurances that she'd figure out something to do to Brand, and even Cory. She was willing to hate them enough for both of us.

I loved Taylor and kissed her cheek; unfortunately, I thought I loved Brand as well.

Chapter 27

I *called Brand often* to make sure he still loved me and hadn't forgotten me. It never occurred to me that he might be in a relationship, or simply be busy with another woman. In my mind, Brand was there, would always be there when I needed him and called. He hadn't forgotten about me, of course. He told me he loved me, which was what I wanted to hear. I wasn't ready to get back with him, but his time and attention was a source of comfort for me, which I wasn't totally ready to be without.

I was lonely and felt like I needed a man in my life. I was used to having a steady boyfriend and someone to rely on. Maybe they weren't always faithful and were mostly assholes, but they were there. I wondered if a relationship with a woman would be any different. Would a woman cheat? Could she be more faithful and committed? Would a woman bring other women, and possibly men, into our relationship? I guess I'd have to find out the hard way, as usual.

Brand and I continued to go out and enjoyed each other. We missed each other and often spoke of it; we just didn't know how to handle it or what to do with it.

Then Brand started talking about us getting back together. But I wasn't sure I wanted that with anyone right now. I wasn't sure what I wanted. I longed for the comfort and security of a relationship with someone I knew;

someone who knew me; someone who knew my situation.

I wasn't sure that I wanted to be in a relationship with Brand again.

The issues that existed when we were together were still there. We had herpes together; that, obviously, hadn't changed and wouldn't. I wanted, needed to talk about it with Brand. I needed to be able to express myself and seek comfort when I was having an outbreak and felt shitty about myself. I wanted to be able to talk to him when I was feeling depressed. I wanted to be able to display the anger and frustration I kept bottled up inside when there was no one to talk to.

I needed to know that he would be there for me.

I told him that I would think about it, about us. I loved Brand; not the hopeless, helpless love I felt for Cory, but a different kind of love, born out of our experiences together. It was a sick, mostly comforting attachment, but it was one that I knew and could depend on.

I wasn't ready to commit yet. Our friendship was important to me and I didn't want things to change.

One night, over drinks at his place, Brand started asking me about children. "So what about us, Eva? What are we going to do? Are we going to be together, or are we going to be friends?"

He's serious as shit and I'm wondering where this is coming from. I couldn't help asking, "You're ready to do this Brand? You're ready to start a family? You think we're ready for that kind of commitment and responsibility?"

I'm thinking about the two children I hadn't given birth to and I didn't really want to discuss any of it. Then he springs on me, "What would you do if I had a baby with somebody else? How would you feel?"

I'm looking at Brand like he's crazy. I'd fucking murder the chick who bore his child before I did. Whether I loved Brand or not, I didn't want another woman sharing that kind of bond with him.

"Where are we going with this conversation, Brand? Do you have something you need to tell me? How the hell do you think I'd feel if you had a fuckin' baby by somebody else?" I'm getting mad and the thought of Brand sleeping with some random chick and getting her pregnant was enraging me. I didn't want to talk about kids. I absolutely refused to think about the two children I hadn't given birth to. Brand didn't know about the miscarriage and the abortion. I'd been too ashamed to tell him and wouldn't bother to bring it up now.

My silence gave Brand the perfect segue into the conversation he wanted to have.

"Damn, calm down, Eva. I'm just asking you a couple of questions." He kissed me and squeezed my arm. "You know, Beth made me promise that I'd tell you what's been going on with the girls." He laughed for a minute before he could even speak. "Brighton doesn't even talk to Dad anymore, he's so fuckin' disgusted with the entire situation. It turns out that the girls' mom's name is Christine, and she's a girl I used to date in high school." At my incredulous look he adds, "Yeah, I know. It's somewhat corny that 'Wayland the playa' would have sex with a girl I fucked with, but that's his shit.

"So he and Christine have been goin' at it, off and on, for the last four or five years. According to Dad, she would disappear and then pop up and they'd pick up where they left off." I'm thinking, Yeah, right, and he never noticed that her body had changed? There were no visible signs that she'd had a baby, and then another?

"Then Christine calls the house and explains to Brighton that she's headed to medical school, on scholarship at Yale University. She claims that Dad brought her to Philly on breaks from the U of Miami while she was getting her B.S. in chemistry. Tasha and Angelique stayed with her mother while she finished her undergrad degree. She only called Dad when her mom refused to keep the girls for another three or four years while she completed her M.D. Brighton cursed her the fuck out and had her crying on the phone. Dad walks in the room while Bright's on the phone with her, and doesn't do anything to stop him. The entire situation is completely fucked up, but what can we do now? The girls are here to stay. At least 'til their mom comes back to get them."

"This is completely crazy, Brand. What was Wayland thinking about? He was actually fucking one of your old girlfriends? How old is this girl? Was he straight up robbing the cradle, or what? Eww…don't tell me your dad's a perv. I can't take it."

"Wait, it gets better. Christine is 25 years old, so that means Wayland has been fucking her since she got out of high school. I only stopped fucking her after she graduated the year before I did. Yo, he's a sick-ass dude. So, she's crying and telling Bright that she couldn't get in touch with any of us to let us know about the girls. And then she finds out that she has this full scholarship to medical school and needs their dad to take them, so she can go. I think Wayland's been paying her college tuition all along and she's hoping that she can beat him for a few more thousand while she finishes medical school."

This was completely bizarre. I wondered if anyone else thought that her excuses were lame or that the entire situation was too strange for fiction. Apparently, guilt and a need for freedom to attend medical school was her reason for now bringing the girls to their father. Christine didn't explain other than she had a scholarship to a medical school at Yale and would be gone for at least three years.

Brand continued, "Brighton confronted Dad and he neither denied nor admitted to fucking with Christine and being the possible father of her children. 'Her children,' as if he isn't likely their father. Bright, being the oldest feels that he has to represent the older kids and almost went off on Dad. Beth said she had to grab Bright before we all were kicked out of the house. He said he was tired of Dad's bullshit. Wayland says that the 'probability is highly unlikely' that he is the father of those two small children, though they do resemble his grown children. Based on that possibility, however, he'd welcome the girls into his home for a time."

Brand ended Christine's tale with her final request of the DeLoache family. "She hinted at the necessity to send money for plane tickets to visit the girls often."

Three months later, Wayland went to family court to establish paternity for both children. The DNA test results were inconclusive, showing that Wayland was a candidate for paternity based on his DNA. The results were inconsistent with his particular DNA but close enough so that he was definitely related, possibly an uncle; some sort of male relative.

It was all very confusing and I wondered why Brand was mentioning his sisters now, when we were discussing the possibility of our future. I didn't care. Maybe I should have.

"That's all very interesting, Brand, but why are we talking about this right now? What do Tasha, Angelique, and Wayland have to do with us? I thought we were talking about us." I let it go for now and attempted to change the subject.

"Brand, there are some things we need to discuss. I love you and have been thinking about the conversations we've had about getting back together. You know, we broke up for a reason and we need to get past a few things before we'll be ready for a commitment again."

"I know, Eva."

"Brand, talk to me. I want us to, honestly, talk to each other. I want you to talk to me. Let's talk about us."

"Eva not now…"

"Brand, please. Show me I was wrong about us the first time."

"Eva, can we please talk about this later?"

It was the usual Brand conversation.

I was disappointed, yet not surprised. I didn't think Brand would ever change. Was he capable of change? Was he capable of the type of change I needed?

I wanted to leave. I should have left then.

Instead, I let Brand make love to me. It was what he wanted. He wanted my silence about our past; about the virus we shared. Unintentionally, I gave that silence to him.

I let him do to me all the things he wanted. I did, for him, all the things he wanted. "Eva, take your clothes off."

I silently took my clothes off and stood before him in my bra and panties.

It was what he wanted.

I let him kiss me on my mouth, breasts and stomach.

I let him turn me around and kiss my neck, back and shoulders.

I felt myself getting wet and cursed my weakness for him.

I let him bend me over and probe my vagina and anus with his fingers and tongue.

I allowed him to push me to my knees and enter me from behind. I heard myself moan with pleasure and struggle to catch my breath.

Brand didn't make a sound. He wouldn't speak to me again until it was over.

It was what he wanted.

I felt him push two fingers into my anus as he fucked me, and I came, crying out.

I felt him pull out of my vagina. For the first time, I heard him breathing hard.

He walked in front of me and put his penis on my lips. It was slick and shiny.

He rubbed himself on my lips and into my mouth. I could smell and taste my scent on him and moaned again with pleasure, despite myself.

He grabbed the back of my head and drove his penis in and out of my mouth, moving faster and grinding harder.

It was what he wanted.

I heard him moaning and gasping for breath. Then he stood perfectly still.

Without warning, his orgasm hit the back of my throat. I tried to pull away but he held my head in place. His hips kept working, filling my mouth and his grip became stronger. He emptied himself into me.

My natural reflex was to swallow.

It was what he wanted.

"I love you, Eva."

I didn't say anything. There wasn't anything to say.

I lay next to him and watched him sleep.

I went home and cried myself to sleep.

Chapter 28

Damn Brand. Damn Brand and his nasty disease. Damn him for what he had done to us. Damn him and his refusal to face up to what was done to me. Damn his unwillingness to own up to the fact that he ruined me for anyone else, yet wasn't willing to make things right between us. He wasn't worthy of me. He wasn't worthy of my time.

Why did I still love him?

I refused to dwell on Brand.

The next day, Monday morning, I went to the office and told myself that I wouldn't think about him.

It didn't work. Everyone assumed I was sick. Then a co-worker came up with an offer I couldn't refuse.

My friend Jess, from work, was constantly trying to hook me up with various male friends of hers. She'd bring in pictures and show me emails of gorgeous men with beautiful bodies, claiming that she knew all of them and that they were available for the taking.

After our weekly morning meeting, Jess told me that she had found yet another eligible bachelor, the perfect man for me. His name was Bryce.

I had seen Bryce, in passing, a few times out with Jess. He was definitely a cutie, with a visibly strong back. He was younger than we were, but was three months away from his Ph. D. and childless. I wasn't looking for love or even guiltless sex. I wanted someone and something to help take my mind off Brand, get over Cory and the desire to ride past his house daily to peer into his windows.

Jess helped smooth the initial meetings by making them group dates and inviting us over to her house for food and drinks. I wasn't really attracted to Bryce, but he was fun and I was embarrassingly desperate.

Bryce invited me over to his house, to get to know each other and spend time alone. I wasn't sure what he wanted or what he was looking for. I wasn't scared to be alone with him, but I didn't want him to get the wrong idea about us either. I did everything I could to avoid going over to his house until I had run out of excuses. By the time I was headed to Bryce's house, it was six weeks later.

Undaunted and too ashamed to back out, I headed over to Bryce's at 2:15 a.m., booty-call time. I knew I was giving him the wrong signals. Oh, well. I decided that I wouldn't stay long.

Stopped at a red light on Upsal Street in Mount Airy, I noticed a car slowly approaching on my right. Not sure of what was coming up behind me alone, so early in the morning; I was prepared to run the red light to get away if necessary.

Much to my surprise, a midnight blue Benz pulled along side of me. You know all possible fear fled my body. Wow. What nice surprises awaited one in the middle of the night.

The driver's side window lowered on the Benz. I immediately lowered my passenger side window. "Good morning." This came from an interesting face inside the Benz. "What brings you out so early this morning?" Nice teeth greeted me from the darkness.

What luck? "I think I was waiting here, at this light, for you," I sang sweetly. My night was looking up already. We exchanged pleasantries through our windows, talking and flirting. I put my car in park and commenced a conversation with Hank, my newest friend.

The traffic light turned green, then yellow and back to red. We sat side by side, in the middle of the street, at the corner of Upsal and Anderson Streets, talking and watching the traffic lights change colors. Poor Bryce was waiting. He would continue to wait. Bryce did not have a Mercedes Benz.

Hank was on his way home to Germantown. He didn't mention where he was coming from. Maybe I should have asked. He was 27 and had a small son. Strike one. Gee. Why wasn't I surprised?

Hank wasn't fine like Cory, or even cute like Brand. When he stepped out of the car, he looked a little short as well. However, this was not the night for pickiness.

Hank and I pressed our luck, never saw another car or, thankfully, the police; and exchanged telephone numbers. Smiling, pulling away at the green light, a disturbing thought struck: was I becoming a whore? Was this how it started? I wasn't sure. Here I was, en route to Bryce's house, and waylaid by Hank the stranger. I was surely on my way to whoredom.

Hank promised to call me the next day and I was off to see Bryce. It was 3:00 a.m. I really wanted to go home.

Bryce was asleep when I got to his house. His mother answered my knock at the back door. Didn't I say I put off this date/meeting as long as possible?

Bryce hugged me and put on his best smile. He then went to brush his teeth. I was praying for a miracle earthquake, tsunami or hailstorm to get me out of Bryce's house and home to my queen-sized bed.

Of course, no natural catastrophe happened upon us and Bryce returned with drinks and replayed the tape of the earlier basketball game. It felt like the date from Hell and I kept hearing his mother walking around above us on the first floor. Did I mention that Bryce lived in the basement? I thought she'd surely bust in on us any minute.

We drank, talked, and watched the replay of the game. I was falling asleep and continuing to pray for nature to give me a reason to leave sooner than later.

Draped across the bed, waiting for an interruption from up above, Bryce snuggled close and kissed me. I wasn't wowed. I kept thinking about Hank and the Benz. Bryce's kiss was stiff and dry. On the other hand, was it my imagination? Was I caught up in Hank's flash and the promise it held? I was ready to conjure up a swarm of locusts, anything, to get out.

I felt badly for Bryce and allowed him to kiss me again. It wasn't any better. In face, it may have been worse than the original kiss. I had had enough. I begged off, promised to make it up to him, and went home.

At home, I quickly changed clothes and climbed into bed. I kept thinking about Hank. There was something quite attractive about him, other than the Benz. It must have been the lips. Yes, his lips were full and sensuous and I imagined them all over my body.

I felt a familiar tingling between my legs. My hands found their way to my breasts and I rubbed my nipples until they were hard. I licked and sucked my nipples until I felt my clitoris harden. I stroked my clitoris and slid two fingers in and out of my pussy until I was moaning and writhing on my bed, alone, in the dark.

I successfully masturbated to the vision of Brand's lips on my breasts, Cory's penis in my mouth and Kristal's lips on my clitoris. Cory came in my mouth; Brand came on my breasts and I deliciously came on Kristal's tongue.

Chapter 29

I *was asleep in* minutes and awoke in the morning with my mind racing. I couldn't believe or understand my behavior as of late. I was thinking of Kristal often and wondered if she was a one-time experience, or if I was interested in women as a full-time gig.

To be honest, I loved having sex with Kristal. Mostly, I loved her soft body, her lips and breasts. I thought about her a lot but was afraid to tell Brand that I was interested in seeing Kristal again. I'd be forced to scour gay bars and clubs to find Mrs. Right, it seemed. It was none of his business, anyway.

For the first time, I thought I might be a lesbian. It was a terrifying thought. I wasn't ready for Gay Pride Day marches and same-sex marriages. I didn't want to explain to my eventual children why our family didn't look like any other family within miles. I wasn't ready for the birds and birds and bees and bees discussion. I'd kill myself before I came out of any closet.

Plus, I liked men, a lot. All types of men.

I decided that I must be bisexual. I obviously liked women and men. I could live with that. Plus, who said I had to make up my mind right now? Didn't people shop around and go on numerous dates before deciding whom they'd end up with? I was no different. I would date men and I would date women. Then I could have the best of both worlds. I was ready for my next conquest.

Or so I thought. First, I had to get used to living and working each day. I longed for the worriless days of junior college, and then Villanova. At this point, my life consisted of working, attempting to exercise and make time for my varied love life.

My job was stressing me and I could barely make it to work each day. Initially, I thought I wanted a desk job where I could sit all day and talk on the phone to my friends. Now I wasn't so sure. The work was mind numbing and I had mastered every task put before me. I felt that I was wasting time and couldn't wait to start school again.

The outbreaks were back and I was depressed each time I felt the pain in my legs and in my vaginal area. I figured out that caffeine and stress brought on the herpes outbreaks so I avoided Pepsi, coffee and Mountain Dew. The stress I attempted to limit but I didn't have much success. I was always worried about the job, Brand, or Cory. I was a mess.

And because I was a mess, I should have thrown Hank's phone number away and concentrated on working on me. I should have ignored his calls and refused to meet with him. Of course, I didn't. I met with Hank at a small Italian restaurant in Glenside. He was slightly taller than I remembered. He brought his two-year-old son with him. Now, there was a cutie. I was won over.

Hank worked in computers. He had a master's degree in something (basket weaving, perhaps) from Brown University. He had been in the Navy. He had a Mercedes Benz. Hank was the man for me.

Hank Jr. sat on my lap and gave me wet, sloppy kisses. Adorable and juicy.

I hoped they were not an indication of his father's kisses.

We ate mini ravioli, pizza and spaghetti; toddler food.

Hank said we needed to make a stop after he paid the check. He'd kept HJ overnight and was taking him home to his mother after our dinner on the children's menu. Hank explained that he didn't normally introduce his son to friends, female especially, so quickly, but he wanted to see me.

Of course, I was flattered and looked completely beyond the fact that he'd brought his small child onto our first date, without informing me. The lights were flashing, the sirens wailing. I still don't know how I missed them.

We left my car at the restaurant and drove HJ home to his mother, who was standing in the doorway, waiting. Upon closer inspection, I turned, horrified, to stare at Hank's profile. I know he felt me staring at him, wondering what kind of drug he'd been on when he met her. He wouldn't look at me so I knew that he knew that she was a beast. Yuck. Maybe Hank needed glasses. She was hideous. Had he really laid down, purposely, and made this adorable baby with that? Had he been drinking the night he impregnated her? The baby resembled neither of them.

I rolled my eyes to the Heavens as she grabbed her baby from Hank and glared into the Benz. At who? Me? I couldn't hear the words but she was pointing into the car, her expressions and body language saying more than enough. I was not interested, nor was I impressed and turned away, looking for a CD to play.

I wanted to slap her. I wanted to slap him for sleeping with her. Surely, he'd been desperate. It was too much for me, especially on a first date. I couldn't wait to leave. Good riddance. I'd had enough of HJ and his mother.

I put on Sade's *Lovers Rock* CD; shit, somebody needed some good love.

I glanced up in time to see Hank kiss his son and walk back to the car, shaking his head and lighting a cigarette. Strike two. He got into the car and sat silently, blowing smoke out of the window.

"Eva, I apologize for Tiffany's behavior. I probably shouldn't have brought you with me. She gets upset when I have Hank around other women. We broke up when he was a few months old, but she can't seem to get a handle on herself. We were arguing because she doesn't want him to come over next weekend. She thinks that we live together and that you'll have a negative influence him. Don't worry, she's harmless. She just can't control her jealousy."

"Sweetheart, truly, she is the least of my worries."

Everything told me to walk away from Hank. He had a child. He smoked. He had baby momma drama. It was nerve wracking.

But of course, the premonition of drama was not enough to keep me away.

Hank appeared for our next date on a motorcycle, a Suzuki GSXR 750. On our second date, we were alone. HJ was with his jealous, worrisome mother. We stopped by Hank's mother's house on our way to dinner. Don't ask.

She was nice enough. A little old fashioned, perhaps. Her living room furniture was covered in plastic. Played out since the early 80s. After talking to her for half an hour, it appeared that she didn't think highly of single women out on dates with men they barely knew. I think she was pushing to be our chaperone. No dice.

I couldn't wait to leave.

We decided on Friday's in Montgomeryville, PA. There was a long stretch of highway, southbound 309, into Montgomery County, made for a fast motorcycle. Too easily, we got up to 120 mph and I was scared to death. I pictured myself flying off the back of that Suzuki, never to be seen again. Fortunately, we made it to the restaurant in one piece.

Over strawberry daiquiris and fried mozzarella sticks, Hank told me about Trina, his live-in girlfriend. Of course.

Strike three.

As usual, I was ready to leave but something in Hank's imploring voice and gaze stopped me. I figured he would be good for a few free meals, maybe a Gucci bag, and that'd be that.

"Eva." Hank's voice was soft and low. "I wanted to tell you about Trina the night we met. I never intended to deceive you. I can understand it may be difficult to believe, but I'd hoped she'd be gone before our first date."

"Really, Hank, don't worry about it. It's okay. I'm fine with it. We can be friends." What I was really thinking, and didn't say, was, 'Don't worry about it, boy, I'll just spend all of your money. Trina, who?'

"Please, don't dismiss me so fast. I want to explain about me and Trina." Hank stopped me from interrupting and continued. "Trina and I have been together for a long time; since we were teens. We've known each other since high school, went to our proms together and everybody expects us to get married eventually. I wasn't sure I wanted to marry her but after HJ was born, she forgave me for cheating and we tried to work on our relationship. We've outgrown each other but neither of us knows how to break it off. I've caught her cheating, she's found phone numbers in my pockets; we somehow manage to get back together."

I really didn't want to hear anymore about Trina. My mind was made up. I sucked down my daiquiri and signaled the waitress for another, with a double shot of spiced rum. I attempted, again, to cut him off.

"Hank. Really, it's okay. I'm fine with your situation. I wasn't looking for a relationship. I'm okay with us being friends." If he didn't shut up about her, I was going to vomit all over him.

"Please, just let me finish. I really want you to understand my situation. I don't normally stop women in the street and engage in conversation, and I especially don't allow women to meet my son. Please, Eva, I don't do this everyday. There's something about you that I'd like to explore." Hank grabbed my hand and caressed my palm. "Let me finish."

My daiquiri arrived. I'd give him 7 ½ more minutes and then I was heading to the ladies' room for a break, and to relieve him of my company.

"About eight months ago, I was fed up with Trina and the relationship. She was having sex with some guy at her job, we had an STD scare and I was through with her. I told her I was moving out and that she could keep all of the furniture and one of the cars. Two weeks later she announced that she was pregnant."

Hank signaled the waitress for a double shot of Hennessy.

"I wanted to ask her who the father was, 'cause I seriously didn't think it was me. It could have been me or some other guys; I didn't know. Then I felt guilty about leaving her, just in case it was my baby. It was her first kid and she was happy and crying. I was miserable and thinking abortion. My mom convinced me that I owed the baby a chance, so I decided to stay."

Hank's Hennessy came and he threw it back.

"I spent as much time as possible away from home, working overtime, hanging out with friends. She was constantly accusing me of cheating and avoiding her. I would come home and she'd be hysterical and try to fight me." He stopped and stared at a spot on the wall behind me for a minute.

"She lost the baby at 5 ½ months. Again, I felt guilty; then I felt happy and relieved that I wouldn't have to be bothered with her for 18 more years."

Hank stopped and shook his head at the memory.

"Then she fell into a depression, starting having anxiety attacks and got fired from her job. She went to her primary doctor, who diagnosed her as bipolar and recommended that she see a therapist and psychiatrist. She was on antidepressants and mood stabilizers. She took Prozac for depression, Ativan for anxiety, and Valium to sleep, and occasionally a few others pills."

Hank signaled for another Hennessy.

"She finally spent time in an inpatient treatment center after she took

22 Valium while I was at work. She claims she wasn't trying to kill herself but she got confused about her pill intake. The doctors at the hospital didn't believe her and kept her for five weeks." Sipping my drink, I could see the anguish in his face.

"My God, this sounds terrible; even to me. I couldn't leave her. I had to wait a while. I'm still waiting."

Damn. I was feeling sorry for Hank. I was feeling sorry for Trina. I was feeling sorry for myself.

Hank switched to Jack Daniels.

I didn't say a word.

"But enough about Trina. Let's talk about Eva. Let's talk about Eva and Hank. I want to get to know you, and I think I can be good for you. Let me make you feel like a woman and make up to you all the wrong that has been done to you by my fellow man."

I wasn't moved. I switched to Bacardi Gold and Coke.

"Eva, if you give me a chance, I will love you. I will give you everything you desire. You will want for nothing. Please, just let me try."

I wasn't overwhelmed.

But I was suckered.

I fell for the bullshit.

He had me.

I should have walked away. I meant to walk away. Nevertheless, I didn't.

What was Hank really offering?

I wanted to hear from Cory. Was he a father yet? Was there a baby? How old was he or she? How old would my baby have been? I was doing the math in my head when I stopped myself. I was on a date with a man who wanted to be here with me. I was here with a man who was interested in getting to know me. Cory didn't want our baby or me.

I caught myself drifting away and forced myself to focus on Hank.

Why was I thinking about Cory?

Hank and I had to finish our date. I had to move on.

Why was this so hard?

I needed some time alone.

I begged off continuing the date with Hank, pleading a massive headache. I really needed some time alone. Hank dropped me off at my new apartment with a nice, lingering kiss. I knew those lips were special.

Chapter 30

Hank was conveniently forgotten when I reached the front door. Heather, from the third floor, was on the steps as I entered the front door. Goddamn, she was cute. I wanted to reach out and touch her body.

I quickly reminded myself that I wasn't in any condition to start a relationship or have even good sex with anyone, male or female.

Of course, I didn't listen to myself.

Hank called me, or I called Hank. Who knows? We got together from time to time to go out and kiss for hours inside her car, outside the apartment he shared with Trina.

I'd ask myself what I was doing.

It was scandalous.

It was such fun.

Then reality set in.

Hank got married two days after our fifth date. I found out when I called his cell phone and his new wife, Trina, returned my call.

I was…angry. I told myself that I didn't have any reason to be. At least I hadn't had sex with him.

I liked him, though.

It was for the best, I convinced myself.

I was home alone, with no one to talk to, no one who wanted to be with me and I wondered what was going on. What was wrong with me? Why were men always cheating? Why couldn't I hold on to a man?

I went into the bedroom and stood in front of the full-length mirror. I stood there turning from side to side, studying my profile and the images I saw there. I stood there, wondering what others saw in me. I saw a cute girl; intelligent, funny and spunky.

Why couldn't I keep a man?

What was wrong with me? Was I too much? Not enough? What were men looking for? Why wasn't I it?

I suddenly pictured Heather, from upstairs, cupping my breasts in her hands, her lips and mouth working magic on my hard nipples. I snapped myself out of it. What the hell was wrong with me? I was becoming a pervert!

I thought of my brothers: handsome young men, witty, intelligent; too bad they took after Mavis. We resembled our parents a great deal; there was no way to deny our gene pool. We were an exact mixture of our Italian American father and our African American mother.

Our skin was golden, so light compared to Mavis' smooth chocolate skin that she was constantly asked, when we were small, if we were her children. During some of our more civil moments, Mavis remarked that people often stopped her and asked if she was our nanny. I think it was insulting, for Mavis, to explain the relationship with her own children to total strangers.

I never considered my mixed heritage or questioned it. It was never discussed in our home. I was the only one of their children who had never seen our father in person. I didn't even know he wasn't black until the first grade. I didn't notice a difference in Aunt Mirabelle until age six when I saw a picture of her and my father as children, standing next to black classmates. Even then, I didn't question it. We lived in Germantown, back Haines Street, the average, urban neighborhood; Mavis looked like every other woman there.

I didn't look different; I didn't feel different; I didn't sound different than anyone else I came in contact with. I wondered if there WAS something wrong with me. Was I too different?

I felt like I was sinking.

I tried to remember what I was like, even six months ago. I had been so sure of myself. I was flying high, close to graduation, making plans for my future. Sure, I'd been concerned about outbreaks, but I'd been sure of me; of who Eva was. There had been no doubt then. Eva knew who she was and what she wanted.

That Eva was self-assured. That Eva had men calling at all times, day and night. That Eva had no problems with her esteem and self-image. That Eva didn't worry that she wasn't good enough. That Eva had her whole future in front of her.

I felt like I was sinking.

I gave into the despair and cried on the bed. I let it all out, cursing men and their abandoning and cheating ways. I cursed myself for whatever was wrong with me. I cursed Mavis for being an asshole, a terrible mother and for marrying a white man who wasn't around to be there for me. I cried, picturing cute couples walking down the street, holding hands, when I couldn't capture the interest of any man for long.

It was too much and I need to talk to someone to make me feel better about myself. I didn't care if they had to lie to me.

Chapter 31

I *called Brand.* He was busy, out with his sisters. They were at Chuck E. Cheese. With the babies? What the hell was he doing with them? He explained that he'd been getting to know them, was spending more time with them since his father spent so much time traveling for business.

"Okay, Brand. That's great. When can I see you?" I didn't mean to be short, but I wasn't interested in Tasha and Angelique.

"Not today, Eva. Once we're done here, we're going to the movies."

I wasn't ready to give up. They had a mother and a father, somewhere. I had no one right now.

"When did all of this happen, Brand? I thought your father wasn't even sure they were his daughters. Did they retake the paternity test?"

I was being petty and felt like shit. The sisters were babies and as far as we knew, Brand was their older brother. He was supposed to take care of them. I was being a brat and trying to foist them off on someone else. I didn't care.

"Well, when can you see me?" I was close to begging. I didn't even give him a chance to answer the questions I was throwing at him.

"Eva, calm down. I just can't see you today. Hold on." I could hear him speaking to one of the girls, telling her to be careful climbing. "Look, Eva, I promise I'll call you tomorrow."

"When, Brand?" I was loud and near tears. I didn't care.

"Eva, I've got to go. Let me call you tomorrow."

"Damn it, Brand, I need you." What was I supposed to do until tomorrow? I felt lost without a man. Any man. I felt like I had no one to talk to.

"Eva…" Brand let my name drag out and I knew then that I was breaking him down and getting on his nerves. "I'll call you tonight after I put them to bed."

"Okay." It was enough for me and honestly, I wasn't being particular about how I got it.

"Bye." Brand hung up.

But it wasn't enough. I needed to talk to someone now.

I called Taylor. She was in Conshohocken at Shawn's parents' house. I didn't want to hear about how happy she was; they were.

I called Bryce. He was home, wondering where I'd been. He said he'd been thinking of me; of course, he'd like to see me.

It was good enough for me.

I made it to Bryce's house in record time and, surprise, his mother was in Atlantic City for the week. I didn't want to talk. I didn't want food or to watch television. I wanted body contact with a man. I wanted to be caressed and lied to. I wanted Bryce to show his appreciation of me through sex and acceptance.

I got everything I wanted and it felt good for a while. I ignored Bryce's stiff, dry kiss. I allowed him to lick my pussy and invade my body with multiple fingers. I stroked his penis with my hands, body and mouth until he came all over me and into me.

Mentally, though, I wasn't into it and kept getting dry despite his arduous and vigorous lovemaking. I finally came after role-playing in my head and pretending, with my eyes squeezed shut, that Kristal was fucking me with a strap-on dick. In my mind, I was sucking and licking her nipples and finger fucking her tight pussy while she steadily worked between my thighs. I was suddenly slick and wet and could feel the wetness run in between my ass cheeks as I rode with Kristal/Bryce's dick until I was crying out, my body involuntarily spastic, gasping for breath. "Damn, girl," I murmured as I drifted back into reality with Bryce.

Bryce was ecstatic. "Eva, I'm so glad you came to see me again. I didn't think you were interested in me, based on your responses the last time you were here." He fingered my pussy, and then played with my nipples, running his slick fingers around and around.

"I know, Bryce, and I'm sorry for not calling you sooner. I've been busy with work, moving and just getting in some me time." I was making it up as I went along. I wasn't feeling this dude who couldn't keep me wet and I needed the image of a dildo-strapped girl to make me come.

Bryce moved my hand to his chest and I played with his chest hair while I planned my next outing to the market for food. "Well, again, I'm glad you called me tonight, Eva. After another week, you probably wouldn't have been able to reach me here and I would have been disappointed to miss your call."

"Oh." What was he getting at? What was he talking about? Sarcastically, I said, "Tell me, Bryce, where you would have been?"

Instead, he got up and moved toward the basement stairs, "Would you like something to drink? I'll be right back. We have soda, juice and bottled water. Your choice." He stopped on the stairs and asked, "Are you hungry?" Laughing at himself, he said, "I'm sorry, I didn't think to ask. I've got a lot on my mind, too."

"Pepsi. Thank you." As soon as he was out of sight, I was getting dressed. He could have that on his mind, as well.

As his feet disappeared on the steps, I looked around the basement, noticing for the first time how nicely decorated Bryce's room was. There was a full bathroom and a stocked wet bar approximately 5 feet from the king-sized bed. I fingered the sheets, looking for my discarded bra and panties in the massive bed. California King. Ralph Lauren down comforter. At least 450 thread-count, I guessed as I searched in vain. The two small windows were covered with matching silk drapes. I walked over to the armoire to look at his jewelry. Diamond-studded Movado. Interesting.

I quickly walked back to the bed and resumed my search. Damn, too late. I could hear him on his way down the steps.

Bryce started talking to me as he moved back down the steps. "You know, Eva, you are the first woman to come to my humble basement abode without making comments about my living situation. A couple of women never made it across the threshold once they realized where we were and where we weren't going; upstairs, that is. I've thought a lot about that as I've waited to hear from you."

In Bryce's hands was a tray laden with food and drink. He handed me a cold Pepsi and a flute of champagne. For himself, there was a Heineken and another flute of champagne. The last of the tray was chilled jumbo shrimp and spiced cocktail sauce.

"Let's toast, Eva, to us. You can't even begin to imagine how pleased I am to be here with you, on this night. I received some good news today and you're the first person I'm sharing it with." Bryce leaned over and kissed me on the cheek. "The developer called me this afternoon and told me that my house will be completed in approximately one week. They're doing the finishing touches and the house will be ready for my final walk-through." He kissed me again. "My mother doesn't even know yet."

"A toast to the new house." We tapped flutes and drank deeply. "Eva, I hope to see you often, in my new house. Who knows, maybe one day it will be our house." I tried to hide my surprise and gulped the champagne.

"That's great, Bryce, and a hell of a secret. Where's your house located?" I gaped in disbelief and attempted to soak in the information he had just shared. "Why are you living here, then, when you could live anywhere?"

"Oh, the details aren't important right now, but I purchased land in Chalfont over 18 months ago and the builders broke ground about six months ago. The waiting has been torture and being cramped in my mother's basement, where I haven't lived since I was 17 years old, is stressing." He reached for the food on the tray and fed me a cold shrimp dipped in cocktail sauce. "Did you know I graduated from high school at 16 and was the youngest freshman, in history, at Monmouth State?"

No. I hadn't known anything about Bryce. I thought he was a loser living off his retired mother. "No, Bryce, actually I hadn't. You're just full of surprises tonight, aren't you? What else do you have hidden away?" I laughed at the next thought. "Is your wife going to jump out of the closet, wanting to join us?" If she was cute enough, I just might like that.

"My point, Eva, is that I have lived here, with my mother, for 20 months and have never told anyone, other than my mother, about my house because most women prejudge my living situation. They assume I'm living here, off my mother, as if I would." He laughed and sipped the champagne. "You wouldn't believe the things I've heard from women about coming here to see me in the basement. It doesn't seem to matter that I'm working on my Ph. D. and make over $110,000 a year. Most women see me in my mother's basement and write me off."

As I'd done, I thought, now ashamed of myself.

"So you see, now, why I am so pleased that you picked today to call me. I would have been here celebrating all alone. There's no one else, I could think, befitting of this momentous occasion, to share it with." He paused in thought. "I was seeing someone a short while ago, but she constantly complained about the lack of privacy, as if my mother would dare come down these steps, without permission, after all I've done for her. This woman wanted me to spend money on luxury hotels every weekend in order to entertain her." He laughed and kissed me again. "She was ridiculous and I can't believe I actually took her to hotels for three weeks straight, to appease her. The sex wasn't even good." He drank from his Heineken bottle and sighed deeply. "You, Eva, are a breath of fresh air. You can't know how often I wanted to hear from you; how I waited to hear from you, hoping that you were different from the rest."

"Bryce. Damn. I'm happy for you. I don't know what to say to you. I'm also glad I picked tonight to come see you." Bryce opened my Pepsi and poured a flute full. "What does your house look like?"

"Oh, it's not much. But while I was working with the architect and the developer, I decided that this may be the only home I ever purchase, and I didn't want to outgrow it when I have a family." He sipped his beer and looked at me.

At this point, I'm dying of curiosity and ask, "And….Bryce, you're killing me! How many square feet, how many bedrooms, bathrooms? Say something! Fireplace?"

"Let me surprise you. Why don't you join me for the final walk—through? You can see everything the same time I see it. We'll be surprised together."

"Okay, let's do that. Thank you, Bryce. I'm flattered that you would invite me to join you on such an important day." I thought of Hank; how I'd been bamboozled by his flashy car and drawn into his personal drama. To think that I'd been missing out on a great guy who actually thought that I was something special. "So, Bryce, what exactly do you do?"

I spent the night with Bryce, talking and laughing until the sun crept into the basement windows. He was a perfect gentleman and didn't touch me, except to caress my hair or shoulder as we talked. I honestly wasn't interested in having any more sex, but I was interested in getting to know him a little more.

Chapter 32

I *went home with* a smile on my face and determination in my heart. I was going to close the Cory chapter in my life. I was going to figure out what Brand meant to me and either open or close his chapter, as well. I was going to block Hank from calling my home number ever again.

My first mission was to be done with Cory. I didn't know how it was going to end, but I needed to start with a phone call.

I called Cory. Then I quickly hung up before the second ring. I was a wimp.

I couldn't help myself. It had been seven months since I aborted Cory's baby. I'd wanted to talk to him. I needed to talk to him. I needed closure. I'd never be able to move on without talking to him and getting the answers to my questions.

I didn't have to wait long.

Two days later Cory called me.

"Hey, Eva, how are you doing?" Cory was casual and informal. I was surprised to hear from him; pleased, I think, but he caught me by surprise. I'd forced myself to stop thinking of him. I literally pried my fingers off the phone each time I picked it up to call him. Some days, it was hard to keep from driving near his house unnecessarily, for a quick peek.

"Cory." I quickly considered pretending that I didn't know who he was, but the word slipped out before I could stop it. I wanted to play cool, distant and uncaring. The almost whine and surprise in my voice angered and embarrassed me. I should have been over him by now. I should have been able to put him out of my head, out of my mind. His memory should have been idle and dusty on some innocuous shelf.

"How've you been?" There was silence on both ends of the telephone. "Where are you living now?" He didn't wait for me to answer and continued, "I rode past your aunt's house the other day. Her door was open and I wanted to stop and say hello to both of you. I didn't see the gold car, so I kept driving."

I could not understand my silence. I had been waiting for this moment for almost a year. I had imagined this conversation so many times in the past. I replayed the imagined repartee in my head, yelling at him, demanding explanations. In these conversations, I was relentless and unyielding; I refused to let go of him once I latched on. I was going to get my answers.

"Eva?"

So lost in my thoughts, I hadn't realized that I wasn't participating in the conversation. I suddenly remembered that Cory didn't like being ignored. Now, why was that important right now? Why was I considering his feelings? When had he considered mine? He had never even called about our baby.

"Cory, why are you calling?" Who was this composed Eva on the telephone? I didn't recognize her.

"Eva, I'm sorry, did I catch you at a bad time? I can call back later."

"How did you get my phone number?" I had apparently turned into a punk because opportunity was speaking in my ear and I was tongue-tied.

"I ran into Taylor at Bookbinder's and she said that you wanted to talk to me. If this isn't a good time, I can call you back."

I was going to skin Taylor and hang her by three strands of hair.

"Oh. Taylor didn't tell me that she ran into you, nor did she mention that she'd given you my number." I paused to clear my head. I didn't want to speak out of emotion but rather be clear headed and strong. "Cory, I'm glad you called me. I'm not going to pretend that I haven't wanted to speak to you for some time. In fact, I've imagined this conversation many times; yet it seems, now, that I'm unsure of how to even approach the subject."

"Eva, I've wanted to talk to you so many times…"

"Cory, honestly, it's too late for that now." I cut him off, abruptly, disinterested in his comments at the time. "The only thing I want to hear you explain is why you left me when I was pregnant with your child. I want to know why I was living in your house, planning to have your baby, while you were out cheating and getting bitch pregnant."

I had to stop and compose myself because I could feel and hear the tears in my voice. I wanted to hang up on Cory before I humiliated myself. I refused to whine and cry as if I'd been pining for him; waiting patiently by the phone, as I had the weekend he left me. I wanted Cory to understand that I didn't want him back. (Did I?) I wanted answers to my questions. I needed to be able to ask and receive without displaying emotion or allowing it to hinder me. I felt as if this was my last chance to get what I needed be able to move on. I ached to finalize and sever the unhealthy connection to Cory and our baby.

"What the hell happened, Cory? What happened to you? What happened to us? How could you abandon the baby and me? Why would you take me to a restaurant to tell me something like that? Why couldn't we talk at home, at our home? You never even gave us a chance. How could you get that bitch pregnant, allow her to keep her baby and tell me to abort mine? Do you know what happened to us? Did you care?" I stopped to catch my breath. "You never called to ask about us," I cried accusingly. "Do you know that I waited, at home, that entire weekend, waiting to hear from you? I refused to leave; I couldn't leave. I waited for you to call me and tell me that you were wrong and had changed your mind."

I was crying, my nose was running but I couldn't stop myself. "I waited for two weeks, loving you, loving the baby I couldn't wait to meet. I rubbed my stomach and cried myself to sleep every night for 14 days." I took a quick breath and continued.

"You don't deserve to know since you obviously don't care but I aborted the baby, Cory; I had an abortion on the 15th day. I was awake and felt every tug, pull and wrenching pain. I wanted to feel the pain and to be aware of what I was doing to our child. I finished the hurt that you started on the operating table. I cried and vowed that I would make you feel the same ache one day. I still want you to feel the anguish I endured on that table."

To his credit, Cory did not interrupt me. He allowed me to vent and cry; to scream and accuse. At some point, my tears were a combination of sadness, anger, and loss. I felt as if I was crying for my baby and myself; I felt as if I was crying for my unknown father and dysfunctional family and home life. The experience was trying and exhausting. It seemed that everything that had ever been wrong in my life was purging itself through my tears.

I finally caught my breath and stopped crying. "Cory, just tell me why. Give it to me straight and let me get over it, so I can move on."

He didn't attempt to make any excuses and gave it to me straight. "I knew she was pregnant and I asked her to have an abortion too. I wasn't in a relationship with her and we had sex, I think, three times. Eva, I swear to you, I was faithful after Therese. I knew how much I hurt you and how tough it was to get our trust back. I don't have an excuse for why I saw this girl again after we met." Cory paused and answered my questions from before. "I saw her a few times, had sex and then stopped calling her back. I know what you're thinking, and yes, I did use a condom."

"Who is she?" I couldn't believe I was asking the question and it didn't matter at this point. Nevertheless, I didn't stop him from answering.

"Her name is Sonja."

"And…?"

"God, Eva, why do you want to know this?"

"Because I do. Because I have to know. I have the right to know. I need answers before we hang up. I don't know if I'll talk to you again and I want it to end here."

"Eva, don't make me do this. Why do you want to know this? It's not going to change anything and I'm pissed at myself for getting involved with her and producing that child." Cory paused and blew out a loud breath. "I barely know her, even now. There wasn't much talking whenever we hooked up. I know she has a 17-month-old daughter with her husband. She didn't tell me she was married until after she got pregnant. She claims they've been separated since her daughter was born. Whatever."

He stopped again and let out a growl of exasperation. "She named her son Cory, Jr. I told her that I already had a son named Corey. This sick bitch said her Cory should be a Jr. since the other one wasn't. Is that crazy, or what? Oh my God, I can't believe I did this to myself. I don't even speak to Sonja anymore and I've made it perfectly clear that I don't want anything to do with her or her junior. I told her to take me to court to set up child support and monthly visitations."

Cory sounded as if her was about to break down and weep for hours. I was so happy I could barely keep the giggle from my voice. He cheated on me, broke my heart and ruined his life in the process. I felt relieved. He wasn't happy and living lavishly without me; he was headed family court and paying for his three nights of fun to Sonja for 18 years.

I was stunned and beyond words.

"Eva, I'm sorry I hurt you. I didn't mean to leave you with our baby to take care of on your own. I'm sorry you had to get the abortion on your own; I'm sorry you had to get an abortion at all. I should have handled us better and I hope you can forgive me."

I didn't say a word.

Cory continued, "I know I hurt you and you probably don't want to hear from me again, but I need to tell you something that I found out after we broke up. I should have called you a long time ago and I feel like shit that I didn't." He paused for a long minute. "Shit, this is hard. Look, Eva, I found out that I have genital herpes." He paused, seemingly unsure of how to proceed. "Sonja must have given it to me; I don't know how it could have happened. The doctor said the virus could travel through a condom and that there aren't always obvious signs. I think you should get yourself checked by a doctor, just to be sure. I honestly don't know if herpes came out of her vagina or her mouth, I just know I got it from that dirty bitch."

I wasn't sure how I was supposed to reply, if a reply was necessary at all. I, again, was stunned beyond words. I'd been exhilarated twice in a matter of minutes. This was better than I had hoped for. Cory was hurting. He was angry. He was branded, for life, by me; by Eva. The lover of state senators and doctors reduced to a statistic. Yes, I had my heart broken and endured the abortion, but he'd live with herpes for life. I couldn't have written a better ending myself.

The rest of the conversation went by in a blur. I was high and floating well above Cory's rhetoric. I was done; I'd been vindicated. There wasn't anything more to be said.

Cory attempted to draw me into a conversation of how I felt about his contraction of the disease and if I'd consider dating him again. He wanted to know how a woman would feel about a man who was up-front and honest about having the disease.

I stopped him short. "Cory, I'm sorry and maybe I hadn't made myself clear earlier in the conversation. I don't have anything more to say to you; I've gotten the information I sought. If you had attempted this conversation seven months ago, things may have been different. Please don't embarrass yourself any further; if not for your sake, then mine. I wish you luck with your new family. Cory, I've moved on; I'd suggest you do the same." I didn't have time for Cory anymore. He'd gotten the best of the worst I had to offer. I was thrilled beyond belief.

Chapter 33

Now that Cory was out of the picture and I closed that chapter in my life, I was ready to move on to Brandon Maxwell DeLoache.

Brand was a lyin ass. His "I'll call you tomorrow" turned into a call three days later. "Brand," I purred into the phone, "where have you been?" Suddenly, the three-day wait no longer mattered. "When can I see you? I miss you, Brandon."

"Eva, I'm glad I caught you. I miss you, too and I'm sorry I haven't called sooner."

"That's okay, I'm just glad to hear from you now. Any chance we can go out somewhere? I just want to talk to you." Now that I had gotten Cory out of my system, I was really feeling Brand and wanted to get moving on things, either way.

"Why don't you come over to the house? We can talk, have a few drinks and go out afterward. How does that sound?" Brand, speaking softly and slowly, was giving me chills and I wondered what he possibly wanted to talk about.

"I'll be there in a half hour. Wear something cute and easy to rip off." I couldn't wait to see him and laughed at my corny joke. "Bye."

When I got to Brand's house, he met me at the door, wearing a short, red, silk robe and tight boxers. He jokingly remarked that he'd looked for one of Bethany's thongs but couldn't find one. He kissed me, holding me close and sniffing my hair. I held onto his biceps, molding my body into his. Here was the Brand that I had been missing; the one I knew and loved, despite our past. I wondered if things could ever be good again.

During our lengthy breakup, Brand had leased a house not far from the duplex he purchased. I hadn't been there yet and was surprised by the size of the house and grounds. Brand admitted that it was leased through the family corporation and that he had to entertain clients, at the house, when they were in town. The kickback was the live-in butler. I didn't think I would ever get used to Brand's family money and their spending habits. Not wanting to be seen by the butler in his tight panties, Brand grabbed my hand and we ran up the back steps to his room on the second floor. Brand's rooms were like a large apartment and completely enclosed, separated from the rest of the house. He had an office, a gym and a full kitchen to himself, rarely leaving the area except to entertain the guests. We ran into his bedroom, giggling like teenagers and slammed the door closed behind us.

Brand pushed me up against the door and kissed me again, softly licking my lips and teeth. He grabbed my head and tilted it to fit perfectly with his mouth. I couldn't remember the last time we had kissed like this. There was no eager foreplay, grinding and groping; no rush to reach the orgasms we usually desired.

"I love you, Eva. I don't think I realized it until I heard the sadness in your voice a few days ago. I realized that I had been putting you off, not respecting the little time we spent together. I realized that I want to spend more time with you. I want to answer your questions and give you what you have been asking of me. I know I've let you down and I want to make it up to you." He kissed me again. "Will you give me that chance?"

God, I wanted to. I wanted it so much, I could taste it. I wanted to give us another chance. I wanted to close our chapter together and move on. "You know I will. When could I ever deny you anything?"

"Good. What are we drinking and where do you want to go?" Brand was trying hard to please me and I appreciated it.

"Let's start with tequila and see where it takes us. Oh, let's order in Chinese and…" I never got the rest of the sentence out when his private phone rang, loudly, rudely interrupting me.

It was Evan, of course. Just when we were moving past the past and attempting to be loving toward each other, my sexual payback rears up and smacks me in the head.

Evan was downstairs, of course. Sure, Brand told him, come on up. Use your key. What? I didn't even have a key. I wanted to vomit and I hoped I could keep a straight face, as I hadn't seen Evan since that weekend in Atlantic City when I sucked the come off his balls and rode his dick like a champion equestrian jumper.

Luckily, Evan wasn't staying and came only to give Brand a truck key for some moving they were doing the next day. Fine ass Evan greeted me warmly, hugging me close. "Sexy Eva," he whispered to me, softly kissing me on my ear. I was tingling and feeling like a whore from one of Mavis' sermons.

Evan made a quick exit, but it was enough to jolt me back into reality and the hurdles Brand and I truly faced. We needed to talk. We needed to communicate.

I sat on the chaise next to the fireplace, resting my feet on the round ottoman. "Brand, order the Chinese food, get us a double Cuervo and sit down next to me. Oh, and take off your clothes. I want to talk to you and admire your body."

After ordering the food, Brand dropped his clothes and walked, naked, to the bar to chill our tequila, just the way I liked. Sitting next to me on the chaise, Brand put his head back and sighed loudly, "Okay, let's have it, Eva. Please get it all out tonight, 'cause I have really been dreading this day and I'm honestly not looking forward to having this conversation. But I owe you this, so let's have at it." He stopped and waited for me.

I had to ask. I considered dropping hints and hedging around the subject, but when it came time, I jumped right in. "Why didn't you tell me you had herpes? Brand, please, let's just get this out and move on. I've been trying to understand. Talk to me."

"God, Eva, I don't even know where to begin. I thought I'd be ready when we got here, but I'm not sure, now. Okay, her name was Jeanine and we were fuckin'. We agreed to keep it casual and keep it between us; no other partners. No big deal, just sex. She had a son, I met her at school, and it was a mutual sex thing. I wasn't looking for much and she wasn't asking for much. Don't get me wrong, I like her; she liked me.

We were good together for a while and I got comfortable." Brand got up and sauntered over to the bar for a refill. I couldn't bring myself to drink. My stomach was rolling and I felt nauseated, but I had to hear it all.

"One night, I called, wanted to see her. She was being real casual on the phone and evasive. I got suspicious and told her that I was coming over. She said it wasn't a good idea and that she would call me in a few. I didn't want to admit it at the time, but I was jealous and it made me furious. I went to her house and she cursed me out through the door. But, I had to see her, so I sweet-talked my way inside. She didn't want me there but I didn't care and I started kissing her; I had to be with her. I guess I was feeling her more than I wanted to admit."

I slowly started sipping my drink. I might need to be numb to get through this.

Brand continued, "I couldn't take her rejection of me, so I forced her to have sex, basically took it. Not quite rape, but close enough. She cried in my arms afterward, telling me that we shouldn't have done any-thing. I remember her crying and her saying, specifically, 'I asked you not to come here, Brand.' Jeanine's pretty and smart and somewhere along the way, I guess I started liking her too much for our agreed terms."

"She asked me to give her some time that she'd call me, and I left. I felt fucked up and waited for her to call me. I can see, now, that she was giving me time to develop symptoms of the virus and after two weeks, she called me. She was back to herself, happy, and we fell back into our regular routine. She never mentioned the reasons for that night and I didn't want to ask, so I didn't bring it up."

"About a week later, I started feeling sick, like I had the flu. I can't remember all of the symptoms now, but I just felt tired all of the time. Then I started itching and burning on my penis, the pain running down into my sac. My legs felt weak and I couldn't shake the feeling that something was wrong. I went to the doctor and he took one look at the bumps and told me that it was herpes. I was floored. I sat back on the table in disbelief and knew. I figured it out almost immediately. It was that night. The night I almost raped her, in a jealous rage, thinking that she had some-one there with her. It was almost what I deserved."

"I confronted her, of course. She didn't deny it; in fact, she didn't say much of anything. She said she was sorry and reminded me that she hadn't wanted me to come over. What could I say? Trust me, I know how you feel, Eva. I felt all of that. I went through the constant outbreaks, the pain, and the worry. I hadn't met you yet, but I knew I'd meet someone some day. How was I supposed to meet someone and get to know them with this shit? How was I supposed to have sex, make love with them, knowing what I could do to them? I told one girl that I had herpes; the first girl after Jeanine. We went out on a few dates and then she wanted to take it to the next level. I thought I was doing the right thing by telling her up front." He laughed at the memory. "She looked at me like I was from Mars, called me a dirty bastard and walked away, for good. That was a great ego boost. She was the last person I attempted to talk to about it."

"I read up on the causes, transmission of the disease, ways to protect myself and a partner. I honestly thought I had it together and took so many precautions to protect everyone. I didn't want anyone to get herpes from me. I wanted to blame Jeanine but I had to place the blame on myself as well."

Brand looked directly at me and I could see the misery and pain there. He grabbed my hands, searching my eyes for forgiveness and understanding. "Eva, I love you and I always have. I never intended to do this to you. I would have never purposely given this life sentence to someone I cared so much about. I don't even know where to begin. I don't know how to ask for your forgiveness. I don't understand why this happened you, and not one of the others, whom I didn't care about.

"I've been thinking so much about you; about us lately. I never want to do this to another person. I'm sorry it was you. I can never truly make it up to you, but I can make things right between us. Stay with me tonight, Eva. Stay here so we can make this right. Stay with me until we make it right. Eva, please..."

The phone rang, of course. Damn. I was probably about to get my engagement ring. It was Tasha and Angelique. Why were they calling Brand at midnight? They were loud, giggling and I could hear Brand laughing with them, warning them to be quiet. "Where's Dad?" He asked them. Now there's good question. Eventually, Bethany caught them, on the phone, and made them apologize to their big brother for interrupting his night. I heard crying and wailing from their side as they refused to hang up. Brand assured his sisters that he loved them and would talk to them in the morning. He hung up and looked at me, waiting for a response.

I wanted to forgive him. I wanted to go back and pretend that we weren't at this point. I wanted to be free of disease and worry. I wanted to love Brand and have him love me in return without guilt or blame. Would I be able to do it? Would I be able to forgive him? I'd surely never forget, but could I move on with Brand and our relationship?

"Brand, let's sleep. We can talk in the morning. I love you, but I need to sleep and think." I pulled him, still naked, over toward the bed. "Dance for me, I got a few dollars. Then I'll put you to sleep the way you like."

And I did.

Chapter 34

We *awoke in the* morning, kissing and cuddling for a while. Then Brand made breakfast and I left to go home. I had a lot of thinking to do and wanted time alone to do just that. I wasn't ready to commit just yet. Not that there were so many other offers on the table. I just needed time.

A few days passed and I heard from Bryce. The walk-through was set for a week from Wednesday. He was checking to make sure that I was going to see his new home. I was thrilled to go and told him so. Bryce wanted to know if I was available to go out before we went to see the house. "I'd be thrilled," I reiterated.

I was going out with Bryce. So what, a few months ago I thought he was an asshole adolescent, living off his mother? He liked me and I thought I might grow to like him. I loved Brand and I wasn't sure what I was going to do with him. However, in the mean time, I was going to enjoy myself.

I considered telling Bryce about the herpes. He appeared to be an understanding person, attentive and he seemed to like me. Would that be enough? I'd have to find out. I decided to tell Bryce after the walk-through on Wednesday night. If there was anything to him, any possibility of us being together, we'd have to take this first leap.

Wednesday came quickly and I wasn't ready to make my confession yet. I had been playing out the scenario in my head, going over possible answers and questions. I often wondered why I was even bothering. Why not just be with Brand and get over it? Brand knew all there was to me: he knew about the herpes, he knew about my attraction to women. What more did I want? Did I really expect another man to accept me with this affliction? More and more, I knew I was fooling myself.

Wednesday afternoon, I was sitting at my desk at work, falling asleep, when Brand and the sisters came to see me and take me to lunch. Wow. Tasha and Angelique were dressed in The Children's Place colored velour sweat suits: Tasha in purple and Angelique in pink. They were adorable, holding onto Brand as if he were their long, lost father.

Bethany was doing a great job with the girls; they were sweet-tempered, respectful and mannerly. Maybe it was because they weren't old enough to know how much money their father had, and that they'd be spoiled rotten by the time they were teens. They let go of Brand, long enough to come over to hug and kiss me hello.

The group took me to McDonald's for lunch. Brand let the girls pay for the food, with a $20, that taking up ten minutes of my break as Tasha, the baby, didn't want to let go of the money and Angelique had to count the change three times, to show that she could. It was cute.

Lunch was terrible and fattening. We let the girls choose our lunch (big mistake) and I was forced to eat cold Chicken McNuggets; salty, droopy French fries, and a strawberry milkshake. Wow. Whenever they were coming for lunch, I planned to be fasting and on a diet.

I kissed their dirty faces goodbye and told Brand that I loved him. I headed straight for the ladies room to relieve myself of that lunch. I didn't want lunch to ruin my dinner with Bryce. I was building up my courage and preparing myself for the eventual confrontation. I practically slept through the rest of my uneventful, boring day and raced home to catch a quick nap, so I would be beautiful for my date.

Bryce called to tell me that he was on his way. I was in the bathroom, brushing my teeth and curling my flat hair when there was a knock at my apartment door. Thinking that it couldn't be Bryce so soon, and besides, he couldn't have gotten past the front door, I walked cautiously to see who wanted me. It was Desiree from the first floor. Damn, why now? This girl was gorgeous and if my calculations were correct, her D-cup breasts were going to fit perfectly in my mouth and hands.

"Eva, hi. I'm sorry to barge in on you this way, but I need some advice and hoped I could talk to you for a minute." She stopped and looked at me closer, noticing that I was dressed to go out. "Oh, is this a bad time? You're going out, aren't you?"

"Actually, I am, but you can come in and keep me company while I wait for my date. What's up? You okay?" I didn't know this girl and I honestly didn't care. I'd been thinking about getting her into my apartment since I moved in. Damn, why now, when Bryce was on his way?

"Not really. I'm stressing and I don't have anyone to talk to, other than my mother, and she wouldn't understand. My oldest sister is in the Navy, stationed in Korea, and she won't be home for two years. My younger sister is only 16 and she's not ready for this conversation. So you're it."

Damn, there were three of them.

She was sitting on my bed and my eyes kept straying to her breasts. I tried listening to her but her breasts kept distracting me. I wondered what she smelled like, upstairs and down. If I had my way, and I intended to, I would slowly slide up and down her breasts, licking and sucking as I went, sliding down further in between her legs, seeking the wetness I knew I would bring.

I snapped myself out of it. Desiree was still talking.

"I broke up with my girlfriend, Angela, last week. We've been arguing about stupid shit: men, money, you name it. This is the third time we've broken up in two months and I'm avoiding her attempts to get back together. We've been in a relationship for three years and she always talks me into seeing her again and getting back with her. I want this to be it. I'm tired of her drama and I need something to keep me busy."

Was I reading too much into this situation? I would love to keep her busy. Why was she here now? She was here for advice, right? Was she feeling my lust vibes for her? This is not what I needed. This vulnerable girl was ripe for the picking, turning to me for advice and I was slowly undressing her in my mind. Hell yeah, I'd help her stay away from her ex.

"Desiree, if you don't mind, how old are you?" I had to know.

"I'll be 23 next month, on the 6th."

"So basically, you've been with this girl since you were twenty years old, too young to settle down with any one person. How many people had you been involved with before her?"

"There were three guys in high school and one girl in college, before Angela."

"Do you think that maybe you've outgrown each other? Is it time for a change?" I looked at her serious expression, listening intently and I felt like a pervert for my thoughts. "I'm thinking that you're young, and maybe this is not your final stop on the relationship train. What about going out with other people? You think you might be interested in dating men again? That may keep your mind off Angela for a while. Maybe you just need a change of scenery." I finally turned away from her to fix my hair for the tenth time. "I've always been fond of saying that the brain is stronger than the heart or libido. So talk yourself out of calling or responding to her when the mood strikes. Give yourself some time to miss her or get over her. You know what they say about what 'makes the heart grow fonder'

"Yeah, I know," she sighed out the response.

"Absence, girlfriend." I turned back to Desiree with a smile. "If you need me to lean on, just come up and knock on the door. Trust me; I'm a specialist in getting over love and relationships." God, I was thinking about offering her a key. I could just see it. Desiree creeping into my apartment, in the dark of night, easing into my bedroom as I slept. She'd stand there watching me as I slept, until she couldn't keep from touching me. I'd awake to soft hands caressing my body, soft lips coaxing moans from my mouth. She'd lay next to me, hugging and kissing me (it's my daydream, of course; my breath is always fresh) until we both become aroused, our hands roaming over each other, seeking an orgasm through mutual masturbation.

The doorbell forced my mind from Desiree and my desire to talk her into my bed. Damn, Bryce. I'd forgotten about him. "Excuse me; I'm sure this is my date." I strolled to the door, let Bryce in the front door and walked him into my apartment. He looked good and smelled even better. I gave him a quick hug and thanked him for coming. We walked into the bedroom where I introduced him to Desiree. "Bryce, this is Desiree. Desiree, this is my date, Bryce." They said hello and Bryce asked to use the restroom.

Desiree stood to take her leave. She surprised me when she walked over to me, put her arm around my waist in a half hug, and kissed my cheek. Her lips were soft and dangerously close to my mouth. She thanked me for listening to her and said she'd see me later. I didn't know what to think. I thought she might have been flirting with me. Maybe it was wishful thinking. I stood there asking myself if I was imagining things when Bryce walked into the room and stood behind me.

"See how good we look together?" Bryce and I were standing in front of my dressing table mirror and we did look good together. We were young, healthy, vibrant and attractive. I turned to look directly at Bryce and thanked him again for coming. I was touched that he thought enough of me to ask me to the walk-through. I wanted him to know. I held his head and kissed him, willing my appreciation to him through my soft lips on his.

Bryce's surprise for me was a reservation at the Pod, an Asian-fusion restaurant in the University City section of Philadelphia. I had been talking about the upscale restaurant for weeks, describing to Bryce their eclectic Asian menu. The décor and ambiance belied the website's description and the cozy dining room and attentive wait staff impressed me. We ordered the seafood special of the day and, from the wine list, a 1992 Beringer Merlot.

When it was time to leave, Bryce carried me to the door. I was stuffed and didn't think I'd make it to the car. Bryce told me that he'd carry me to the car but he wanted a return payment later that night. I thought I knew what he meant and leaped into his arms for my ride to the parking garage.

Chapter 35

Traveling westbound on I-76, I initiated my return payment by releasing my seatbelt, opening his zipper and using my mouth to bring him to a quick orgasm before we reached Lincoln Drive. Bryce recovered well, swiftly maneuvering the Chevy Suburban around the curves, moving through Germantown and Mount Airy. We reached Northbound Route 309 within minutes and Chalfont in half an hour.

The house stood on a cul-de-sac surrounded by beautiful landscaping. The two-story, brick single had a two-car garage and a separate garden shed. The developer walked Bryce and I through the front door and into the foyer, leading to an open floor plan where you entered the family room to the left and living room to the right. A fireplace flanked each wall in the rooms, providing extra warmth for cold winter nights. The hardwood flooring glistened and I swore I could see myself in it. The kitchen, dining room, mudroom and half-bath were situated in the back of the house, sharing the same Greek-inspired tile.

The kitchen was beautifully decorated and I secretly hoped I'd get the chance to create a meal for Bryce in it. The center island was covered with copper; it had two oak cabinets and rolled on casters. The Viking refrigerator, double oven, gas range, and dishwasher were covered in stainless steel. The oversized cabinets surrounding the ovens and range had the same oak as the center island.

Upstairs were four bedrooms, which shared two full baths. The master suite was the size of my apartment, equipped with his-and-hers walk-in closets. The master bath contained a sauna tub, double sinks, separate shower stall and a completely enclosed toilet.

Bryce appeared unmoved by the sheer size of the home, taking features for granted, that had me gaping behind his back. Of course, Brand's family home was twice the size but I wasn't aware that Bryce could afford such luxury.

The unfinished basement led to an enormous back yard, covered in grass and small, perimeter trees, planted strategically to offer privacy from neighbors. Bryce spoke quietly with the developer about minor adjustments and said good night, walking him around to the front of the house.

I was lost in thought when suddenly Bryce was standing behind me, his arms around my waist. "So what do you think, pretty Eva? You think this will do for a man living with his mother? I'm planning to build a swimming pool in the area over to the left. To the right, I'll build a patio, including a barbecue grill and possibly a hot tub. I'm still deciding and Bob's going to speak with the architect about how to accomplish everything." Bryce kissed my neck, grinding his hips into me. "So, do you think you could stand to spend a few nights, here, with me? Tell me what I have to do to make you say yes." He palmed my breasts from behind, continuing the motion with his hips. I was ready to say yes to anything.

Oh God! I had forgotten. My plan to tell Bryce about the herpes was completely forgotten until his hard penis, pressing up against my ass, quickly reminded me. I took a couple of deep breaths, walking away from Bryce, to collect my thoughts and build my confidence. I couldn't believe I was here. I couldn't believe I was doing this! Why was I doing this? I didn't need Bryce or his house. I didn't need this headache. Why was I suddenly the voice of reason? Sure, the sex turned out to be great, where was I going with this?

"Bryce, we need to talk." I turned toward him, slowly moving closer, but not too close. I was well aware of men and their tendency for violence. Maybe this wasn't a great idea after all. Where would I go if he kicked me out or beat me up? I thought back to the man I spent time with all evening and the night we spent together in the basement. I owed someone the truth. I should have started with Cory. I should have told Bryce sooner. I had to move forward and I decided to start here.

"Actually, Bryce, I need to talk to you. I have something to tell you about myself; something that I should have told you a few weeks ago. You are only the third person I've uttered these words to." I laughed at myself, before I cried. "Honestly, I wish someone had given me the same consideration and told me before it was too late.

"But I'm rambling and that's because I'm really dreading having to tell you this, but I told myself that tonight would be the night." I took a chance and moved closer to him. Now that I was here, I would do it right. "Bryce…" whirling around, I covered my face, thinking that I wouldn't be able to do this after all. Damn it. Was this how Brand felt? Had he really considered telling me, or had that been a lie? Why had this shit happened to me?

"Bryce," I continued again, turning around before I changed my mind, "I have genital herpes." I looked at his face, waiting to see his reaction, preparing to flee for my life, if necessary.

He didn't say anything for a long moment. I watched, in fear, as his emotions played across his face. I'm sure I saw shock, surprise, anger and disbelief, as well. Bryce reached out and grabbed my wrist, as if he knew I was preparing to run. "Eva, why are you telling me this now? I can understand not telling me the first time you came to my house; we didn't do anything other than kiss. Why didn't you tell me the second time you came to my house? Didn't you think I would want to know before we made love?" He turned around to look out at the vast backyard. "How do you know you have herpes? Are you just finding out? How long have you known?" He caught himself, realizing that he was squeezing my wrist, and releasing it. "Wait, do you think I gave you herpes?"

"No, Bryce, I know you didn't give it to me. I already know who gave it to me." I paused to look directly at Bryce, now that it seemed he wouldn't be killing me on the spot. "I found out a two years ago when I had symptoms that I had sent me to the doctor. My ex-boyfriend, Brand, got herpes from someone named Jeanine and never told me until I confronted him with it." I didn't know what else to say. "I'm really sorry, Bryce. I don't know what else to say to you. I'd appreciate it if you would drop me off at home."

"Wait, Eva, why are you telling me this now? Were you having an outbreak when we made love?" Bryce stood looking at me and then turned to walk away. When he turned back and saw that I was not following him, he came back and grabbed my wrist, pulling me with him.

We sat at a stone bench facing each other; Bryce finally let go of my wrist. "Tell me, Eva, what you want to accomplish by telling me this information. Why tell me now? How many people have you told? What did you think I would do when you told me? What do you think I will do, now that you have?"

"I don't know what to think right now. I still can't believe I told you. I've been worrying about this conversation, this confrontation, since the night we spent at your house. I've been dreading this, hoping you would forgive me, hoping you'd still speak to me and not kill me for deceiving you." I could feel the tears coming and didn't try to stop them. "I still don't know why this happened to me. Karma maybe. Partly I blame myself because I haven't been a great person, partly because my boy-friend was an asshole and didn't give me a choice or the option to choose my own fate.

"Honestly, Bryce, I wasn't sure of what you'd do when I told you. I was ready to run, to defend myself, physically, if necessary. What do you want to do now?"

Bryce thought for a moment, then said, "I'm not going to pretend that I'm not pissed right now, Eva. I'm not going to let you off the hook easily, regardless of how you got herpes. You had no right, especially knowing how you felt when it happened to you, to make love to me without telling me what I was exposing myself to. Like you, I had the right to make my own choices. You're very lucky we didn't have this conversation about five years ago or my reaction would have been quite different, and not in your favor.

"But it's not five years ago, and I'm a little more understanding now. Luckily for you, I've been through this before so other than the dishonesty on your part, I'm not particularly worried about the herpes."

I stared at Bryce, unsure of how to ask the questions I was dying to ask. All I could squeak out was, "What?"

"I know about herpes, Eva: How you get it, how to spread it, how to protect yourself from contracting it. I happen to know all of this because

I used to date an older woman who had it. I met her about three years ago, in Chicago at a conference. We worked for the same company: I in Philadelphia, Carla in Mobile, Alabama. We had this immediate sexual attraction to one another. We spent the first night together, drinking and having dinner, intending on making our way up to my room."

"During our last drink, Carla told me she had something to tell me before we made our way upstairs. She admitted to being promiscuous in her twenties and getting involved with someone who was the proverbial older, married man. She didn't find out that he had given her herpes until she was giving birth to their first child, when the obstetrician noticed the outbreak near her vaginal opening. Before she could begin pushing, the OB advised that she have a cesarean instead. She'd never had any symptoms or any idea that she'd contracted any type of disease. Later she learned that her child could have been born blind due to complications, and that she could have taken medication to help avoid any of it, had he been honest."

"Once she left the hospital, she went to the library to research the virus. She was more concerned about possible damage to her child *in utero* than she was herself. She learned that she was one of the very few who never have symptoms, and learned how to live her life with herpes and how best not to spread it to others."

"We never made it to my room that night but we sat up until dawn, talking. I was concerned but never turned off. We talked about it for three days and then we had protected and unprotected sex. We slept in each other's rooms for the rest of the two-week conference and went home. Every month for two years, she sent plane tickets for me to come to Alabama until about a year ago, when she met someone else and got married."

"So, again, I know all about it. What I don't know, is what you're about. I'm disappointed in you, Eva. I was really hoping that you were different from other women. Is there anything else that you need to tell, since we're here being honest? Let's get it all out right now, okay?" Bryce reached over to rub my fingers. I wondered if this meant that he'd forgive me and we'd be able to move past this stage.

"That's all of the important information, Bryce. Since we're talking, I'll admit that I had a miscarriage about 18 months ago and an abortion approximately a year ago. I guess it sounds terrible and really whorish but I want to be honest with you." I contemplated telling him about the crabs and microwaving my underwear, but I didn't want to go overboard and scare him completely away. I thought I had confessed enough.

"Bryce, I'm glad we had this conversation and I can more than understand if you don't choose to see me anymore. I can't control this thing and I've been lucky so far, but I would hate to give you herpes. I don't know if I could live with myself and you'd hate me forever." I didn't mention giving herpes to Cory, because he got what he deserved.

"Eva, you didn't answer my question: Where you having an outbreak when we made love? Is that the reason for this confession? Do I have something to worry about, right now?"

Chapter 36

I *felt sorry for* Bryce and myself. No one should have to go through this; it was a fucking nightmare. I hated Brand at this very moment. This was terrible and I couldn't imagine going through this again, with any other man or woman.

"No, Bryce. I seem to have the virus under control lately, with medication, avoiding stress when possible, and staying overall healthy. I wasn't having an outbreak then, nor am I having one now. Most times, I can tell when one is coming on and avoid having sex or sexual contact with anyone." I let the tears that had been threatening, fall down my face. "I feel really fucked up, Bryce, and I didn't know it would be this hard. I feel like shit, having deceived you."

"Calm down, Eva, it's all right. We'll find a way to get through this. I couldn't have been completely wrong about you. Make me a deal, okay? Let this be the last time we're dishonest with each other. Let's do things differently, from now on. Eva, I like you. I think I might like you even more, now. Trust me, I know how hard it was for you to come clean and tell me about the disease. I'd still like to see you and we'll be extra careful. I'd like to see where this could go."

I couldn't speak. This was a real breakthrough. I never believed anyone would understand about the possibility of getting herpes from me. I covered my face and cried from the relief. "Bryce, I don't know what to say. I wasn't expecting this type of reaction. I honestly thought we'd be fighting, physically, by now. I don't know how to thank you for being so understanding. I never intended to deceive you and I hope you can forgive me." I took a chance and kissed Bryce's cheek. "Do you think you can forgive me?"

"Let me think about it for a while." He paused quickly and said, "Well, I think I may be able to be persuaded, depending on the persuader and what she's willing to do. Do you know anyone like that? Someone who needs forgiving for being a bad girl? Someone who fucked this boy crazy last time and is trying to scare him away now? Who could she be?"

I laughed, joining in the third-party conversation, "I think I know somebody like that. I think I know a certain girl who's in need of forgiving. I think this girl would be willing to do almost anything to get back into this boy's good graces. I think a certain boy could almost name his desires and have every one of them met, tonight. I don't think this girl would have the nerve to say no."

"I didn't think so. Eva, honestly, do you think we need to use protection? Do you want to? I must be crazy, but I like you. I think I like you enough to take a chance with you."

Bryce took off his jacket. "Come here, Eva, you naughty girl. Come show me how sorry you are and how much you want to make it up to me. I'm done with this conversation; I want you to put something else on my mind and make me forget. You think you can do that for me?"

"I'm almost positive I can."

"Pick a room for me, Eva. You choose a room and we'll make love in it. Whichever room you choose will be our special room and every time I'm in it, I will think of you and remember this night. I want you so badly and I think you know it. I want you here with me but I don't think you're ready yet; I'm not sure if I'm ready yet. I'm patient and I'll wait for you, as long as you choose me in the end."

I was speechless, emotional and moved by Bryce's words. I took his hand and led him into the house, up the basement steps and into the family room. I kissed him as I removed his shirt. My lips lead a trail from his mouth to his chest as I moved lower to remove his pants. Across his stomach and lower until I reached his hard penis and stopped. "Tell me what you want, Bryce. Tell what you want me to do to you so I can please you."

My hands reached around and massaged his ass, my fingers moving suspiciously close to his anus. Bryce allowed me to play around his anus, rubbing around the tight hole, until I attempted to penetrate him. He moved my hands back to his penis, covering my hands with his own. "Fuck me, Eva, with your beautiful mouth and that tight little cunt you've been teasing me with. I want you to suck my dick like you own it and ride me until I come deep in your pussy."

"Oh, do you?" On my knees, I pulled his boxers to his knees and slowly licked his penis around the head, into the tip, up and down the veins that stood out. I moved in between his legs and sucked his balls, pulling each one into my mouth, rolling it around with my tongue. I stopped and peered up at him, "Like this?" I sucked his dick into my mouth, lightly biting, concentrating on the head as my hands stroked his shaft. "Or like this?" I French-kissed up and down, sucking lightly on each side, never placing it in my mouth, but leaving wet kisses as I went.

Bryce's hands were in my hair, palming my head, squeezing me, almost hurting me, driving in and out of my mouth. My lips were sore and swollen, my mouth cramping. But I wouldn't stop. I couldn't stop as the night had turned out to be too perfect. The mood had been just right.

I stopped before he came in my mouth and led him to the wall, where I peeled of my clothes and stood before him, bent over, ass in the air, and holding onto the mantle of the unlit fireplace. I pulled him to me and guided his penis into my wet, dripping pussy and heard him sigh as he slid right in, pushing himself forward until he hit my wall. "Don't move; let me do the work." And I did, riding his dick, moving myself forward, backward and around, sliding him in and out of my pussy, using my Kegel muscles to squeeze his dick, making him moan out loud. His hands found my hips as he started losing control, fucking me ruthlessly, growling with each thrust, moaning and muttering under his breath. I caught something like, "Fuck me. Take this dick. Want it in your ass. Want…cum in your mouth." Bingo.

Moving faster and harder, I put my hands on the floor, throwing my ass back on his dick as if I would die without it. "Bryce, don't come in me," I panted out. "Tell me when you're about to come." No response from him. "Bryce, tell me before you come." I was near orgasm and felt the familiar tingle, mixed with slight pain, as the orgasm tightened my vaginal muscles, making Bryce's penis feel larger, longer. My orgasm hit my legs, stomach and clitoris, stopping me from moving, as Bryce continued to work toward his. I heard him yell out, "Eva, fuck it, I can't stop it! Eva, I'm coming." I felt him struggle behind me as his hand fumbled to pull his dick out before coming in me.

I moved forward and quickly turned around to face him, watching as Bryce stroked his dick, hips jerking forward, as he coaxed the come out of his penis. I sucked until I felt the pulsating vas deferens bulge and let go as Bryce's come shot into my mouth. I watched him as he came, watching him watch me catch his come in my mouth, and on my lips and chin. His gaze was glazed, a secret smile on his mouth. I could see his unspoken delight as he watched himself come all over me.

Smiling, mouth full, I looked around for a place to spit; finding none, I stood facing him and swallowed his semen. Bryce grabbed my face between his hands, kissing me, murmuring that he couldn't live without me; that no one had ever made love to him this way, asking me to stay the night. His final question: Where had I been all of this time? Good question; I didn't have the answer. We stood there, kissing, licking and mixing our fluids between us, until we caught our breath and fell to the floor.

We performed an encore in the master bedroom and sauna tub. After falling asleep on the floor in two separate rooms, we decided to call it quits and drove to Philadelphia at 4 a.m.

Chapter 37

Bryce dropped me off at home with a sweet, soft kiss and a promise to call me later. He said I had sucked the life out of him and he needed sleep before he could fuck with me some more. I thought it was cute and giggled my simple ass into the apartment, where I immediately thought of Desiree.

I definitely needed sleep. And maybe a psychiatrist as well.

I was dreaming. It was a scary dream and I didn't like it. I was alone and running. There was noise in my dream that didn't belong. There was a lion chasing me around Germantown, but only at the XH bus stops. I was cornered at Germantown Avenue & Walnut Lane and the lion was steadily advancing. I heard myself screaming, loudly, as if that would scare off a wild animal. But when I stopped screaming, the sound continued. I checked myself in my dream. I had definitely stopped screaming. So what was that noise?

Damn that telephone. Oh, God. This phone was going to be the death of me. I felt as if I'd been sleeping for 10 minutes and I was about to give hell to some poor, unsuspecting caller. I peeked at the clock. Wow. It was 10 a.m. Six hours of sleep as opposed to 10 minutes. Well, it felt the same.

"Hello?" Please, let it be the wrong number.

"Wake up, pretty girl. Where have you been?" It was Brand. Damn,

I wondered if he was looking for me last night. I hoped not. I didn't have my story together and I was too tired to attempt to make up one now.

"Here sleeping and trying to get more sleep." I wanted to talk to Brand, just not right now.

"Well, you don't have to get up now. We have dinner reservations at 8:00, so be ready by 7:00 and make sure you look good. I have something for you and I think you'll like it. No, forget that, you'll love it. Go back to sleep, pretty girl. I'll see you tonight." Brand blew me a kiss into the phone. "I love you."

Eight hours later, I was dressing for my date with Brand. I'd purchased a burnt orange linen suit by Lord & Taylor a few weeks earlier. My hair was wild as ever, but Brand apparently liked it that way. I stepped into a pair of black, leather wedge sandals and sprayed Red onto my throat, wrists, and behind my ears.

I kept thinking about Bryce and our amazing night. I still couldn't believe that I told him about the herpes. The thought was as equally as scary the next day. I smiled, thinking of our wild night together. Bryce had been so understanding, and we moved past my confession as if it hadn't happened. It had probably been the second worst day of my life. I didn't think I wanted to ever tell another living soul that I had herpes. I'd go to drastic lengths to avoid having to say those words to anyone other than a doctor. How was I going to have a baby? Never mind.

Brand picked me up at 7 p.m. and surprise, our dinner reservation was at the Pod. Was this some kind of joke? Brand had never mentioned the restaurant. This couldn't be happening. What had I gotten myself into this time?

The very same host seated Brand and I to a table in a dark corner. The waiter greeted me by saying, "It's good to see you again, madam." I glanced at Brand but he was preoccupied and didn't hear the comment. This night couldn't possibly get any worse.

Over dinner, Brand sat next to me and kissed me whenever I didn't have a mouthful of food. I started to relax after I realized that Brand had no idea that I had just been at the same restaurant the night before. With another man. A man whose dick had been, 24 hours ago, all over and into the same lips he was kissing tonight. I had to suppress a giggle.

Brand ordered champagne and asked me to make a toast. "Toast,

Brand, and all that we've been through. I'd like to get past the difficult times and concentrate on the future." We tapped flutes and took a sip.

"Now it's my turn. Eva, I asked you here for a specific reason, tonight. I've been thinking about us and what you mean to me. I've taken you for granted in the past, but I want to change all of that after tonight." I watched him nod to someone and get out of his chair to kneel in front of me. As I sat there, dumbfounded, the very same waiter materialized next to Brand with a small, black tray in his hands.

I watched Brand reach over and pick up a black box before turning back to me. "Eva, I love you. I want to make you happy and give you everything you desire." Brand pulled a ring out of the box and, kissing my left ring finger, placed a large marquise diamond ring on it. "Eva, will you marry me?"

I sat in the chair, momentarily stunned. There were, at least, three karats on my ring finger. Brand was still on his knees in front of me, grinning at me and the other patrons who were whistling and clapping. Oh, my God, what was I supposed to do?

Brand studied my face and surprised reaction. What about Bryce? What was I doing? Was I crazy? Of course, I was crazy. Why was I hesitating, was the question. Wasn't this what I had hoped for? Hadn't I been on this mission to end my misery? I would be Mrs. Brandon Maxwell DeLoache; respected, envied. I couldn't wait!

"Hell, yeah. Brand, of course I will marry you." I laughed, thinking that my problems were at an end. I was going to marry Brand. I'd never have to worry about herpes or confessions again. "When do you want to do this?"

Chapter 38

I *was on the* phone, screaming Taylor's ear off. Brand had dropped me off at home and had some running around to do. Fine with me. My days of complaining were over. He could do whatever he wanted to do. Except fuck other chicks, that is. "Girl, he got on his knees and pulled out this diamond ring! And the people in the restaurant were staring at us as if we were crazy, and then they started cheering once they saw the size of the diamond. Shit, I felt like cheering when I saw the ring, myself. Girl, wait 'til you see this shit! You know Brand might be an asshole, but he don't do nothin half-ass. This diamond is fucking ridiculous, and I can't wait to see them hatin-ass bitches. They thought they hated me before." I cracked up. Taylor just laughed at me.

And then my other line rang. So lost in my conversation with Taylor and twirling in my living room, silently choosing which furniture I'd keep and which I'd toss, that I didn't look at the caller ID. Still laughing, I barely told Taylor to hold on and clicked over. "Yeah."

"Eva, what's up, baby? Where you been? It's only been 24 hours or so; I know you didn't forget about me already."

Words stuck in my throat that didn't even begin to describe the feeling of dread.

"Bryce."

"Yeah, that's what they usually call me. What's up?"

"I'm on the phone with Taylor." I felt like English was suddenly my second language.

He wasn't getting it. I must have really put it on him last night and dulled his senses. Oh, shit! What was I thinking? I just got engaged to Brand and I was out fucking Bryce last night!

"Okay, and so get off. Let's go out. My buddy's having a party at the Marriott. It's invitation only. Throw on something sexy and I'll swing by in 45 minutes."

Why was I hesitating? And Taylor's on the other line.

"Bryce…"

"Eva, you're wasting time and I'm hungry. I want to see you. No sex this time. I'm beginning to think you want me only for my body." He paused for dramatic effect that was totally lost on me in my frame of mind. His tone was somber. "Seriously, I'd like to see you again. I want to make up for the time we missed out on when we were apart. Plus, you owe me somethin to make up for the time when you weren't calling me."

Words were stuck in my throat and Taylor was still on the other line.

Bryce continued talking but I was no longer paying attention. I was listening to myself, thinking of why I wasn't hanging up on Bryce, instructing him to never call me again.

"Eva, you still with me? You think you can be ready in half an hour to 45 minutes?" He sighed, used to my shenanigans. "Be honest; give it to me real. Do you need an hour?"

I heard myself saying yes.

What was I doing? Was I going out with Bryce? What was I thinking? What would I do with my ring? Was I supposed to take my engagement ring off?

"Give me an hour, Bryce. I'll look beautiful for you." I was straight tripping. I knew I was going to regret this night and what ever I planned to do. But that didn't stop me. "Do we have to go to the party? Can't we do something else? Please." I wasn't completely crazy. I would not be caught out in public with Bryce anymore. "I just want to spend time with you." I was so fake and surely soon to be busted.

"Fine. Whatever Eva wants, suits me just fine. One hour, Eva." He banged on me. Whatever.

I clicked over, thinking Taylor was gone; long ago tired of waiting and had hung up on me. And none too nicely, I'm sure. Surprise. She was still waiting.

"Bitch, this better be good. You had better tell me that was Dwayne Wade and he dropped his main chick for you. I swear Eva, you better be marrying a millionaire and taking me along for the ride."

Taylor was a little annoyed.

"Sorry, Tee, that was Aunt Mirabelle. She wants me to come over for dinner tomorrow. You know she never wants to hang up."

It was true. Mavis told me I had a forked tongue, capable of delivering tremendous damage and lies that would destroy nations. Okay, so maybe she went a little overboard. But she was pretty pissed at the time. I think that was the time she called me 'hot in the ass'. Yes, Mavis cursed. I wonder what her Christian friends thought of that.

"Anyway, Tee, I gotta go. I'm gonna go stare at my ring a little while longer and wait for Brand to call. If I'm still up, he said he would come by." I was turning into a hot mess of a liar. I NEVER lied to Taylor! Well, maybe I withheld a few truths from her; but straight out lying to Taylor is something I didn't do.

I hung up and wondered what I was getting myself into. I also wondered if any of this would prove to be worth the trouble.

I ran to the shower and got beautiful for a man other than my new fiancée.

Chapter 39

An *hour later, we* were on our way to New Jersey. I told Bryce I wanted seafood from Benihana in Cherry Hill. My favorite type of restaurant – food cooked right in front of you at your table. Shrimp tossed into your mouth by your very own chef. It was almost like being treated like a beloved pet dog at premium price.

I hoped I didn't see anyone I knew or knew Brand.

Two Blue Hawaiians and a Long Island Iced Tea later, we were stuffed and headed for Bryce's house. My heart flip-flopped, my conscience tore me a new asshole, and yet I rode with Bryce up the long stretch of NB Route 309. I knew I would fuck him again, at least one more time.

I knew I would. I knew it was wrong, but I would fuck Bryce once more. Why? I kept asking myself, but I had no answer. I just knew it would happen. A part of me wanted one last chance to get back at Brand. The other part advised me that I was crazy to play with fire and risk losing what I claimed I lived for; a chance to marry Brand and put an end to my misery.

"Kiss me, sexy. What are you thinking about? You look like you're a thousand miles away. Where you been all night? You've only partly been in my company since I picked you up. What's up, Eva?"

I stretched across the Suburban and kissed Bryce's cheek. I was washed with a wave of guilt and attempted to scoot back over to safety but Bryce had other plans. His hand found the back of my head, I was now facing his bulging penis, and my mouth started to water despite myself. My clit jumped and I tugged at his zipper as his hand massaged my neck.

But I couldn't put it in my mouth as I had on so many other occasions. I felt gentle pressure from Bryce and decided to compromise by licking the head, showering it with small pecks. So unlike the Eva that usually slobbed his knob as if it was the last piece of candy on earth.

Bryce was satisfied and when he kissed me once we were parked in his garage, I didn't pull away and kissed him back. I sucked his tongue and ran my fingers over his head, knowing that this would be the last time we would be in this position. He moved me back into the passenger seat, climbing over the front seats and settled into the large and luxurious back seat cavern.

"Come to me, sexy."

I moved into the back seat with him. It was almost like being in a small room. Or maybe it was the Blue Hawaiian and Long Islands in my system.

He tugged at my clothing from top to bottom, kissing skin as he went, licking my ears, eyes, nose and mouth. When I was naked, he repositioned himself so that I was on the leather back seat and spread my legs. I felt his fingers run down my legs, moving toward my hard sex and slip two fingers into my pussy. His fingers made sounds as they entered me and I raised my hips to get him further into me.

His lips found my nether lips, sucking my clitoris as if it was sweet nectar. I pushed my hips into him, seeking to make myself one with his mouth. I wanted to get everything possible out of this last hurrah with the man whom I counted out and didn't give a chance, initially.

I pushed and pulsated against Bryce's mouth, driving myself mad as I fought to come. I would reach the goal. I had to. This master deception had to be worth it. I would not come this far to be denied.

Yet I was. After each attempt and riding Bryce's tongue in every way imaginable, I faked the most outrageous orgasm and gave his mouth a rest. I felt him fumble out of his clothes and attempt to slide up my body to enter my vagina when I completely froze and found some sort of conscience.

We needed to use a condom. I could not go any further this way. This I could not do. Despite the fact that I was even on this date, I would not sleep unprotected with Bryce when I was promised to Brand. Some sense of morality, I know.

"Bryce, I'm ovulating. We need to use protection." This was a first. We'd never considered using condoms, not even when I confessed about the herpes.

"Eva. You're killing me. Don't do this shit to me. I promise I'll pull out."

"Bryce, I can't take this chance. You got condoms in the house?" I was sitting up and flattening myself against one door, as far away from him as possible. I would fuck him, yes, but I would do so on my terms.

"Yeah, I think I got a few in the house somewhere."

I grabbed my clothes, which were strewn about the cavern, jumped out of the truck and walked, naked, through the garage door into the kitchen. Bryce followed; half dressed and completely pissed with the prospect of not getting some ass, and probably even more so because I asked him to use a condom when he'd never hesitated to have sex with me, even when he knew about my disease.

Oh, well. Either he was finding a condom or he would be ass-less tonight.

"I can't believe you would pull this shit on me tonight." He grabbed my hand and practically pulled me from the kitchen through the house toward the stairs leading to the second floor.

Maybe I hoped he had a condom for my own good. Bryce didn't look very happy. Now I wanted to fuck.

He picked me up when we got to his bedroom door and I went flying onto the bed. That shit turned me on. "You better hope I can find one, Eva, and that it's not expired. You are gettin fucked tonight, trust me." He tossed his drawer in the night table. Everything was flying out except a condom. "We can do this the hard way, or you can make it easy on yourself."

I rolled over onto my back, closed my eyes and started rubbing my clit. I had news for him. I was gettin mine tonight, even if I had to get it myself. I must have been deep into my masturbation 'cause I never heard him find the condom and slip it on. I felt him land on the bed next to me and he sat me on his dick all in one motion.

"Bryce." I had no words. I wanted to come.

"Shut the fuck up. I can't believe you made me wait, lookin for this fuckin' condom." He grabbed my face and kissed me, roughly handling my breasts. "You gonna pay for that shit."

And make me pay for it, he did. Bryce rode the shit outta me, even though I was the one on top. His hands were working some kind of magic on every available body part. If his hands weren't on it, his mouth was on mine and all over me.

"Bitch. I'm about to come."

Who was this new Bryce? His potty mouth was turning me the fuck on and I braced my legs against his hips and rode his dick, rubbing my clit against his shaft.

"Fuck me, Bryce, I wanna cum all ova this dick."

I watched him jerk into motion and felt him up in my womb. Damn, I was gonna miss this dick when it was all over.

"Cum with me, Eva." He was breathing hard, had my ass cheeks covered with his hands, helping me ride him and pushing my hips down as he pushed up. "Eva, take this dick and cum with me." His breathing was ragged and his voice hoarse. One hand cupped my head and he kissed me softly while he moaned into my mouth.

I felt his body jerk stiffen. That was my cue to ride his pulsating dick over the edge into my own madness. Damn, I was gonna miss this dick.

And as I floated back to earth, simmering from my orgasm, I felt the slightest sting deep inside my vagina. Puzzled, I pushed myself off Bryce's dick and stared at the torn condom on his soft penis.

I kept staring as if the action alone would change the past 20 minutes. "Bryce, take me home.

It's pretty fucking amazing how easily I can forget certain information and pretend as nothing ever happened. My tryst with Bryce was behind me. I was so moving on.

Once Bryce dropped me off, I put my ring back on and hopped into bed. I couldn't wait to see Brand. I sent Brand a 'miss n luv u' text so that he'd know I was thinking about him on our momentous night.

There was absolutely no way in hell I was dragging this engagement thing out. Six months, tops, I wasn't giving Brand the chance to back out or change his mind. Now that he'd proposed to me, there would be no opportunity to escape.

As I drifted off, I put my wedding plans into action, making mental notes of what I needed to accomplish within the next six months. In my mind, I began a 180 day countdown, broken down by month, of what I'd like to accomplish and how.

Trust me, that man was going nowhere without me. I planned to make sure I was pregnant before we walked down the aisle. He'd pay the next time he screwed me around; literally and figuratively. With the first DeLoache grandchild, I was guaranteed a place within their family and would do what ever I needed to do to keep it that way.

Brand and his nasty-ass herpes! He ruined my life and now he would make sure that the rest of my disease-ridden life was the most comfortable and elegant that Wayland and his clan could provide.

Oh, don't get me wrong. I loved Brand and his family. But, Brand and I knew the truth of our situation. He owed me, and I would get what was due me — one way or another.

Yeah, my plan was to get Brand hitched as soon as possible. I needed to stay focused, lest I became lax. I had to remember that his behavior had been unpredictable in the past. And, that unpredictability often included other woman in singles or in groups.

Could he be trusted? One part of me wanted to run to Las Vegas and do the damned thang! The other, less sure side, wondered if a wedding between us would ever take place. I felt like I had come to a crossroads. I wanted to get married, would plan it, but damn it, I would do me. Eva would get hers and do what she does best!

I wanted to picture Brand and I as a perfect couple. I wanted to believe that nothing would change that. I wanted to believe that marriage would be the cure for our problems. Maybe he would be faithful. Maybe I could finally forgive him for giving me herpes. Simply put, I wanted this wedding to fix everything.

But, I still didn't trust him.

Chapter 40

I *was up at* the crack of dawn. Giddy, elated, and part disbelief prevented me from getting much sleep. I almost jogged to Borders to pick up every magazine that remotely looked like "wedding preparation." By late afternoon, I had lists of vendors, and appointments to view the reception site, and several others to choose a wedding dress, our wedding rings, a florist and photographer.

I was becoming a DeLoache in style, trust me.

A few quick phone calls to Brand secured the name and address of the jeweler who created my 3-karat masterpiece. I should have been grateful for the gorgeous ring, looking forward to adding a matching wedding band to my engagement ring. Instead, I wondered how long it would take to drive to Mount Joy, Pennsylvania, locate Koser's Jewelers, and meet with Scott Kay, jewelry designer.

Two days later, I would visit The Night Kitchen in Philadelphia to have my dream cake made. I pictured a four-tier, German chocolate confection with butter cream frosting and coconut filling. It sounds delicious and I know you're dying to get your own invitation.

The countdown began....

Month 6

"Auntie, I'm so excited. I can't believe that Brand finally asked me to marry him. I love him so much. This is like a dream come true."

I went to Aunt Mirabelle's because I wanted to tell her face-to-face about the proposal, and because I hadn't seen her in quite some time. It was almost like a guilt trip and announcement in one. I honestly felt like shit when I didn't spend time with her, since she had been more like a mother to me than Mavis. Mirabelle had been my single parent 'cause, Lord knows, the other two weren't shit.

"What about your mother and brothers? Have you invited them to the wedding, Eva?" She couldn't help but ask, I know. Aunt Mirabelle knew I couldn't stand Mavis and felt completely indifferent towards my brothers, but she would do the right thing.

"I've considered inviting the angels, but Mavis is off my list. I will not allow her to ruin my day. Auntie, you know how she is. I can imagine her upsetting me on my day and I don't want the drama. I'm sorry, but I just can't do it. I'd like you to stand for me, since Daddy won't be there. Please accept my decision, Aunt Mirabelle, even if you don't understand or agree with my reasoning."

Okay. Brand was acting right. I was mostly acting right. I searched for the perfect place to stash my feelings, so that my happiness wouldn't depend on Brand if he decided to back out on our wedding and relationship. Lord knows, I loved him. I truly worshipped and adored him. When I wasn't with Bryce, that is.

Bryce was calling on a daily; he was relentless and soon I gave up trying to avoid his calls. I was still angry from my engagement night, when he first balked at the idea of using a condom. Then the raggedy rubber broke inside of me and ruined my night. I mean, the very last thing I needed was an unforeseen drama coming by way of unexpected sexual stimuli.

But I knew my anger would abate, soon. I wouldn't stay angry with Bryce, especially when he was the next best catch to Brand. I wanted so badly to get my mind around true love for a lifetime. Mavis' sermons (admonitions) were often in my mind and permeated throughout my thoughts. Fornication. Adultery. Bastards. Sin.

Yes, I'd gotten over the anger from our sexual mishap and had to think of how I'd allow him to make it up to me. I'd gotten the latest email from Coach.com and they had some bangin'-ass new merchandise. I went to the website, ready to spend. When their delivery options proved to be less than desirable, the Coach store at the Willow Grove Mall sufficed. A Coach Hamptons Hair calf Large Hobo, a Signature Stripe Fedora and Black Jasmine sneakers in a size 7 ½ later, my good feelings for Bryce returned with vigor.

No, of course I didn't tell him about my engagement and promptly hid my ring when he came calling. Pulling up to the Willow Grove Mall with Bryce reminded me of my relationship with Cory, when I took similar chances of being caught red-handed by Brand. Sometimes, I really wondered about myself.

I literally dressed in costume to go to the mall. Hair down, long bangs in my eyes, dark Jackie O glasses. I didn't quite resemble myself. Even I had to look twice when I glanced in the mirror.

We slipped into Coach at approximately 9:20 p.m., ten minutes 'til the mall closed. The place was deserted. I perused the shelves; Bryce paid with the Gold AMEX and we were out the door within eight minutes. The talkative cashier took longer wrapping the merchandise in tissue paper, than we had in selecting and paying.

After I'd gotten over the anger, I decided to commence my sexual relationship with Bryce, orally only. I wasn't taking any chances with the goddamned condoms again. We'd exchange cunnilingus and fellatio whenever we convened.

Mission accomplished.

I couldn't remember the last time Brand bought me a designer bag, hat and shoes at any store so I showed Bryce my appreciation in the dark parking lot, on my knees as he leaned up against the Suburban. Yes, folks, outside.

I got such delicious thrills kneeling in front of him, knowing passersby could see us. Kissing him (lips not quite as dry anymore, thanks to Carmex), grinding on him in the night air was stimulating. Pulling his turgid member out, admiring the chocolate tone and pre-come running down his swollen head was intoxicating.

Licking the cum from inside his urethra, tasting his thick, salty cream was erotic. Having Bryce moan and grab my head, pushing himself into my throat was more than one human should bear. Using his hands to maneuver my head as he stood perfectly still, his stiff dick in and out of my throat had me coming on myself.

I was tired, mouth slack and sore, using my entire body to keep up with his rhythmic hips. I unbuckled his belt, opened his button and pulled his pants down to expose his scrotum. Pushing his legs apart, I pushed my head between his legs and French kissed his perineum, running my tongue over the slightly sweaty skin.

"I want you to catch it, Eva." I paused to look up into his face, contorted with pleasure and fascination. "I'm comin'." He held his dick in one hand, my head in the other as he stroked himself into an orgasm. I knelt, eye-level and watched the first spurt of semen shoot out, catching the side of my mouth. The second and third spurts were better aimed and met my swollen lips. I looked up again to see Bryce watching me, his mouth open, guiding his dick over my lips, rubbing the creamy substance around my mouth.

I used my hand and tongue to clean up.

So engrossed in my sexual extra curricular activities, I had forgotten that we were outside, in public. Bryce, too, seemed to have forgotten because he quickly pulled me to my feet. He grabbed me in a bear hug and showered me with sloppy kisses.

"You keep doin that shit, Eva; I just might have to marry you." With that, he hit the alarm/unlock button of his remote and nudged me into the driver's seat. "You drive."

I couldn't wait to wear my Coach ensemble for Brand.

I reviewed my wedding plans as I drove the gigantic Suburban down the single lane of Route 611 back to the city. My appointment to tour the reception site required a trip to Bensalem, PA the following week. The PenRyn Mansion Belle Voir Manor boasted fully restored Victorian estates with brick patios, grand entrance columns and 2000-foot, tree-lined driveways and award-winning chefs from the top US culinary schools.

Chapter 41

Month 5

Bethany screeched into the phone. "Eva, I'm so happy for you and Brand. I'm happier for him, because he's getting you. You poor thing, I'm not sure what you're getting out of the deal." She laughed at herself. "Please let me help you do something. I'm finally getting the sister I've always wanted. At least, until Bright finds some floozy who'll take him off our hands. You know what it's like having only brothers; though I can't imagine anyone having worst brothers than me."

I laugh along with Beth, wishing I felt more of her enthusiasm. For some reason, I thought her brother was going to try to get out of the wedding. "Beth, I'm actually calling to ask you to be one of my bridesmaids. I'm only having two and Taylor will be my maid of honor. I'll get you in touch with Shawna, the other bridesmaid, and you two can compare notes."

"Eva, I'd be honored to take part in your bridal party. I can't wait to get in touch with the other girls and start the fun." She rambled on for a few, but I only half listened. I almost wished Bethany and I were closer, and that she knew at least a tiny bit of my history with her brother. She was absolutely clueless when it came to the mess Brand and I managed to make.

"Listen Beth, I gotta run. I'll send you an email later today with the details about the dresses, shoes and jewelry. Oh, and I'll include the consultant's information, the calendar and our itinerary. Thanks, love. Bye bye."

Chapter 42

Month 4

"Eva, I gotta go to this job interview on Tuesday afternoon. I need you to drop Shawn off at her doctor's appointment and I'll pick her up after I get this damned job."

I almost choked on my Honey Nut Cheerios and had to jump up to keep one from going down the wrong pipe. "What? You've got to be kidding me, Tee." Now that I wasn't choking, I laughed. "You? A job? Yeah, right, who's gonna hire you, and to do what?" Taylor had been at a junior college for five years.

"Look, trick, I ain't askin' for no comments from the peanut gallery. Since ya nosy ass had to ask: I have an interview at a juvenile detention facility in Norristown at 2:30, and I can't do both."

"Okay. If they hire you, I'll make sure no kid of mine ever goes there." I couldn't help myself and laughed again. When I heard Taylor gear up to start in on me again, I quickly added, "All right. I'll take her. You just get a damned job so you can take care of your girlfriend, 'cause she ain't gonna keep letting you fuck her for free."

"Whatever. Just 'cause you gotta pay for your pussy, don't put that shit on me. You gotta work that pussy, don't let that pussy work you.

Anyway, just get Shawn where she needs to be by 4:30 and if you can't make it, call one of us, and I'll see what I can do."

"Alright, Tee, just get off my back."

"Shawn, it's Eva. I'm around the corner. Are you ready?" I was on my cell phone, late picking Shawn up from Taylor's house. I felt like slapping Taylor for having me play limousine driver to her girlfriend.

"I'll be just a few more minutes, Eva. Just come in for a minute. I left the door open. I'm so sorry; I promise I won't take long."

"Shawn, I'm already running late, can't you move any faster?"

"I promise. Just come in for a few minutes."

"All right, I'm parking now." I could have slapped the shit outta Shawn and Taylor. I was thinking that we'd never make her appointment and Taylor would surely blame this on me, somehow. I got inside and sat on the arm of the couch, listening to Shawn walk around upstairs.

"Eva, do me a favor, please. Can you get this for me?" Shawn appeared in the living room, shirtless, holding her bra together in the back. I looked at her pretty face, her D cups hanging out of the bottom of her bra, and my clit awakened, hard and ready.

Her nipples were hard and I watched her breasts, swinging loosely in her unhooked bra. Was it my imagination, or did she just strike a pose in the doorway? I must have been trippin'. With every step and saunter, her breasts fell further from the cups.

I sat there, dumbfounded and mesmerized.

Shawn stood before me and bent to give me a hug. My arms hung limply at my sides, daring myself to reach out, not trusting myself to touch her when my clit was responding like a live missile, ready to destroy.

Her hands stroked my hair and her head turned as she placed a kiss on my cheek. My hands stayed in place but my head responded of its own accord and I met her kiss halfway. Her mouth settled on mine in a light, quick kiss. She stepped away from me, looking, hands on her hips, her head cocked to the side.

Her hands found my clit through my jeans. She stroked my pussy, moaning as I sucked her nipples into my mouth, one at a time. Shawn was stroking my clit, drawing sighs from me as I was caught up in the sight and sounds of my lips drinking in her lush cleavage.

Then she was crouched before me, her hands pulling at my jeans. Something inside my head screamed, "Stop her!" But my hips went along with my jeans, in accordance with her movements to rid me of them. Her lips were on my clitoris before my pants were completely down. Shawn's small, pink tongue disappeared into my swollen lips, locking onto my clit, sucking it softly. I barely had the opportunity to grind my hips into her face when I lost control and exploded on her tongue.

She continued to suck softly and I rolled into another orgasm, smothering her as I pulled her face-forward into my vagina, screaming as a third ripped through me. I pulled her up before I busted again and kissed her lips. Although no woman had ever brought me to a multiple orgasm, I didn't have time to cherish the moment; Taylor was creeping into my thoughts.

I remained in place, my head hung low, wondering what I was doing kissing Shawn in Taylor's house. And then her breasts were bare, in my face, her nipples a dark rose against caramel skin, hard and smooth. Pushing her breasts together, she used her fingers to guide them to my lips, opened, ready to receive. I pushed her hands aside, roughly grabbing her breasts in my hands and rolled my tongue around the areolas.

Thoughts of Taylor and Brand threatened to break into my conscience and my hands roamed over her breasts, down her flat stomach and into her thong, slick from wetness. I don't know when she unbuttoned her jeans but her pussy lips were pushing against her thong, enabling me to rub in between her lips, pushing my middle finger into her pussy, feeling her warm wetness. I sucked her nipples hard, finger fucking her until I heard her gasp and push against my hand, languishing in her pussy. "Come for me." I managed this as I moved from the right nipple to the left, inching slowly back and forth.

I allowed the thought of Taylor gushing about Shawn's preference of being finger-fucked while eating her pussy. I used my mouth, fingers and hands to please her, patiently awaiting the luscious sounds Shawn emitted for Taylor when I was on the phone.

"Come for me, Shawn." I pulled her face down and kissed her lips, darting my tongue in and out of her mouth, sucking her lips and licking her teeth. I felt her responding to my sexual assault. I grabbed her hair from behind and yanked her head back, pushing her down further on my finger inside of her.

I heard her muffle a scream and say, "Taylor."

I drew her nipples into my mouth to escalate the sensations of her orgasm and rode her waves, caressing her body as I told myself that I didn't care what I was doing.

Shawn made it to her doctor's appointment on time: She'd called ahead and told them she'd be more than half an hour late, so they scheduled her for a later appointment. What a crafty and beautiful wench.

I reviewed my wedding plans as I drove home. Anne Barge of Fontana's Bridal Salon in Scarsdale, NY would design my dream dress: strapless, diamond white, silk Mikado, slightly altered, and replacing tacky rhinestones down the back, with Swarovski crystals.

Chapter 43

Month 3

I *simply decided not* to think about it. I could rationalize my sleeping with Bryce on occasion, sucking his dick outdoors, whatever. But I could not wrap my mind around eating Shawn's pussy in Taylor's house and LOVING IT!

She was fucking beautiful and soft. She smelled good and her skin felt like silk. Oh, God, how would I face Taylor ever again?

As usual, I simply put it out of my mind.

I called a recommended wedding consultant, Miss Joanne, and began the real preparations to bind Brand to me forever. We toured the reception facility for a third time, noting minor details that we'd somehow overlooked previously. Miss Joanne followed up with the dressmaker, the florist, the bakery and any other minor and major details I didn't care to make.

I had to take a break from men and women. Somehow, Desiree had gotten my phone number and was calling non-stop. I could probably thank Aunt Mirabelle for that minor miracle as well.

I was all fucked out. At this point, Brand wouldn't to stay married to me because my pussy would be hanging inside out on our honeymoon.

Month 2

"Hello."

"Evangeline Arianna LoDolce." Mavis was on my phone. What the fuck? I could not even begin to imagine how she got my phone number at Brand's house, how she knew I was living here and why, now, she'd chosen to contact me.

My mind immediately flashed to my visit and conversation with Aunt Mirabelle, three months prior, at her home. I could hear the question, 'What about your mother and brothers?' I wanted to scream then, 'What the fuck about them?' At the time, I wanted to walk out of her door but out of respect, I'd refrained and gave the most politically correct answer I was capable of.

I snapped back to the present.

"Mavis." It was all I could muster past my lips. My lungs had squeezed every drop of air from my body. "What can I do for you?" I was professional, detached and cold.

"Your aunt informed me that you are preparing for your nuptials to a young man named Brandon." She sounded like a machine.

No, Mavis had never met Brand and if she was waiting for some sort of explanation or and invitation to suddenly meet him, she'd be waiting until Hell froze over.

"Your brothers feel slighted and are hurt that you'd not consider their feelings regarding such a momentous occasion. But, you were always a selfish child and I'm not surprised that you've carried that particular trait into adulthood. I see that Mirabelle hasn't fared any better than I in raising you to be a proper young lady."

I forced myself to breath slowly. I needed to allow the steam building inside my head to evaporate slowly. The phone was inching ever closer toward a loud bang in her ear. I refused to feed into Mavis' bullshit tirade, as it was the same sermon she delivered countless times during my youth.

"Okay. Please get to the point, Mavis."

"In any event, Evangeline, I take responsibility for the absence of your father in your life and on your special day and I insist that one of us attend your wedding. Mirabelle has informed me, as well, that you've asked her to give you away."

Damn, had Aunt Mirabelle kept anything to herself? I didn't even want to know how all of this had gone down.

She continued, "I'm sure you are unaware that I am currently as associate pastor at Freedom Bible Church of Faith, and I insist in presiding over your nuptials. Evangeline, I'm sure you aren't happy to have my involvement but Mirabelle showed me the invitation and I have taken it upon myself to secure Freedom's sanctuary for your chosen day."

Was I in the fucking Twilight Zone?

"I'm sure you would rather that I fulfill your unspoken desires to uninvite me from your wedding, but that will not be the case. I allowed you to vacate my home, at 16 years of age, against my wishes. I gave into your petty demands as a child, Evangeline: I will not be denied this."

She had to be fucking kidding me.

She continued, "I have spoken to a Mr. Wayland DeLoache; Brandon's father, I presume. I advised him that, as your birth mother, I would not allow you to bar me from participating in this wedding. He quite agrees with me on this. I will pay for my meals, as well as for Ethan, Christopher, and Marcell. You needn't worry yourself regarding our transportation to and from the events, as I have seen to those details as well."

What the fuck was happening here?

But she wasn't done. "I have conversed with your wedding consultant, Miss Joanne, and I will say that she is a delightful woman and quite knowledgeable about her chosen profession. We agree that six months to plan and execute this wedding seems a bit rushed. We also agreed that another six to nine months would have greatly benefited your plans, but I assured her that this is your typical, irresponsible and impulsive behavior. She has a much greater understanding of your personality now that we've spoken at length."

Someone get the cyanide, because this bitch needs to die today!

She still wasn't done. "I know you find it difficult to believe, Evangeline, that I love you and have your best interests at heart. I love you as God has instructed a parent to love a child. You are my only daughter, and you may feel that I was harder on you than I appeared to be on your brothers."

You got that fuckin' right! Yet, I maintained my silence.

"I raised all of my children with Christian values to be loving, kind, respectful and above all, holding absolute reverence for the Lord." She actually stopped to take a breath. "And with that said, Evangeline, I trust that you will be an honorable Christian wife, loving and faithful, to your husband."

The bitch couldn't even keep HER husband!

"I will see you on your wedding day, Evangeline. Goodbye."

I need a fuckin' drink. Hell, no. Make it a double.

Chapter 44

Brand thought the shit was funny. He couldn't believe the way I'd been steamrolled by Mavis. He couldn't stop laughing. Brand also wouldn't agree to my pleas to elope to Mexico. Fuck him — let him marry Mavis.

Bryce understood my ill feelings toward Mavis and her angels. He just didn't know that my ill feelings were about them planning to crash my wedding. I didn't care whether they were paying for their own meals and limo or not. It was the fucking principle.

But that was not important as I was laying on my stomach on Bryce's California King waterbed. He was peeling off my bikini bathing suit bottom with his teeth, kissing each centimeter he exposed.

In between licks and soothing kisses, he murmured appropriate comments and noises in agreement. We'd been in the outdoor pool and Jacuzzi, frolicking and going crazy with the oral sex.

"I love you, Eva. I swear, you make me come just by talking to me and when you put that mouth anywhere near this body, I'm ready to sign away my life insurance, 401(k) and the deed to this house. You keep this shit up and you gonna have to marry me, girl."

"Yeah, right. You ain't ready for this, Bryce. You can barely take me on an occasional basis. What would you do if you had this pussy next to you, night after night? Your ass would go crazy, that's what."

I got up and paraded around the room naked. He loved my body and I showed it off every time I saw him. I got down on my knees and crawled around, swinging my ass from side to side. I knew I'd have his tongue up in it before the night was through. He was a supreme sucka for this pussy.

Wait 'til he got this ass for real.

"Bryce, you know they say all that glitters ain't gold." I stopped by the fireplace and lay on my back with my legs spread. "Come get this pussy, Bryce, and make it yours. Put your dick in my mouth and fuck me until I'm choking. Make me your bitch."

Don't let this pretty face fool you, Bryce. For every action, there is a reaction.

Chapter 45

Brand and I spend a sex-filled weekend at the Hilton Hotel at the Philadelphia International Airport. We reserved our usual suite, and ordered room service and fucked non-stop for three straight days.

We decided to abstain from sex for the last month before the wedding. Yeah, right, I couldn't wait to see how that went over. Brand pulled out all the stops for this weekend getaway, though. He brought lotions, cuffs, a dildo for my ass so I could get the thrill of being fucked by two men at the same time (he could either read my mind or I was talking way too much in my sleep).

What he needed to do was be careful of what he introduced to me, 'cause my sexual appetite had grown by leaps and bounds and was on the verge of full-blown, out-of-control (or was it already there?).

Brand called room service and ordered steak and shrimp, medium well, French bread and a bottle of house champagne.

"Come here, wife."

I almost melted into a puddle and slithered across the floor. The words were like a mood enhancer slipped into my drink. My love came flowing down my body and I crawled across the room to him.

He rubbed a clear gel over my breasts, rolling my nipples between his fingertips. I feel a slight stinging sensation, both pleasure and the tiniest ounce of pain. Before I could stop myself, I was moaning and rubbing my nipples over the rough stubble on his cheeks, over his lips, searching for contact with his tongue.

"Tell me how this feels, Eva. Tell me how much you're going to love this shit when you become Mrs. DeLoache."

I was out of my mind and willing to do anything to prolong this wondrous pleasure. "Oh, God, Brand." I moaned through my words, eyes closed, grabbing at his clothes and body. But he had other plans for me and stayed out of my grasp; instead, tormenting me with his teeth and tongue.

Eyes closed, I didn't feel him apply more gel until his hands were on and inside my pussy at the same time. I felt a sting and then my body was on fire, my legs tense and shaking.

Brand's lips, teeth, hands and arms seemed to be everywhere at once and I felt orgasmic all over my body. My limbs were shaking, strange noises were spilling from my mouth and I was caught between a place of undeniable pleasure and sinful pain.

"Oh, my God, Bry…" I caught myself milliseconds before I screamed out Bryce's name. And with the realization came an abrupt halt to my body-consuming orgasm, sure to have put me in a frame of mind to be faithful to Brand forever.

I was slipping away.

"Eva, baby, what happened? I thought you was about to either come all over me or die. Don't stop, baby, come for me." Brand was trying his hardest to slowly fill my pussy with his semi-hard dick.

But the flowing river source that runneth over mere minutes ago was rapidly drying, slowing Brand's ascent into Evaland.

Shawn's creamy pussy popped into my mind and I could taste her sweet nectar on my tongue and envisioned licking her come out of her pussy, slowly savoring the mixture of her arousal and juices on my lips.

Brand was whispering that he loved me, and telling me how he wanted to please me in various ways. His dick stayed semi-hard and his attempts miserably failed to enter Evaland.

Then Bryce's eight inches was in my ass and I tongued Shawn's pussy with further determination as I felt an orgasm on the horizon and bucked my body harder in search of my distant goal.

Suddenly Shawn was in between my legs, a 7-inch dildo strapped to her small waist and SHE was stroking my pussy, successfully easing into Evaland, thrust after thrust. Bryce was matching Shawn, stroke for stroke, in my ass.

My flowing river source again runneth over as the sensation of two holes filled with hardened flesh (even if one was plastic), was an overload on my sexual senses. I don't know where I busted first, but one orgasm was followed by an ear-splitting scream as another busted out of both holes and saliva ran from the corners of my mouth.

Shit.

I had been fucked; thoroughly, mindlessly and skillfully.

I felt Brand stiffen and then heard him emit a groan.

Damn, I couldn't wait to get married.

Chapter 46

Month 1

Okay. I was down to the final month. I almost couldn't believe I was actually here. I couldn't believe we'd made it this far. Or had we?

Brand and I started our abstinence kick yesterday. The wedding was set for 29 days from today. On July 2, I would formally become Mrs. Brandon Maxwell DeLoache. Herpes was no longer a concern of mine or a danger to others, so long as I kept my list of sexual partners short and confined to those present within the last six months.

And in honor of my commitment to Brand and marriage, I'd do my damndest to remain faithful and celibate.

Wait. Who said that?

Week 2

"Eva, what the fuck is this shit?" Brand had my cell phone in his hand, flipped open to reveal my text messages. He read aloud, "'when can I cum 4 u again?'" He looked enraged and capable of homicide.

"What da fuck is that supposed to mean? And who is sendin' you this kind of shit fourteen fuckin' days before we get married?" He was advancing as I was retreating, holding the phone up so I could see the provocative text message. "I swear to God, Eva, if you are fuckin' around on me, you're gonna find yourself marrying this nigga on your wedding day." Brand looked ready to commit that homicide and I could deduce that I was high on his shit list.

I honestly had no idea of what he was talking about, so I futilely attempted to snatch the phone from his hand, but he raised it above my head. "I don't know who the fuck you're talking to, Brand, but I'm not going to stand here and take this shit from you, when I don't know what you're talking about." I was exasperated and felt the beginnings of fear as Brand's eyes danced in a lethal recognition of prey caught in defeat.

"Give me the goddamned phone, Brand. If I can't defend myself, I'll leave until you come back to your senses and talk to me like I'm the woman you're going to marry in fourteen days." I was bitchin' inside. Had Desiree or Bryce slipped a text message in under the radar and I failed to notice it, hence, no deletion?

"Take this bullshit! I swear to God, Eva, I'm not havin' this shit this time around. I knew you would do something like this. You can't keep your fuckin' legs closed, and you and that nigga too stupid to keep that shit quiet."

Brand threw the phone at me. It hit the carpet at my feet and I reached down to retrieve it. I pulled up the text and immediately recognized the number. "You know, you could've asked questions before comin' at me like this. This is some real, live bullshit, Brand. This is Kristal's number, asshole."

I felt disrespected and was ready to spit fire. "You remember Kristal, right? Burberry trench coat, Gucci sandals, Victoria's Secret bra and panty set. Let me refresh your memory: Kristal eating my pussy at your apartment and you masturbating over us on your bed."

"Whatever, Eva. What is she doing texting you? You messin' with this bitch now? Oh, I see. I'm supposed to believe she's just texting you this type of shit outta the blue."

"Fuck you, Brand. I ran into her in New York, when I was being fitted for my wedding dress. We stopped to speak and exchanged numbers. She mentioned that she's been living in Brooklyn for about a year. She asked about you and that was that."

Brand just stood there, looking stupid. I could tell he was trying to decide whether I was telling the truth. If I was, my coincidental meeting was his fault, as he was the one to introduce us.

I was ready to catch a case.

"You're the one who hooked me up with that bitch, and now it's a problem that sends me an innocuous text that you misunderstood and blew out of proportion." I wasn't letting this go without a fight.

I took a breath to calm myself.

"Brand, why don't you take a walk and check me when you're level-headed and ready to apologize."

I turned my back to him, to let him know that the conversation was over.

I still don't know what that text meant and why she was sending it to me now.

Yeah, we made up. But I'm thinking, "Nigga, you introduced me to this shit."

Be careful what you ask the fuck for.

Chapter 47

Day 5

"What's up, Tee, where you been?" I hadn't heard from Taylor in a few days so I called, expecting to hear tales of fucking Shawn senseless in some context or another. Thoughts of my fucking Shawn were a mere blip of a memory.

"I'm alright, I guess. I don't know. Somethin is bugging the fuck outta me and I can't put my finger on it. But I know it has somethin' to do with Shawn. She ain't right, or I'm trippin', or somethin'. I think she might be seeing somebody on the side."

I was almost afraid to ask Taylor for the specifics. I had a feeling that they had something to do with Shawn calling my phone at odd hours of the day and night. I wasn't sure if she was calling me to say that we were wrong and our interlude could never happen again, or to ask me to indulge in my eat game again.

And as I wasn't sure what I might say or do, I felt it best to just ignore her calls until I could say with certainty that I no longer had the desire to grow a dick and fuck her senseless.

"Tee, what exactly are you feeling? I mean, could you be paranoid and imagining things, or do you have some hard proof that you could confront her with?" Did I really want to hear this?

"I don't have any hard proof, but I think she's fuckin' with somebody else. I know, I'm trippin', 'cause it ain't like I'm really into chicks, but I gotta feeling that it's a woman that's got her attention. Don't ask me how I know, but I'm not crazy and she hasn't been the same for a couple months."

"Tee, don't do anything rash." Had I really said that?

"Don't worry, Eva. On the strength of your wedding, I'm not goin' to drop that ass; but if I find out this bitch is eatin' pussy somewhere else, it's a wrap."

"I don't know, Tee. You said you're the first chick she's been with; maybe she's getting used to the whole relationship thing; she might be a little uncomfortable and doesn't know how to tell you." I was grasping at straws.

"Yeah, well, she got a few more days to get her act together, or I'm goin back to niggas and say 'fuck bitches.' You help me keep my eye on her at the wedding, 'cause you know how hoes be. Alright, man, get off my phone. I'm trying to get my maid of honor shit together and you are wastin' my time. Ciao."

And with that, she was gone. How was I going to live this down? In the end, would Shawn prove to be worth my friendship with Taylor? Was I going to be able to maintain my friendship with Taylor after this?

Chapter 48

Wedding Day

My wedding day was finally here. The headache, worry and anxiety have all abated with the knowledge that later today, I would be Mrs. DeLoache. I could finally breathe again.

I was up at 6 a.m., calling and texting Taylor, Shawn and Bethany. An 8 a.m. limousine would take the bridal party to the Borgata Hotel and Casino in Atlantic City. Wayland's present to us was a day at Spa Toccare, located inside the hotel.

My spa package included a Botanical Republic facial, Aqua Latte Foaming Milk Bath, Healing Stone Therapy massage, manicure and pedicure. I hadn't seen the price list and figured I didn't really need to know. This is how the DeLoaches handled their business and I would learn to get used to it; or die trying. My stylist was making the trek to Spa Toccare to sweep my hair into a chignon, with curled tendrils framing my face and veil.

We had separate but connecting rooms at the plush hotel and a scheduled lunch in Taylor's room at 11:30 a.m. We would have time for a brief rest, dress at the hotel, and the limo would take us directly to Mavis' church.

Yeah, Mavis had won that round. I couldn't fight Mavis, Wayland

and Mirabelle. They had collectively railroaded me and I finally, quietly, acquiesced. Fine. Fuck it. Mavis could do her thumping and in the end, I'd have the prize. Let her think she was doing something.

Out of sheer exasperation, I'd stayed with Mirabelle for the last week leading up to the wedding. Brand eventually apologized for his insufferable behavior and the make-up session came too close to breaking our vow of abstinence. Then we began arguing again.

Plus, I wasn't really feeling the way Brand had spoken to me the day he found the text. I mean, I still meant to get married; nothing would stop my pending wedding and subsequent marriage to Brandon, but I was seriously considering having him eat Bryce outta my pussy on the honeymoon.

Speaking of Bryce: That nigga wouldn't take no for an answer. We'd been together for the last four nights and I'd been getting my shit off as if it would be the final supper of oral sex.

Taylor, Shawn and Bethany got to Mirabelle's by 7:30 and we double- and triple-checked our dresses and accessories, makeup, etc. These would be my final hours as a single woman and I didn't want anything to go wrong.

Ah, Bryce. I wondered, during my milk bath, where he was. I wasn't sure how I felt about him today. For the last two days, I'd managed to put that night out of my mind. What happened to the ring? Okay, this is actually scary 'cause I couldn't quite put my finger on the exact details of that night.

Day 2 Rewind

"Eva. Where have you been? I've been calling you all day." It was Bryce, sounding worried, yet sweet and honestly concerned. "Why don't you come see me tonight?" I didn't really want to do this with Bryce tonight. I was getting married in two days. I was trying to do the right thing, but it kept eluding me. Then that same thing propelled me out of the safety and security of Mirabelle's home each night, into his truck or some other place and his hard-ass dick in my mouth.

"Bryce, can't this wait another day or two?" I know; I ain't shit. In another day or two, I'd be on my honeymoon to Punta Cana and I wouldn't have to worry about this drama for a spell. See, I tried to do the right thing.

"Humor me, please, Eva. This won't take long, I promise. I just want to see your beautiful face and besides, I have something for you." The bastard knew just what to say to get me out of the house and my lips on his dick.

And that was how I ended up with Bryce, two nights before my wedding to Brand, when I had absolutely sworn off my reckless behavior. I made my way to his house, all the while asking myself what possessed me to act so carelessly. I would have skinned Brand alive if I knew that he was even looking at other women at this time.

Bryce met me at the beginning of his driveway, dressed impeccably in natural stretch wool pants and Loro Piana cashmere. I couldn't help but smile in his direction as I pulled into the opened garage door. He was devilishly handsome and his oral game had only improved in the month of abstinence with Brand.

"Damn, girl, it took you long enough to get here." He helped me from the car and pulled me into a long, warm, welcoming hug. Despite myself, I hugged him back, wondering if this would be the last time I would spend with Bryce. His body had grown to fit mine during the time we'd spent together and I felt security and love oozing from his body, wordlessly, into mine.

I reached up on tiptoe to kiss him. Oh, he'd come so far. It was almost be a shame that we wouldn't eventually be together. Our babies would have been gorgeous. Pretty, petite girls, just like their mother and rough, built boys like their daddy. I had to snap out of this fantasy shit.

"Eva, I love you and I'm glad I got you to come out of the house. You need to relax, and I have the perfect remedy. You seem so stressed lately and since you won't tell me anything, I did what I thought was best for both of us." He took my hand and led me into the house through the garage door.

He walked through the kitchen and into the formal dining room that we never used except to have loud, raunchy sex occasionally. "There's a bottle of Moët in the fridge; can you get it for me? I'll be right back."

Later, I'd feel idiotic that I hadn't seen any of the signs from Bryce, so caught up in preparing for my wedding. Completely unprepared, I opened the fridge. Yes, there was a bottle of Moët, chilling for optimal consumption.

And around the neck was a jewelry bag from Tiffany.

Call me Scarlet O'Hara, because I almost fainted and fell sideways into the refrigerator door. And then Bryce was behind me, his chin resting on my right shoulder, his arms encircling my waist.

An open Tiffany blue box rested in his hands and a pear shaped, pink diamond engagement ring winked at me. My first thought was, Goddamn, that's a big-ass, pink diamond. My second thought was, Oh, no, this can't be happening.'

And then Bryce slid down my body and turned me around to face him. He was on one knee, pulling the ring out of the box. My mind told me to bolt but my body stood perfectly still. I hate to admit that I wanted to see this scene played out.

"Eva, I've told you in every possible way that I love you. I know we haven't known each other very long and I sense that you've been pulling away from me these last few months, probably unsure of my intentions for us. I feel like I've known you for years instead of months, and you have to admit that the sexual chemistry between us that is unparalleled."

Bryce kissed my hand. "I know we have a lot to learn about one another and I'm willing to take all the time you need to grow to love me. Take this chance with me, Eva. Take the chance to love me and grow with me."

Bryce kissed my left ring finger. "Eva, accept this ring as a promise to marry me when the time is right. No pressure and no, this isn't a ploy so you'll have sex with me again." We both chuckled at that one. If he only knew.

"I love you, Eva, and I want to marry you when the time is right for both of us." He looked up at me, patiently.

"Bryce…" I wouldn't say yes. Yet, I wouldn't say no, either. I didn't know what to do. Part of me thought this was a chance of a lifetime and that I could marry Bryce without guilt and an ugly past behind us. There were no secrets lurking in the dark to come between us.

How different might things had been if Brand had been honest up front? How different would our relationship have been if he hadn't contracted herpes at all? What the fuck was I thinking? I was getting married to Brand in two days!

Then I thought, fuck it; men did this shit all the time. Men strung two or three women along for months and years, promising to marry all and eventually marrying none. Why shouldn't I profit from two loving, committed relationships, as long as they never found out about each other?

I heard myself say, "Bryce, I do love you and I'm flattered that you're asking me to marry you. But, I'm not ready to get married right now. Why don't we hold off for a little while? Let's make this a promise ring and we'll see where we are in six months."

I heard Bryce breath a sigh of relief. He slid the winking, pink diamond solitaire onto my finger. He stood up, towering over me, and picked me up. With my legs around his torso, I kissed him and then considered throwing myself under the nearest train.

For the next hour, we kissed, cuddled, and talked about a supposed future that I knew would never take place. And then he made love to me, sweetly, lovingly, honestly. I cried afterward at the unfairness of it all. I cried softly for the Eva I used to be before Brand and a disease that changed my life, and took away the opportunity for a different future.

I didn't think at all on the way home.

Bryce sent flowers to Mirabelle's house the next day. I told her they were from Brand and went to look at the pink diamond in my jewelry box, in the same place the marquise sat when I was with Bryce.

I was getting married the next day.

Chapter 49

Wedding Day
12:00 PM

Everything went perfectly at the Borgata. Lunch was catered from their main kitchen, thanks to Wayland. We stuffed ourselves, knowing we wouldn't see food again until later tonight. I caught a 30-minute nap and then allowed Taylor to dress and accessorize me into the princess I'd always dreamed I'd be on this day.

We were picture perfect as we entered the limousine, complimenting one another one minute and then giggling like schoolgirls the next. I believed the fairytale was finally happening to me. I think the bridal party was more excited than me.

3:00 PM

We arrived at the church with more than an hour to spare for our 5:30 p.m. service. The bridal party shielded me from prying eyes, or an accidental glance by Brand. I was ushered into a sitting room off the main sanctuary and attempted to calm my nerves.

"Eva, sit down and try to relax. I'm going to find Brand and Evan and make sure they're ready. I'll look for Miss Joanne to make sure every-thing is in its place, or if she needs something from you." She walked over to Shawn and kissed her. "Shawnee, baby, I'll be right back. Keep Eva company and don't leave her."

Shawn made appropriate mewling noises for Taylor, as she always did. But as Taylor left the room, I felt Shawn's eyes burning into my veil. I refused to turn around. I sent out a silent prayer: Please, Bethany, don't leave this room.

And as if she heard the opposite of my words, Beth jumped up. "Eva, Shawn, I'm nervous as hell and I gotta pee like a race horse. Shawn, please don't leave her alone; Taylor would kill us both and I'll be right back." With a rustle of peach silk, she was gone.

I closed my eyes to offer up another prayer and then changed my mind. I didn't know what I might get instead. When I opened them, Shawn was standing before me. She reached out to caress my face and I willed myself not to look at her or respond to her touch.

"Eva, I've been calling you. I know you've gotten my calls, yet you don't answer them." Her hands trailed down my chin and lighted upon my breasts. My nipples were instantly hard and I silently willed someone back into the room.

"Taylor doesn't know that anything happened between us, and I in-tend to keep it that way. I wish it were you I met that night. I don't believe you'd be getting married today, if that were the case." Her fingers outlined the swell of my breasts, so perfectly outlined in my strapless gown. "Oh, I know you're not gay; you are, after all, marrying a man in a few hours. I'm not gay either, if that's any consolation, and neither is Taylor. But I'm thinking about changing my mind about that. I want you, Eva, but I'll have Taylor if you insist on being faithful to Brand."

She ran one finger into the bodice to caress my breasts and my nipples threatened to come through my dress. She was whispering in my ear and I was ready to run from the room as I felt wetness seep into my silk panties, dyed to perfectly match my dress. "Shawna," I managed to push out.

"Eva, Brand is here..." Bethany rushed back into the sitting room, flushed from excitement. She stopped in the doorway, staring at Shawn's finger in my bodice and, I'm sure, the exquisite look of lust on my face.

I sat up, ready to offer an explanation, but the words failed me. Shawn simply withdrew her hand, walked across the room, and settled on a chaise. "Did you hide the tag from my bra, Shawn…?" Even to me, the question sounded flimsy and contrived. I closed my eyes, ready to send up another prayer and then changed my mind.

Bethany flushed even further and stepped out of the room, I guess to collect her thoughts. I didn't want to know what she was thinking about the cozily sexy scene she happened upon. She stepped back to the doorway. "Eva, Brand and Evan are here. Taylor's greeting guests until she locates Miss Joanne. I was looking for my dad and your Aunt." Her words trailed off and she entered the room and sat as far away from Shawn as she could without being out of the room.

I heard my cell phone ringing in the Coach Hamptons bag. Needing to break the tension in the room, I made a big fuss of reaching into the bag to answer the phone. Oh no, it was Bryce. I hit the ignore button and prayed he would leave a message and not call back. I especially could not handle any more drama today, before I got married.

Shawn got up to leave the room. As she passed my chair, she stopped and stared at me until I returned her gaze. "Eva, think about what I said. And if we don't get a chance to talk again before the ceremony, congratulations and my best wishes to the bride and groom. I'm going to find Taylor and see how I can help."

Chapter 50

4:00 PM

Once she was gone, Bethany rushed over to me and grabbed my hands.

"Eva, are you okay? What happened after I left the room? Did she say something to upset you?" She looked into my face, hopefully mistaking my visible guilt for pre-wedding anxiety. "Is she a lesbian? Was she coming onto you? You know, I don't like her. I felt like she was staring at me all day. I felt really uncomfortable when we were changing out of our clothes at the spa."

My cell phone signaled a new voicemail. It began to ring again instantly.

"Beth, no, really, I'm okay. Shawn was helping me with the bra that I should have tried on before I bought it from Macy's. Don't worry; everything's fine. Will you do me a favor, please? Can you find Mirabelle and have her come to the sitting room? I'd like just a few minutes to myself." I could see the hesitation in her eyes and wondered if she was afraid to leave me to the clutches of Shawn. My cell phone rang again. If she only knew.

"Okay, Eva, I'll go for a few minutes, but I'm coming back. I don't want that girl upsetting you on your wedding day." She walked cautiously to the door and looked back at me questioningly.

"I promise I'm okay, Beth. Just do this for me, please." My cell phone was ringing again.

She was gone and I answered Bryce's ring. "Bryce." I was whispering and felt smarmy, like a baby snatcher.

"Eva, what the hell is going on? You haven't answered my phone calls all day. I finally drove to your aunt's house, 'cause I wasn't sure what was going on. You are my fiancé and I think I have the right to know if you're sick or in the hospital. I just assumed something had happened to you. What's going on at the church?"

My heart dropped at the realization that he knew where I was and I'd have to give him some semblance of an answer.

"Eva, tell me the truth: Did you tell your aunt about our engagement? If you need more time to break it to your family, I'll have to understand, but I felt like there was something else on her mind when I asked her if she knew where you were."

My God, why had I accepted Bryce's ring? Why had I gone to his house that night? What the fuck was wrong with me? How had all of these contingencies converged today? What next: Evan has an epiphany and confesses to Brand that I fucked him like a rodeo girl that night in Atlantic City? Wasn't it bad enough that Shawn was coming onto me at my wedding? Beth is thinking she's gay and probably wondering what was up with me as well.

"Eva, baby, tell me what's going on. I made plans for us to have dinner with my mother tonight, so we can tell her about the engagement together. If you want to wait, we don't have to tell her tonight. Talk to me, Eva. You've been closed off from me for months. Let me help you through whatever it is."

The lies spewed forth from my lips without hesitation. "Bryce, we're at the church at a christening for my little cousin. It's nothing, really. We should be done in an hour or so, let me get back to you about tonight." My mind wasn't even racing anymore. I was sweating; probably ruining my dress and feeling the walls close in on me. I knew someone would open the door any second and I'd have to explain why I was on the phone, having this conversation.

"Bryce, baby, just give me a little while and I'll call you back and explain everything. We'll have dinner with your mother another night. We'll talk about everything tonight." I faked answering someone calling to me. Covering the receiver, I called out, "I'm in the bathroom; I'll be right out."

"Bryce, I promise I'll call you when this is over. I love you."

Chapter 51

5:00 PM

Taylor stormed into the sitting room. "Eva, everybody's here and the organist is playing music. Brand looks like he's going to cry, while Evan looks like he ate the Cheshire cat. Then Brand's sister pulls me outside on the steps and tells me that Shawn upset you and was touching your titties. What the fuck is she talking about? Shawn is looking at me as if she doesn't know what I'm talking about; she's looking stupid. What happened when I left? Damn them! I can't believe this shit. I told them not to leave you alone and now this."

"Tee, calm down. Everything is fine. Bethany came in the room as Shawn was helping hide this tag from my bra; it was showing on the side and she tucked it back in. It was as simple as that." I pushed out a laugh. "Then when Shawn left to find you, Beth asked me if Shawn was a lesbian and trying to hit on me. Can you believe that shit?"

Taylor narrowed her eyes suspiciously. "Are you serious? She asked you if Shawn was gay? Ain't that a fuckin riot. What did you tell her?"

"Tee, please, just let it go. I just want to get married to Brand and be done with all of this drama. I knew we should have eloped. Go and make sure everything is perfect for me. Thank you, Tee.

I love you. One day, I'll do all of this for your wedding."

5:45 PM

 The organist began playing the wedding march and I was gliding down the aisle on the arm of Aunt Mirabelle. At the altar, I could see Brand waiting for me, looking like my knight and savior. I didn't care what happened after today. I was getting married and that's all that mattered.

 I tried not to look at Mavis, dressed in full regalia, looking like an actual minister. For once, I tried to muster some feelings of respect and gratitude. Never mind, too much work on my day. Let her marry me so I could be done with her for good.

 I caught Evan's eye as I slowly marched down the aisle. As Brand's best man, he stood next to the groom lookin' good as shit! Calm down, Eva, get your thoughts together. Okay, I know he was not giving me the eye and doing his best lip-licking LL impersonation.

 Damn, those lips felt good on my clit.

 I tried to avoid Shawn's eyes but her gaze caught my eye and had me stumbling. She ran her hand over her breasts, making slow, lazy circles around her nipples. She knew everyone's eyes would be on the bride. Saucy wench. I knew what she was signifying and my clit jumped again.

 Damn, those lips felt good on my clit.

 I caught Taylor's eye as I continued on my march. She looked stricken, caught somewhere between a smile and a grimace. Then she glanced at Shawn and caught the last finger lap over her breasts. She immediately looked into the crowd and I saw her gaze fix on one particular individual. I'm sure she didn't realize that Shawn was signifying to me, her best friend.

 Had I really fucked three people from my wedding party?

 Aunt Mirabelle and I reached the end of the carpet laid out for my march. We had come to stop at the altar, where she wiped a tear and handed me over to Brand. I wanted to kiss him right then. The crowd be damned! Didn't they understand what this day meant to me? Did they understand all that I had gone through to get this man here? Forget them; this day was all about me.

 Mavis stepped forward and joined my hand with Brand's.

"Ladies and gentlemen, we are gathered here today to join this man and woman in holy matrimony. I digress for a short moment, as this is a particularly special day for my family and me. This beautiful young woman is my daughter, Evangeline Arianna LoDolce, and I couldn't be happier or more proud to join Evangeline with Brandon on this day."

I watched Taylor's eyes narrow and peer into the crowd. Maybe Shawn wasn't flirting with me and there was someone else out there. Despite this being the part of this day I've lived for, I was dying to turn around and see what Taylor was looking at.

"Our loving couple has written their own vows and will recite them as a symbol of their love and commitment to one another. Brandon, we will start with you. You may begin."

Brand turns to me, still holding my hand. We've been practicing our wedding vows in between arguments over the last few months. We knew the ceremony was thrown together and perhaps a little non-traditional, so we wanted to make it as special as possible.

"Eva, in the presence of God and these, our friends, I take thee to be my wife, promising with Divine assistance to be unto thee a loving and faithful husband, so long as we both shall live. I will be yours in time of plenty and want, in times of sickness and in times of health, in times of joy and in times of sorrow, in times of failure and in times of triumph. I promise to cherish and respect you, to care and protect you, to encourage and stay with you, for all eternity."

Mavis beamed at Brand as if he was her star pupil. I almost expected her to kiss him for me. "Evangeline, you may begin."

My heart was beating and I hoped I made Brand as proud of me as I was of him. His vows were honest and filled with such emotion! I cleared my throat and took a deep breath.

"Brand, in the presence of God and these, our friends, I take thee to be my husband, promising with Divine assistance to be unto thee a loving and faithful wife so long as we both shall live."

There was a rustle and a burst of murmuring from the crowd. Taylor's face turned white and her eyes threatened to pop out of her head. The entire wedding party stood motionless and stared behind us, and a flash of anger surged through me toward the person trying to steal my glow on my day.

I wasn't having it, nor would I give that attempted usurper the pleasure and acknowledgement of interrupting my wedding ceremony. I raised my voice and continued without missing a beat.

"I will be yours in time of plenty and want, in times of sickness and in times of health, in times of joy and in times of sorrow, in times of failure and in times of triumph. I promise to cherish and respect you, to care and protect you, to encourage and stay with you, for all eternity."

At this point, Evan stepped forward, staring seemingly right through us, his fists clenched and a murderous look in his eyes. Brand turned around, still holding my hand, and followed Evan's eyes as Evan walked past us to meet this unseen foe.

I still did not turn around to validate or acknowledge this intruder.

Evan reached the stranger first and I could hear him confront the unknown person. "What's up, brotha? I don't think you belong here. This is a private ceremony and you weren't invited by Eva or Brand."

I knew that this was tame for Evan, compared to his lively and colorful language spoken on a regular basis.

"Eva." It was unnaturally quiet in the sanctuary. Completely non-plussed and at an absolute refusal to stop my wedding, I tuned the voice out.

"Eva." I could hear the emotional voice behind me. No. This was not happening. I wouldn't admit to myself that Bryce was standing behind me, calling my name at MY wedding to Brand.

"You can't be here to marry Brand after all you've told me about him. Eva, how are you about to marry Brand, when you accepted my engagement ring two days ago?"

Brand took a step away from me, still following Evan's gaze.

"Eva, turn around and tell me what the fuck is going on." Bryce sounded as if he was near tears.

I stood motionless, afraid to turn around and meet Bryce's gaze.

Chapter 52

Bryce's voice was emotional. "I know you're not marrying this nigga, after what you told me he did to you. He ruined your fuckin' life, Eva, and you're giving him your entire life to continue to mess up." Bryce was trying to get past Evan. "Eva, we've been together for almost a year. You took my ring and promised that you would marry me two days ago."

Brand looked at me as if he didn't know who I was. "Eva, who the fuck is dis clown, comin' in here, talkin' about you was about to marry him? I know you ain't that fuckin' stupid."

I heard fabric rustling and knew, without looking, that the verbal confrontation between Bryce and Evan had changed to physical. I heard a shout from the crowd and then fists meeting skin.

Brand released my hand and sucker-punched Bryce from the side, catching him off guard. Stunned, Bryce caught Evan's foot to his ribs on the way down. They attacked him, taking turns kicking him as he tried uselessly to defend himself.

Brand was out of breath and breathing hard. "Pussy, I should kill you, comin' in here like that. Fuck makes you think you could come in here and talk to my girl like that?" Evan was standing to the side, watching with a sly grin on his face.

I heard Bethany make a noise and then she was quiet. I couldn't turn around to see what happened to her.

Brand was cursing, calling me names and kicking Bryce like a maniac. He truly looked as if he intended to kill Bryce, on the floor, in Mavis' church.

The wedding guests started rapidly dispersing. Someone shouted, "He's got a gun!" and pandemonium broke. People were jumping over pews and knocking over slower guests in attempt to reach the sanctuary doors.

Taylor ran to stop Brand from kicking Bryce. "Evan, why are you just standing there? Stop Brand before he kills him! Do something! Somebody help me." She grabbed at Brand, only to be pulled away by Evan.

Mavis stood, immobilized, at the altar, whispering and then alternately shouting, "Evangeline, what have you done? The blood of Jesus! Evangeline I taught you better than this. The blood of Jesus! Evangeline, what have you done? The blood of Jesus!"

It was enough of a reprieve for Bryce to stagger to his feet. Then, Evan was all over him again. Bryce was trading punches with Evan and hit Taylor in the process. Brand was immediately back in the fray, cursing Bryce for hitting Taylor.

Taylor was in the mix, looking like a super lightweight. Evan was delivering kidney shots to Bryce's midsection. As he bent over from the pain, Taylor pimp-slapped him from the side.

I had to do something. I put out a hand to assist…someone. I didn't know what to do. I could hear Mavis moaning and wailing in the background. Her words were alternately indecipherable and then crystal clear. "The blood of Jesus!"

Bryce was bleeding everywhere, Evan had a cut on his eye and Brand had blood running from his mouth. Taylor would bitch-slap and kick Bryce after Brand and Evan hit him. She mainly stayed on the outside but managed to get a few punches in.

I felt a hand on my shoulder and whirled around to defend myself. Shawn's body was molded against mine and her other hand, hidden from view, was caressing my ass. I felt my clit jump as I tried to forget the feel of her lips on me. "Now that you won't be marrying Brand, you can return my calls and we can spend some time together. I want to make you cum like I did before. You remember, don't you?" She kissed my open mouth and stepped toward the fight to pull Taylor out.

I looked behind me. Brighton was kneeling over an unconscious Bethany, who'd fainted after the first couple of blows. Poor thing.

"The blood of Jesus!"

Wayland and Winston, his younger brother, climbed over people and pews and broke up the fight, pulling Brand and Evan off Bryce.

Bryce fought against Winston as he was pulled down the aisle. "I love you, Eva. It didn't have to happen like this." He coughed up blood through swollen and busted lips. "You know where to find me when you have enough of that nut-ass nigga you about to marry."

Then to Brand: "Brand, we can do this again when it's just you and me. I'mma see you again on the bricks." Winston hauled Bryce out of the sanctuary and into the street.

"The blood of Jesus!"

Brand walked over to me, standing in the exact same spot that I had, moments ago, spoken my vows. He laughed in my face. "You're a tramp-ass whore, Eva! That's why I always treated you like one. I'm not even surprised that some nigga came in here, at my wedding, to kick my ass over you." He spit out a mouthful of blood. "I told you to marry that trick-ass-nigga you were fuckin' with."

He turned around and motioned Evan to follow. Evan wiped blood from his nose and blew me a kiss as he followed Brand out of the sanctuary.

Brighton had roused Bethany, who was sitting on the floor. "Bright, what happened? Where's Brand? Eva, is that blood?"

Bright went out after Brand, bumping my shoulder and arm as he passed, pushing me forward. "You better watch your back, bitch."

Oh, God. Brighton fought women as if they were men.

"The blood of Jesus!"

Taylor and Shawn had disappeared. I'm sure Shawn was some-where tending to Taylor's wounds.

In the end, I didn't have Brand or Bryce.

I was still standing in the same spot, clutching my wedding bouquet, in my wedding dress. A few nosy guests stood on the pews, whispering amongst themselves, waiting to see what would happen next.

As I realized that the rest of my wedding would not take place and my world faded to black, I could hear Mavis shouting, "The blood of Jesus!"

Dear Readers,

The sexual behavior of the character of the book is pure fiction. But to millions of Americans Herpes is all too real. The author gives all due respect to the grave seriousness to the rising tide of unchecked, sexually transmitted diseases (STD) in the urban community.

The publisher and author, as a matter of public health, do not endorse gratuitous and unprotected sexual relations, or the willful and deliberate sexual transmission of any communicable disease.

Even more than AIDS/HIV, Herpes is prevalent in the human population. As much as 80% of Americans have been afflicted by Herpes Simplex (HSV 1), Herpes Zoster ("Shingles"), Epstein-Barr (Mononucleosis) and Genital Herpes (HSV 2).

Herpes is most often triggered by emotional, physical and mental stress and by a compromised immune system. Oral and general Herpes can be transmitted sexually and from mother to child by blood and have accounted for countless suffering for those afflicted.

Symptoms include: Cold sores, legions on cervix or vagina, irritation or sores on penis, painful intercourse and/or discharge from penis or vagina.

If you suspect that you have been exposed to the Herpes virus and/or are currently experiencing its symptoms, please seek competent medical attention as soon as possible.
For more information, please visit the following websites:

www.GenitalHerpes.com
www.manageherpes.com
www.herpeshelp.com
www.niaid.nih.gov/factsheets/stdherp.htm
www.kidshealth.org/parent/infections/std/herpes.html

BOOK CLUB QUESTIONS

1. If you were casting a movie, who would play the main characters?
2. Do you know any one like Eva? How are they like her? How are they unlike her?
3. Do you think Eva's a good person? Would you be her friend?
   Why or why not?
4. Do you know anyone living with an incurable virus/disease? If yes – How did that person deal with it?
5. Can you relate to any of the emotions and/or actions Eva displayed throughout the book? Why or why not?
6. Can you relate to situations she found herself in? How would you have handled things differently?
7. Explain 3 separate instances when Eva made poor choices and what you would have done instead.
8. Do you feel sorry for Eva? Why or why not? What did you feel for Eva throughout the book?
9. Did Eva stir strong emotions in you? If no - Why or why not? If yes - What were they and why?
10. Why do you think Eva had such a poor relationship with Mavis and her brother's?
11. What was the significance of Mavis' spiritual life and how did it affect Eva?
12. Why do you think Eva was attracted to men like Brand, Bryce and Cory?
13. What do you think of Eva having only one close friend?

ESSENCE BESTSELLERS
WIFEY
AND
I'M STILL WIFEY
BY
KIKI SWINSON

NOVEMBER 2007
THE TRILOGY ENDS WITH
LIFE AFTER WIFEY

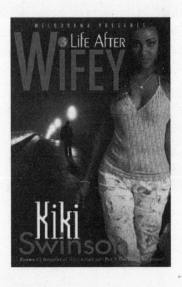

FEBRUARY 2007
THE CANDY SHOP
BY
#1 ESSENCE BESTSELLING AUTHOR
KIKI SWINSON

NOVEMBER 2006
STRIPPED
FROM THE DESK OF JACKI SIMMONS

NOVEMBER 2006
IN MY 'HOOD
by ENDY

SEPTEMBER 2006
CROSS ROADS
CARL PATTERSON

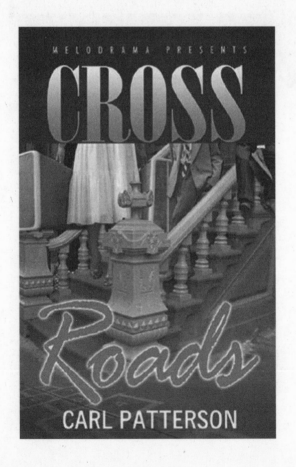

JANUARY 2007
EVA FIRST LADY OF SIN
by STORM

NOW AVAILABLE
A TWISTED TALE OF KARMA
AUTHOR
AMALEKA McCALL

NOW AVAILABLE
MENACE II SOCIETY
VARIOUS AUTHORS,
**AL-SAADIQ BANKS, MARK ANTHONY,
CRYSTAL LACEY WINSLOW, ISADORE JOHNSON
J.M BENJAMIN**

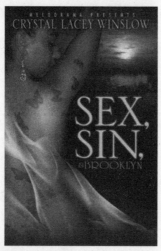

ORDER FORM
(PHOTO COPY)
MELODRAMA PUBLISHING
P. O. BOX 522
BELLPORT, NY 11713-0522
(646) 879-6315
www.melodramapublishing.com
melodramapub@aol.com
Please send me the following book(s):
THE CRISS CROSS ISBN: 0-9717021-2-8
WIFEY ISBN: 0-9717021-3-6
I'M STILL WIFEY ISBN: 0-9717021-5-2
A TWISTED TALE OF KARMA ISBN: 0-9717021-4-4
MENACE II SOCIETY ISBN: 0-9717021-7-9
SEX, SIN & BROOKLYN ISBN: 0-9717021-6-0
CROSS ROADS ISBN: 0-9717021-8-7
IN MY HOOD ISBN: 0-9717021-9-5
STRIPPED ISBN: 1-934157-00-7
EVA FIRST LADY OF SIN ISBN: 1-934157-01-5
THE CANDY SHOP ISBN: 1-934157-02-3
ALL ABOVE BOOKS ARE PRICED AT **$15.00**

UP CLOSE AND PERSONAL ISBN: 0-9717021-1-X
THE POETRY BOOK IS PRICED AT $9.95

@ 15.00 (U.S.) = _____
QUANTITY

Shipping/Handling*   = _____

Total Enclosed   = _____

PLEASE ATTACH, NAME, ADDRESS, TELEPHONE NUMBER(for emergencies)
_____
Please enclose $3.95 to cover shipping/handling ($6.00 if total more than $30.00
AND under $50.00)

FOR BULK ORDERS PLEASE CALL THE PUBLISHER.
To pay by check or money order, please make it payable to <u>Melodrama Publishing</u>.

Send your payment with the order form to the above address, or order on the web.
Prices subject to change without notice. Please allow 2-3 weeks for delivery.

WWW.MELODRAMAPUBLISHING.COM